"Jada, I thank you for indu ... n, his
soothing voice putting her ...
know that I don't normall ...
made an incredible c ...
Luca ha 'n't .icip ...
her would be. He wan.ed to b ...
back.

"I—I never do this. But I don't know . . . I was almost
speechless when you shook my hand. I know stuff like
this doesn't happen every day."

He fixed his blue eyes on her, trying to decide how
direct he should be, before continuing.

"Let me tell you right away . . . I am fifty years old. I
was married for ten years and I have been divorced for
ten years. I don't have any children. I haven't had a
serious girlfriend since my ex-wife—just a few affairs that
ended badly. I don't play games. And I have never dated
a black woman."

ALLEGRO

ADORA BENNETT

Genesis Press, Inc.

INDIGO LOVE SPECTRUM

An imprint of Genesis Press, Inc.
Publishing Company

Genesis Press, Inc.
P.O. Box 101
Columbus, MS 39703

ISBN: 13 DIGIT : 978-1-58571-391-2
ISBN: 10 DIGIT : 1-58571-391-0
Manufactured in the United States of America

First Edition

Visit us at www.genesis-press.com
or call at 1-888-Indigo-1-4-0

DEDICATION

To my parents, Mary and Patrick, who told me that all dreams are possible with hard work and faith.

To my classmate and friend, Whitney, who inspired me to try.

To my personal "Board of Directors": Andrea, Ruth, Sheila, Kim, Colette, Antoinette, and Al—good friends who cheered me on and kept me in line.

CHAPTER 1

"Oh, Lord," Jada groaned, frowning at her ringing alarm clock. "It just can't be 5:30 already." Morning seemed to her to be arriving earlier and earlier with each passing day. And the days were getting longer and more intense, which is why she had committed herself to starting each day with a forty-five-minute workout, minimum.

Jada threw back the covers and looked approvingly at her taut arms and nearly flat stomach. "I've definitely come a long way, but there's still room for improvement!" So she coaxed herself out of bed and headed for her workout room. After turning the TV to the morning news, she jumped on the treadmill, resolving to make this the best possible day.

Her forty-five-minute penance passed so quickly she decided to go for the full hour. Soon after, she was showered, styled, suited in Max Mara and stepping out in the brisk mid-March air, on her way to Honoraria, the advertising agency where she worked as vice president of client services. At forty-five, she was one of the older VPs and the only person of color with a management title in the entire agency. Many articles have been written about the paucity of blacks and other minorities in advertising; Jada lived that reality every day. She didn't obsess about it, but she knew that the eyes of the few black, Hispanic and Asian young people in the company were on her. In some cases they were openly rooting for her—asking to join her team or volunteering to work on task forces that she chaired. In other cases, support was more covert; regardless, Jada felt the responsibility of being "the first" on her shoulders and did not intend to let them, or herself, down.

Her rise to the top had been the result of long hours and her great skill at honing in on strategy and working closely with the creative team to develop highly effective advertising. Few of her peers were willing to give as much of themselves to get ahead. While working her way up the ladder, she had forgone weekend getaways and socializing with her friends. Moreover, she used her time more productively at the office. She raised her hand to take on projects no one else wanted; she stayed later than everyone; and she took pains to cultivate important business relationships inside and outside the agency. Success in the client services business had a lot to do with buzz: the better your buzz, the more likely you were to be included in potentially lucrative client pitches. As a black woman involved in what was until recently an old (white) boys' club, Jada knew that crafting the right image was vital to her success. She was always impeccably dressed and always on time, and she *never* let her hair down around her colleagues. Jada had seen too many rising stars cut down by one bawdy evening out drinking with the guys or one off-color joke told to the wrong person. Only rare exceptions were given second chances after such indiscretions; Jada could not risk that she would be one of the lucky ones.

No one at the office knew anything about her personal life, not that there was much to know. While in school, she studied! She had dated casually, but back then, getting married was the last thing on her mind. She'd wanted to finish college with the best grades possible and to get the best possible job. It hadn't occurred to her to "snag a man" as many of her friends had done (though she knew that most of them were now divorced single parents). After college, she had lots of dates, but most of the men were either intimidated by her job trajectory or not that serious about being serious. Her timing always seemed off when it came to men. It was a good thing Jada never felt desperate about being single, because in the blink of an eye, both thirty and forty came and went with nary a man in sight.

She took some comfort in knowing that she was hardly alone. Many of her friends were in the same boat, and each had found her own way of dealing with solitude. Some slept with any man they could get regardless of his status—married, single or something in between. Others decided they would just work late, eat at elegant restaurants and shop obsessively, leaving little time to even think about a relationship. But Jada was in a different place. She never let aloneness get her down, and she was determined not to let herself go. She might not have been quite as svelte as the First Lady, but her five feet, ten inch frame was pretty well toned; she had worked hard to lose the twenty-five pounds she had gained after turning forty. It had taken her over a year to do it once she finally set losing the weight as a goal. Now, she was older but definitely better; at forty-five, she could still turn heads. In the meantime, now that she had achieved some success, Jada enjoyed hanging out with her friends when she could, indulging in a weekend get-away with them or on her own and making the most of her life. If she didn't have a man, she still had a life, and it was a pretty damned good one.

Honoraria was one of Boston's top three advertising agencies. Their client focus was companies with over fifty million dollars in annual revenue. Many of their clients were service focused, but consumer brands and high-tech businesses were also represented in their portfolio. Formed in the late 1970s by two New York admen who wanted to become big fish in a smaller pond, the agency had a certain edginess that either attracted or repelled potential clients. Over the years, Honoraria had created some of the most memorable local and national advertising campaigns for TV, print, online and direct mail. It was what was known in the industry as a hot shop. The offices were housed in a stately building near the heart of downtown Boston. Neither soaring skyscraper nor townhouse, the building had an urban charm that made it a cool place to go every day.

Jada enjoyed working in the downtown area because she got to see such a cross-section of the city during the day. Wealthy people with their fancy cars and expensive suits rubbed shoulders with students, office workers and people of more humble means. The neighborhood had an excitement and a tension that complemented the office environment.

Honoraria occupied two entire floors of the building, with account management on one floor and the creative and media teams on the other. When clients walked into the sleek, ultra-modern reception area at Honoraria, they knew they were at an agency that believed their work made a difference for their clients. Television ads were projected onto the walls in a continuous silent loop. Print and online ads flashed on opposite walls intermittently, along with press clippings about the agency's creativity. The visual stimulation kept visitors captivated because there was always something different to see. Jada found it hard not to feel energized whenever she walked through the door.

As a vice president, Jada had finally worked her way to a larger office near the corner. She'd taken great care in decorating it—toning down the high-tech look and adding touches from her personal art collection: fashion photographs by Gordon Parks and striking pieces by famous local African-American artists Alan Crite and Paul Goodnight. It gave her office a warm, individual style that she liked, but it had set tongues wagging; no one had seen anything like it. Until Jada came along, no one had felt they had the license to break from the sleek, minimalist style of the reception area. It had never occurred to her to ask permission before redecorating. It *was* her office. Besides, it was important to her that her work space projected the warmth and professionalism of her personality. A few of the partners had made comments about it to her but no one ever suggested that she tone it down. Soon after, some of the other directors and vice presidents started adding more personal touches to their offices. She had unwittingly started a mini-revolution, and her innocent defiance of the status quo endeared her to many of her colleagues.

"What's on today, Annie?" Jada asked as she walked into her spacious office, pausing to hang her jacket behind the door. Annie, a slightly portly woman with long, silver-streaked light-brown hair, a sharp mind for numbers and dates and a devious smile, had been her assistant since she joined Honoraria as a manager five years before. They were a powerful team. Annie understood how Jada worked and was great at anticipating what she'd ask for next. Over the years, they had found that the morning update was the best way to ensure that they both had a clear understanding of what to expect throughout the day.

"You're free until ten, and then you have a new client-overview presentation with a company called Allegro."

"Allegro?"

"Yes; they design corporate interiors. It's an Italian company and they're in the midst of setting up a US office. They have revenues of about two hundred million over there, and they want to launch here with a strong business-to-business campaign. It seems they could bring in a decent amount of business if we're lucky enough to get them to sign with us."

"Sounds good. This should be an interesting one."

"Oh, one more thing: They requested that they only meet with client services for this initial meeting—no creatives, no media people. I think it was the principal who called to set up the meeting. He said they just want to see what the agency is like—no dog-and-pony show for this round. So it's just you and them."

Jada chuckled. "It sounds like they know the routine. That's interesting, too."

"Here's a little file I've put together on them."

"Thanks, Annie. You read my mind."

"We've been at this for a long time."

"Yeah, I guess we have."

Jada retreated to her office to study the file. Annie watched her go to her desk and smiled. She was by far the best boss she'd ever had. She wasn't a pushover by any means, but she was kind and compassionate. She listened to suggestions and was neither afraid to admit mistakes nor reluctant to give someone else due credit. Annie liked working for her so much that she had decided long ago that she would follow her to another agency if she ever left Honoraria. The chances of ever getting to work for another Jada Green were slim to none in this business, and she was getting too old to deal with the young prima donnas who were coming up at the agency.

Annie only wished that Jada had more of a life outside work. Even though she was only a few years older than Jada, their lives were worlds apart in so many ways. She was white; Jada was black. When the city's demographics began to change years ago, Annie's parents had moved their family to the suburbs and now she only came into town to go to work. Jada was the quintessential city girl; Annie had been married for over twenty years and enjoyed a quiet life with her husband, Joe, and their two teenaged sons. Sadly, Jada was single. Perhaps she was just an unsophisticated woman who wanted everyone in the world to be married, but she always wished Jada could find herself a nice man. She was such a nice person!

Annie was probably the only person at the agency who knew any real details about Jada's life, which was often the subject of watercooler chatter. Did she lead some glamorous life outside the office? Was she a lesbian? Was she just obsessed with work and unable to maintain a relationship? No one seemed to have a handle on what kind of man she would spend her time with (assuming she wasn't gay). Annie found it fascinating that people considered Jada such an enigma, since in her view few people were as transparent as Jada Green. Annie knew exactly the kind of man Jada needed in her life: someone who was just like her—smart, personable and as interested in his job as he was in friends and family.

Annie had racked her brain trying to think of a few nice men she could introduce to Jada, but Joe's friends certainly weren't her type, and the only other men she ever met were ones who came to the office. But she knew for sure Jada would never date anyone who had anything to do with her job; she was too straightlaced about office associations. So, since she herself had no options to offer and a relationship at work was not an option, Annie was at a loss as to how to help improve Jada's love life. Maybe it didn't matter. Annie loved her husband and her two boys, but she had learned that marriage wasn't all it was cracked up to be, anyway.

Jada flipped through the Allegro catalogue, marveling at the different styles of corporate offices that the company designed. Headquartered in Turin (or Torino), Allegro also had offices in Lyon, Hamburg and Birmingham, England. So they liked the second-city approach; but even still, why Boston? Why not Miami or LA or Chicago, cities with strong reputations for outstanding commercial design? Though she was not one to question a company's business strategy, she was curious nonetheless.

"Hmmm. They've had five years of growth, a few of them double-digit, so what do I know?" Jada wondered out loud. Time passed quickly, and it was soon time to greet the principals from Allegro: President Luca Alessandri, Creative Director Fiorella Fontana and Chief Operating Officer Hugh Laws.

"They're here," Annie announced from the doorway.

"Great. I'm on my way. C-Room, right?"

"You got it."

"Thanks, Annie."

Jada gave herself a final once-over in the mirror, smoothing down her sleek bob haircut and fixing a slight smudge in the makeup that she had applied to highlight her spectacular brown eyes.

She walked up to the trio seated on the sofa in the reception area and said, "Mr. Alessandri?" whereupon a tall, clean-shaven man in the middle of the group stood up.

"Hi, I'm Jada Green, vice president of client services. It's nice to meet you," she added, now taking a closer look at the man. *Wow, he's one good looking man,* she couldn't help thinking.

"Please . . . call all of us by our first names," the man said, "I am Luca."

Jada quickly acknowledged the other members of the team and then motioned them to follow her, saying, "Right this way."

"Luca, are you coming?" Fiorella asked, noticing that he'd frozen in place.

"What? Yes, of course," he replied, picking up his briefcase and wondering what had just happened to him.

Jada led the way to conference room C, giving herself a pep talk along the way:

Focus, girl, focus! Do not blow this meeting over a stupid schoolgirl reaction! By the time the group had reached the conference room, she had pulled herself together enough to venture another look at Luca. Tall and fit, but not overly muscular, he wore an impeccably cut dark blue suit with a champagne-colored shirt, a color combination that only a confident man could carry off. His eyes were striking—the deepest blue framed by almost girlish eye-lashes. She knew from his bio that he was a bit older than she. His wavy, jet-black hair was longer than the fashion of the day and graying slightly at the temples. Jada wondered if he colored it.

Similarly, Luca was sizing her up and also chiding himself for being distracted.

Luca Alessandri! You are a fifty-year-old man and president of this company. Act your part. But his instant attraction to this woman was perplexing. She was beautiful, but hardly the most beautiful woman he'd ever seen. Still, no woman had ever left him this flustered. There was something about her, something he could not yet define. She had great style, yes, and she was tall and had a nice shape—not like a model, but a woman. Jada's voice interrupted his reverie.

"Even though Honoraria is one of the most acclaimed agencies in the region, we don't rest on our laurels. Our creative team of writers, art directors and online experts are some of the best in the business. We have a media team that knows how to build strong, cost-efficient plans that incorporate direct mail, online—a variety of elements from the media mix. We believe in pushing the envelope, and in testing new and innovative approaches, so that we can deliver breakthrough creativity and the strongest business results possible."

This woman is as sharp at business as she is attractive. He nodded approvingly and said, "That aligns nicely with our company philosophy. Allegro was started by my father as a spinoff from a company he began with my uncle. Their company had installed the first personal computers in offices around Italy. My father saw an opportunity to create a business that offered office redesign in conjunction with the installation of new technology. It was a risk, but it paid off, since personal computers required office spaces to be redesigned. We still have many of our original clients. Allegro designs their offices when they move and we work with them to ensure that their space works as they grow. We have a variety of clients—from fashion houses to high-tech offices." He smiled. "We even work with advertising agencies. We are always trying new approaches to ensure that when a client comes to Allegro, they get the most innovative ideas for their space."

Jada was impressed. Luca's love for his work was impossible to hide. She loved talking with people who had a passion for their work.

Despite Jada and Luca's initial jitters, the meeting went well. Fiorella and Hugh asked relevant questions about top-level attention to accounts and turnaround time. Jada highlighted all of Honoraria's strengths, especially their depth of talent and experience building brands. Luca had little to say, but this seemed more like his letting his team shine rather than disengagement on his part.

"I have one question for you, Luca, if you don't mind . . ."

"Please."

"Torino, Lyon, Hamburg and Birmingham, England . . . why Boston?"

Luca paused before answering. "Because I like it," he said, looking Jada straight in the eyes.

Jada shifted uncomfortably. His eyes were like blue lasers, and even though his cryptic response contained nothing off-putting, she somehow found it unsettling.

Luca kicked himself as soon as the words left his mouth. He was going for witty and charming, but the words made him sound more like a rich, spoiled asshole. He *did* like Boston, but he never would have picked the city as his US headquarters if he hadn't thought it had a depth of untapped talent at art schools and universities in the area . . . and a desire not to be seen as New York City's dowdy cousin. Why hadn't he said that? But it was too late. If he tried to explain all of that now, he would risk looking foolish in front of Fiorella and Hugh. Luca was rightly concerned that they might already be thinking he was behaving strangely. In any case, he suspected, Fiorella sensed that he had been struck by Jada's presence. She was a woman, after all, and women tended to see such things way before men usually did. So he used one of his favorite cover-ups: more discussion about business.

"Thank you, Jada. This was extremely thorough and helpful. We are seeing a few other agencies and then we will make a decision on which ones we are going to ask to do a pitch. Also, I appreciated your willingness to meet with us without all your colleagues. If we decide to have your agency pitch to us, we definitely want them all there, but for this initial meeting. I appreciate just having a conversation as we did."

"It was my pleasure to meet with you and your team this way. I actually agree with your approach, though I should say we usually have everyone join in unless the client requests otherwise."

Luca wished that he could think of a way to prolong the meeting, but he was at a loss as to how, finally saying, "We'll be in touch."

They said their goodbyes, with Jada handing each of them a folder emblazoned with the Honoraria logo; Luca worked it so that he was the last out the door.

"Jada, thank you again." He shook her hand and smiled, revealing the tiniest dimples. He felt his heart flutter when they touched and again when he looked at her.

"You're welcome, Luca. Please call me if you have any questions at all. My card is in the folder."

Still smiling, he said, "I will."

Jada saw them to the elevator and then rushed back to her office.

"Are you okay, Jada?" Annie asked, a little worried. Jada seemed flustered.

"I'm fine," she replied and closed her door—something she rarely did when she was in her office alone. She took a few deep breaths and started dialing. There was only one friend to call to break down situations like this one: Katrina Culver. They had been friends since they were little girls and couldn't have been closer if they were real sisters. Jada had always known her as Renie, but she'd gone formal in her latest incarnation as a graphic designer for a studio downtown.

"Can you talk?"

"Yeah. I've got a few minutes. What's up?"

"I met this man . . ."

"STOP! Girl, when you're our age, you don't call a girlfriend out of the blue and say 'I met this man!' Gimme some context: I was dreaming I met this man; I hit a car and I met this man; I—"

"Okay! I get it, and you would have, too, if you'd given me ten seconds."

"Sorry. If you can't tell, I'm excited."

"Fact established. May I—"

"Go ahead. I'm zipping it now . . . all ears."

"Anyway, he is a potential client. His name is Luca Alessandri. He—"

"Ooh. Italian. You know Italian men love black women . . ."

"Renie!"

"Sorry. Not another word."

"He's about my age—maybe a little older. He is the president of the company. He . . . I don't even know what to say. When I saw him, I was just blown away. He's really good-looking. He almost threw me off my game."

"Wow, knowing how buttoned up you are, he must have been something."

"Renie, I really don't know what I'm going to do! I don't think I've ever been in the presence of a man who's got me so . . . I don't even know what the word is!"

"Shook up?"

"Yeah. Shook up works. Confused. I want this account, but I don't even know how—I'm just all off balance! How will I be able to work with this man?"

"Whoa, Nellie! You only did an agency presentation. You don't even know if he'll ask your agency to pitch."

Jada sighed. "Of course he will. I can imagine the other shops they'll meet with. We'll be asked to pitch."

"Well, aren't you the confident one?"

"When it comes to what I do, I guess I am. What I'm looking for is advice on how to manage this . . . crush."

"Just focus on the job, I guess."

"Huh?"

"Well, you're so focused on getting the job done that you can proudly tell me that you'll get to make a pitch, so just maintain that focus on the goal whenever you have to deal with him, and keep your distance from him as much as you can unless you want to jump his bones!" Renie fell out laughing.

"That's not even funny."

"Well, you said he's good-looking. Is he married?"

"I don't know. He didn't have on a ring."

"That was a little bit of a trick question. I wanted to see if you had looked."

"Renie, I *always* look—even if I think they're dead ugly."

Katrina laughed. "Yeah, me, too. But if he's single, why not see what can happen? Ask him out for a drink."

"Renie, you know that I don't have anything to do with *anyone* on my job—especially clients or potential clients."

"Well, I don't know. Maybe you need to rethink that. Shit, everyone else is doing it, why not you?"

"I'll give you three reasons: Black. Female. VP. I can't even think about it."

"I hear you. So just play it cool. You can do it. You do it every day."

"Thanks for talking me off the cliff, Renie."

"You can call me any time."

CHAPTER 2

Luca went back to his hotel room at the Ritz to unwind and call his father. After meeting Jada, he had been off balance all day and desperately wanted to regroup. It had been a long time since he'd been so intrigued by a woman. Thoughts of her had driven him to distraction throughout the rest of his meeting-filled day; God only knows what he had done to feign attentiveness. He pressed his fingertips to his temples, took a deep breath and dialed. Luca's father, Lorenzo, was not only his business partner but also his best friend, and as CEO of Allegro, he would want to know how the day had gone. And as Luca's closest confidante, he would likely offer some perspective on his son's intense attraction.

"*Papà, come stai?*"

"I am okay. My English is getting rusty, so I'm going to practice with you now."

"That's good." Luca laughed.

"How was it today? You saw four agencies, no?"

"Yes. We have two more we want to meet, and we will then ask three of them to pitch to us."

"*Va bene . . .*"

"English, Papà! It was your choice."

"Okay, okay. Tell me what's wrong."

Luca stared at the phone. How did he do that? Could there be a more intuitive man on earth than Lorenzo Alessandri?

"Nothing, really."

"Luca, you were never a very good liar."

"No, I'm not. There was this woman at one of the agencies—Honoraria. Papà, she took my breath away."

"Ah, she's beautiful."

"Yes, but not like a fashion model or anything, though she was impeccably dressed—extremely stylish. She's got this extraordinary presence; you can't help but notice her. She has such passion for her work; she reminded me of me! I became excited about what we can do while listening to her. I could have sat there all day. She is in her late thirties, or maybe forty. And she is black."

"Oh."

"I don't think I've ever been so struck by a woman."

"How did she react to you?"

"I don't know for sure. I think that she had a similar reaction. I don't know."

"Why a black woman?"

"I don't know, Papà. There's just something about her. I want to know more about who she is; it's strange."

Lorenzo was quiet for a long time, thinking, *It's not so strange, my son. It's called* amore a prima vista—*love at first sight.* It happened to others, but it was somewhat of a shock to hear his son talk of such things—especially at his age. He had been married years ago, but it was clear to Lorenzo that his son had married his wife, Mirella, because he believed that it was what he was supposed to do. They were married for ten mostly unhappy years. In the end, it was Lorenzo who pushed his son to end it. He hated to be around Luca then. There had been almost no joy left in his beloved son's eyes as he fought with all his energy to make his marriage work. They never had children, which had been a disappointment for Lorenzo; he and his wife, Olivia, had wanted grandchildren so desperately! After having had only one child, Lorenzo had hoped that Luca and Mirella would have had at least three. But that was not to be. And now, this: a black woman, and one almost as old as Luca! If this attraction developed further, he could officially kiss his dream of grandchildren good-bye. He didn't like it at all, but he did like to hear his son sounding genuinely intrigued by a woman. That had not happened in a long time.

"Papà! Are you still there?"

"I'm here; I was just thinking. Do you have this woman's phone number? What is her name, anyway? I don't like referring to her as 'this woman.' "

"Her name is Jada. Jada Green. She is a vice president at the agency Honoraria."

"Jah-da? Like the Italian, Giada? How do you spell it?"

"J-A-D-A. The first 'a' sounds like the last 'e' in '*elegante*.'"

"So call Jada up and ask her out for dinner or drinks. You have important questions you need answered. Honestly, Luca! You've obviously been working too hard lately."

"I guess so."

"Let me remind you, old man: If you want a woman, go get her!"

Luca laughed. "You're right, Papà. I will. Thank you. *Ciao*."

"*Ciao,* my son."

Lorenzo tapped his pen on his notepad. He had to make a call.

CHAPTER 3

It had been a hectic day. From the moment Jada walked through the door, people had been on her case. Now her boss had called her in for a status update on new business. Gene Bradley was a man dancing on the line of middle age. Of average height and somewhat pudgy, he had a double chin and a wide gap between his two front teeth, which gave his slightly weathered face a youthful look. All of his clothes were about a size too small, and he wore overpowering cologne that caused everyone to take a step back whenever he stopped to talk. Jada wished she could just stand in the doorway and have her conversation with him from there. He was sitting behind his enormous, glass-top desk. She took a seat in one of his treasured Philippe Starck chairs, across from him.

"What's happening with Allegro?"

"I don't know, Gene."

"What do you mean, you don't know?"

"They were having up-front meetings with five other agencies and will pick three to pitch. He said he would call."

"No follow-up on your part?" Gene asked.

"Gene, he said he would call. It hasn't even been twenty-four hours. I don't think it makes sense to pressure him. It makes us look desperate."

"Well, you know your stuff, but if this one goes away I'll have to question your judgment on this."

Great, Jada thought. *After five years here and almost three doing this job, my judgment gets challenged over a phone call.*

"We're in good shape, Gene," Jada said as calmly as she could.

"Good. I hope so. Be sure to keep me posted on what happens. We really want this business."

"Gene, believe me, no one wants this account more than I do."

"Well, I'm glad to hear that."

"If that's it . . ." Jada got up to leave.

"Yes, I think that covers it."

Jada was fuming when she got back to her office, but before she had a chance to take a breath, the phone rang. She looked out her door to see if it was going to get picked up. No Annie. Jada snatched the phone up.

"Jada Green," she snapped. "Hello?"

Luca took a deep breath. *Bad timing.* He almost hung up the phone without saying anything. "Did I reach you at a bad time? You sound very busy. This is Luca Alessandri."

Jada had recognized his warm, baritone voice the moment he spoke, and hearing it brought an inexplicable calm over her.

"Luca, I'm sorry. I was just frustrated when I answered the phone. I shouldn't have taken it out on you."

"No apology required. I think everyone has those moments at one time or another during the day."

"What can I do for you?"

Luca was silent for a moment, her question having sparked a myriad of imagined things Jada could do for him.

"Ah, I was hoping I could invite you for a drink. I had some questions . . ."

"Oh, I'm really sorry I left you with questions," she said, instantly going into self-doubt mode. Luca sensed he had unintentionally hit a nerve.

"No, it's nothing like that . . ."

"Oh?"

"I'm sorry, Jada. I've gotten off to a bad start. I do have questions, but they are about you. I am only here in Boston for a short while, but I cannot go back to Italy without meeting you."

"I don't understand . . ."

"Jada, I want to get to know you. I would like to take you out for dinner, or at least a drink."

Jada could feel her heart racing. Why was this happening? It was bad enough that she found him distractingly attractive; now she was going to have to make a difficult choice, no matter what she decided to do.

"Luca, I'm flattered, but as a rule—"

"I know. As a rule you don't have any dealings with either clients or colleagues, I would imagine. From what I have seen of you, I wouldn't have expected anything less. I should tell you I have already decided that Honoraria will be in the pitch."

"Excuse me?"

"You're in the pitch. This is about me getting to know you."

"That makes it worse! We can't even *pretend* to talk business now."

"If anyone you know sees you, it's a business meeting, but we will know differently."

Jada didn't know what to say. She had no explanation for her intense attraction to Luca and no rational reason for being so tempted to defy her own personal code of ethics to go out with this man. But she was going to go out on a limb and trust her intuition, which told her this was a man she would regret not getting to know if she let this opportunity slip away.

"Say yes!"

"Against my better judgment, yes. Where shall we meet?"

"I am a tourist of sorts, so to impress me, you would invite me to the Top of the Hub so that I can enjoy the amazing view from one of the city's tallest buildings . . . and I will."

Jada felt herself blushing. She looked around to be sure that no one passing by could see her.

"Okay. Top of the Hub it is," she whispered. "Is six o'clock okay?"

"Perfect. I'll see you then. Jada?"

"Yes?"

"Do not worry. I would never put you in an uncomfortable situation. I am an honorable man."

"I know . . . I think you are . . . I mean . . . I'll see you later." Jada hung up the phone. Her head was spinning.

What was she doing? She picked up the phone to call Luca back and cancel, but immediately hung up without dialing. Why not have drinks with an attractive, interesting man? He was right. If anyone saw them, it would look like a business meeting. Jada could hear Renie cheering her on: "Go for it, girl!"

CHAPTER 4

Luca got there early. He didn't want to miss seeing Jada walk into the room. Actually, he had been to the Top of the Hub many times before, but it seemed like the perfect cover for a non-business business meeting. He looked over at the elevator just as she walked off. Their eyes met and they smiled.

He stood up. In heels, she almost matched his six feet, two inch height.

"Jada . . ." He kissed her on either cheek. "You look beautiful." And he meant it. She seemed even more attractive than he had remembered. He took in Jada's delicious curves, shown off in her head-to-toe grey ensemble: a light cashmere sweater set belted over thin wool trousers with a matching bag. The look was both relaxed and sexy—much more so than the polished, professional outfit she had worn the day before. She could compete with any woman on the fashionable streets of Milan—and win. Her cropped hair was pulled back off her face—a look that could be severe on some women, but on Jada it served to complement her heart-shaped face, making her dazzling brown eyes stand out even more.

"Thank you," Jada said with downcast eyes.

"Shall we take a table? I asked them to hold the one over there so that we can enjoy the view," he said, pointing to the table with the most perfect view of the airport and the harbor.

Jada smiled. "Sure." They walked over to the table and he pulled out the chair for her and positioned his own so that he could look directly at her but still enjoy the cityscape that had supposedly brought them there.

"Jada, thank you for indulging me," he began, his soothing voice putting her at ease. "I want you to know that I don't normally do this. I just . . . I felt like we made an incredible connection. I couldn't ignore it." He wanted to hold her hand. Luca hadn't anticipated how strong his desire to touch her would be. But he held back.

"I—I *never* do this. But I don't know . . . I was almost speechless when you shook my hand. I know stuff like that doesn't happen every day."

He fixed his ocean-blue eyes on her, trying to decide how direct he should be, before continuing.

"Let me tell you right away . . . I am fifty years old. I was married for ten years and I have been divorced for ten years. I don't have any children. I haven't had a serious girlfriend since my ex-wife, just a few affairs that ended badly. I don't play games . . . and I have never dated a black woman."

Jada swallowed hard and fought the strong desire to flee. She had heard of men putting it all out there up front, but this was almost more than she knew how to handle.

"Wow."

"Sorry. You just got great insight into my business style: all out in the open. But I'm really not trying to scare you."

"Luca, I have to tell you, that's a lot to put out there in the first ten minutes."

"I'm really sorry, Jada. Why don't you try it? Just put the most important things to you out in the open."

"I'm still processing what you just said. Hmmm. Okay . . . But my story is much more boring. Let's see . . . I'm forty-five years old."

"No!"

"Yes, I'm forty-five."

"You don't look it at all."

"And I hope it stays that way for a long, long time!" she exclaimed, quickly adding, "I'm one of the seventy percent."

"Seventy percent?"

"Yeah, that's the estimated percent of professional black women who are single. I can't even tell you the last time I had a date. Years . . ."

"You're joking."

Jada shook her head slowly. "Believe me, I wouldn't joke about that."

Luca couldn't stand it; he had to hold her hand. He wanted to kiss her so badly that he was actually trembling. "That can't be possible . . ."

"Possible? It's my reality, Luca. No dates, no affairs that ended badly . . . nothing."

"Jada, I—I don't know what to say. You are beautiful. You are smart and successful. I don't see how . . . I don't understand American men!" He took a deep breath. *Calm down. You really* will *scare her away if you don't watch it,* he cautioned himself.

"I think you are an amazing woman, that's why I felt so compelled to get to know you."

"I don't know what to say . . ."

"Say anything. Tell me more about who you are and what you like to do."

"Well, I've worked at Honoraria for five years."

"You like it, then?"

"Most of the time, yes. I really like the different types of clients I get to work with. Over the years, I've had banks, hospitals, one of the city's hot, new boutiques and a large charity on my roster. It keeps things fresh."

"Did you always want to go into advertising?"

Jada smiled wistfully. "Actually, no. Once upon a time, I wanted to be a fashion designer."

"That explains it."

"Explains what?"

"You have a very unique flair for fashion. For example, you're wearing a sweater that is a classic; you've probably had it in your closet for years. But your trousers are contemporary; I bet you bought them this season."

"I did. Tell me, how do you know so much about clothes?"

"Because, once upon a time, I wanted to be a fashion designer, too."

"You're kidding!"

"No."

"So why didn't you do it?"

"Well, I considered doing a lot of things before I decided to study architecture and commercial design at university. I took a few fashion design classes but that was it."

"That's too bad."

"Not really. I love what I do. I think that designing office interiors allows me to use my appreciation of fashion."

"I'm sure you do."

Luca laughed. "Some clients really need help with everything—from what equipment they need for their office to what color the rugs should be. It's a lot of fun. Just like you, I find every client is different; it's impossible to get bored."

Their conversation paused in awkward silence as Jada thought about how easy it was to talk with him and Luca considered how forward to be about what he was feeling.

"Jada, I think you are an amazing woman. What's happening here is something special. I cannot walk away, because I'm old enough to realize that life is too short and these feelings aren't ones that come along every day . . . I am a man who is used to getting what I want, but this feeling just cannot be one-sided. It's just too strong."

"Luca, we just met." She tried to pull her hand away from his, but he wouldn't let go.

"I know. That makes it different, but that doesn't make it less real."

"What you want just can't happen, Luca—no matter how attracted I might be to you. You're a potential client. You live in another country. I read your bio, so I know a little bit about you, but you don't know *anything* about my life."

"I know, Jada. Please . . . tell me everything."

"Where should I start?"

"At the beginning."

"Well, I was born here in Boston. I have two brothers. One lives here and the other in New York."

"What do they do?"

"They're both engineers. Darren is at Bose. Their headquarters is just outside Boston. He's single. Craig lives in Manhattan and works in New Jersey—a reverse commute. He's married with two children—a boy and a girl. Darren is two years older than me; Craig is two years younger. Do you have any sisters or brothers?"

"No, I'm an only child."

"Really?"

"Yes. It's just me."

"What's that like?"

"Well, it's all that I've known. I'm very close to my parents. My father and I are in business together and he's my best friend, too. It's strange to many people, but my father has always been there for me as a parent, as a business mentor and as a friend. He is seventy-three years old and as time goes on, I become more and more aware of his mortality. I don't know what I'll do without him. My mother is also wonderful. She's a beautiful person inside and out; I know you would like her very much. My parents married when they were teenagers, and they have the kind of relationship that everyone I know wants to have. They are friends, lovers and confidantes. My father can be . . . well, difficult. He is a terrible flirt. I don't think he has ever cheated on my mother, but perhaps he has come close. Anyway, I don't think my father keeps any secrets from her; he shares the good and the bad with her."

"Wow. I don't think my parents have the same kind of relationship at all . . ."

"Really?"

"No. They've been married for a long time, too— over fifty years—but I don't think any of us feel that they have the kind of relationship that you just described. They love each other, and get along pretty well most of the time, but . . . I don't know, they aren't particularly affectionate."

"That's a pity."

"Yeah, but at the same time, I think they love each other in their own way. I mean . . . I could never describe my parents as lovers. The thought of it grosses me out."

Luca laughed. "Jada! Older people make love, too, you know! Some people might consider us to be older people, and I know that I still enjoy making love with the right woman."

Jada blushed. "I know . . . still, they're my *parents*. I have a hard time thinking of them . . . that way. No more talk about my parents. I have a question for you."

"All right, I'm ready."

"Tell me something you enjoy that I might find surprising."

"That's a good question, but an easy one for me. I like romantic movies. Here in the States you call them 'chick flicks.'" He mumbled, "I really resent that name."

"Chick flicks?"

"Sure, a man can appreciate a good romance, too. I love them all—classics like *An Affair to Remember* and more contemporary ones like *Love Actually*. It's a nice, relaxing way to spend an evening."

Jada looked at the tall, strapping man facing her and stifled a giggle, imagining him tearing up watching *Titanic* or *The English Patient*. "I suppose so. Still, I'm surprised."

"Well, what about you? What do you like that I would find surprising?"

"I don't know if it's that surprising, but I love dance. Ballet, modern, ballroom; there's something about the art form that really enthralls me."

"Did you ever study dance?"

"For a short while when I was a little girl. But I get much more out of watching it than I ever did taking lessons. The timing, the coordination, the testing of physical limits: dance has it all."

"Hmmm. I don't really care for it, but I never thought about it that way. One day soon, you'll have to take me to a dance performance."

"But you just said you don't like it."

"Maybe experiencing it with you will help me to see it all through different eyes. I want to share in the things that you enjoy." Jada thought that was one of the sweetest things anyone had ever said to her.

Squeezing her hand affectionately, he reassured her, "I sincerely want to get to know you."

And so it went until they were told the Top of the Hub was closing. They'd had a couple of drinks, the last one mostly untouched. After Luca paid the bill, they exchanged personal phone numbers and prepared to leave.

"Where are you parked?"

"Down below."

"I'll walk you to your car."

"You don't have to, Luca."

He took her hand and gazed into her eyes.

"Yes, I do."

They made their way to the elevator for the long journey to the lobby. Jada was sure it would be a long time before her feet would actually touch the ground. She couldn't remember the last time she'd spent a more enjoyable evening in the company of a man who was only interested in knowing all about her. Throughout the night, women passed by their table, quite openly trying to get a closer look at him. But he kept his attention focused on her, making her feel that she was the center of his world.

Luca was happy not to have to share the elevator with anyone, using the opportunity to steal his first real kiss. It took some coaxing before Jada opened her mouth to Luca's probing tongue; when she finally did, he felt her knees weaken. He held her close, reveling in the feel of her shapely body through the soft cashmere.

"Jada, I—" His words were cut short by the opening of the elevator door.

"We're here," Jada said, pulling away from him.

Luca sighed. "Yes, I see," he said, his tone betraying more than a little frustration. "Where is your car?"

"Just over there."

As they walked slowly through the quiet garage, Luca took her hand but quickly decided it was not enough and put his arm around her waist.

"Tonight was so special to me."

"Me, too," Jada said, looking up warmly at Luca. He stole another kiss. It was gentle, loving and passionate all at once.

"I don't want to leave you," he said, but felt Jada instantly tensing up.

"Luca, I—" He put a finger over her lips.

"Shhh. I told you, I am an honorable man. I will tell you again that I want you more than anything, but I know that now is not the right moment. We have business we have to deal with, and we'll take some time to get to know each other more. But I believe that we will be together sometime soon, and I want our first time together to be as long as we want it to be—not just a few hours."

Jada leaned on his well-toned chest. "Thanks for reminding me that it's way past my bedtime. You've cheated me out of my beauty sleep."

"Sleep, yes; beauty, no." He stole one last kiss. "Good night, *amore mio*. I'll call you tomorrow."

"Okay." He took her key, opened the door for her and stood watching until her car disappeared from sight. Then he walked slowly and happily back to his hotel. Clearly, whatever he had felt for women in the past could not have been love, because he had never experienced this combination of lightheadedness and omnipotence.

CHAPTER 5

Jada could barely focus on the drive home. It had been an amazing evening. And while she knew up front that she was attracted to Luca and he to her, she had not anticipated feeling so connected to him after having just one evening of drinks and talk. What had she gotten herself into?

At home she undressed and made a cup of herbal tea. She needed to think, as she was in an almost hopeless situation. She could never date Luca if he selected Honoraria as the agency of record for Allegro. At the least, she would have to hand the account over to another team leader. It would be ethically unacceptable for her to manage the account if they were seeing each other. But she wasn't even sure if moving aside would be enough.

"Jada Green, *what* are you doing?" she asked out loud. She couldn't stop herself from thinking about possibilities, just like she'd done with Ken, the last man she'd dated many moons ago. No sooner had they met, she was already thinking about where their relationship was heading. *Why* did she always do that? This was a man who didn't even live in Boston. So what if he seemed to be interested? What future could they really have?

She sat drinking her tea, her mind replaying the kisses in slow motion. It had been so long since a man had kissed her that way. God, it felt good, she thought, recalling the faint scent of his cologne when she leaned on his chest just before they parted.

Jada turned on the TV in an effort to try to stop her memory of the evening from becoming all-consuming, but it was like putting one sandbag in place against a tidal wave. Despite her best efforts, Luca was all she wanted to think about. Then her phone rang.

"Hello?"

"Jada?"

"Luca, hello!"

"I'm sorry. I told you that I'd call you tomorrow, but I couldn't wait. Technically, it *is* tomorrow already."

Jada laughed.

"I made you laugh. So you're not angry."

"No, of course I'm not angry."

"I just wanted to make sure that you got home safely and to tell you again what a nice time I had tonight. All of my business questions have been answered, thanks to you."

Jada chuckled. "Well, I'm glad to hear that, Mr. Alessandri."

"Yes, but I still have many, *many* questions about you."

"Luca, we have a problem. I really had a wonderful time with you tonight. God knows, I don't think I've ever had a night like this one. We seem so in synch with each other, but it kind of scares me."

"That's a good thing, though, isn't it?"

"For us? No."

"Why?"

"Because we *can't* be involved with each other. We just can't."

"I know that we can't *right now*, but once I make a decision . . ."

"Luca, this is an impossible situation for me. If you select my agency, I can't work on your account. That would be ethically wrong, and it would be bad for both of us, but especially for me." Jada considered whether she should relate everything on her mind, finally deciding that she had no choice. "You're not from here, so you may not be able to appreciate how big a deal what I'm going to say is to me."

"Go ahead."

"I am a black vice president—the only one *ever* at Honoraria. I have to guard my reputation ten times more than my coworkers have to."

"Okay. I understand that. I do. But what if I select your agency and someone else manages my account?"

"Even though I may have brought in the business, I would get no credit for it and I would be ostracized by my peers for being involved with a client. No one would believe that we weren't seeing each other right from the start. Remember what I said about my reputation?"

"Okay. What happens if I give my business to another agency? I will be honest and say that I was really impressed with Honoraria, and, as long as the pitch was good, it would have been my first choice. So I'll go with my second choice. What's wrong with that solution?"

"Nothing personally. But professionally, it kills me. My boss is expecting me to bring your business to Honoraria. If you go elsewhere, it just means that I lose a lot of credibility that I didn't deserve to lose. He's already told me that if things go wrong, he will have to question my judgment on how I handled the account."

"I see. Jada, I don't want to disrupt things for you on your job, but I cannot let this go. What can we do . . . Jada? Are you still there?"

"I'm here," she said softly.

"*Amore mio* . . . please don't close the door on us already. I understand everything that you've said, I really do. But there's got to be a way to make this a win-win situation."

"I don't know . . ."

"You don't know?"

Jada could barely contain her frustration, and she spoke harshly. "Look, Luca, I really do like you. But I can't deal with this right now. It's much easier for us to just call it a day, having enjoyed a fun night in each other's company than for us to let this go any further, so I'm going to say good night." She knew she wasn't committed to the words even as she spoke them, and she made no attempt to hang up the phone, so it wasn't a surprise when Luca picked up on her ambivalence.

"You're wrong. Have dinner with me tomorrow."

"Luca, did you hear anything I just said?"

"I did. I'm ignoring it. Have dinner with me."

"I can't. I won't."

"Then have lunch with me."

"No."

"Drinks?"

"Luca, I can't do this."

"Jada, we have to keep a connection somehow. How can we do that if you won't see me?"

"We can do what we're doing now."

"What?"

"We can talk on the phone. I'm fine with talking on the phone. I like talking to you."

"She wants to talk on the phone," Luca muttered under his breath.

"I'm sorry, I cannot be seen anywhere with you until after the pitch and after you've made your decision. We're off limits. Depending on what your decision is, we'll take it from there. That's the best I can offer, and I can't believe I've let you talk me into that much."

He sighed. "Then I guess it's what I'll have to accept. I am a patient man when I have to be."

"Luca, I'm going to go to sleep now. It's almost three o'clock in the morning. I am going to pay for this big-time tomorrow—later today."

"I wish I could be there to hold you until you fall asleep."

Imagining what that would be like, Jada said, "Well, it wouldn't take very long. I'm exhausted."

"Good night, Jada. I'm still going to call you later."

"I know that I sounded horrible earlier. I'm sorry. I'll look forward to talking with you whenever you get the chance to call."

"Jada, I understand. I really do. Maybe I haven't experienced everything that you're talking about, but that doesn't make your feelings any less real to me. *Ciao, amore mio.*"

"*Ciao,* Luca." She hung up, turned out the lights and went to bed.

CHAPTER 6

When she awakened at 5:30 a.m., Jada didn't feel the least bit rested. She considered sleeping through her daily workout, but thought better of it. After forty-five minutes on the treadmill, she felt a little more energized than she'd expected she would be after only two and a half hours of sleep.

"Oh, God, let this be a reasonably calm day at the office," Jada beseeched the universe. "I really don't have the juice to deal with any madness today."

Pondering what to wear for the day, she quickly settled on St. John. "When in doubt go for the clout," she told herself, pulling out a classically tailored navy-blue knit suit flecked with pink, which she enhanced with a blue and pink silk blouse. She completed the look with pearl accessories and navy blue Bally pumps. She finished her makeup, took the flat iron to her hair and was out the door and in her office by eight o'clock.

David Heath was the first person she saw as she walked in the door. Her rather portly colleague, with his frizzled beard and thick coke-bottle glasses, turned and walked in her direction when he saw her.

At fifty-eight, David was the oldest vice president at the agency. He joined Honoraria a decade after the agency opened its doors, during the glory days of 1980s advertising. Back then new clients lined up at the door, and a good portion of the account management role was entertaining clients. Few were better at schmoozing than David Heath. He often reminisced about those golden years and relished the close ties he'd forged with the agency's partners.

He was not one of Jada's favorite people. There was always a current of passive-aggressiveness in his exchanges with her that gave Jada the creeps. Still, David was never overtly unpleasant, so she kept her true feelings about him to herself.

"Ugh. The day is *not* getting off to a good start," Jada mumbled under her breath as she headed to her office, all the while thinking, *Please, just keep walking, keep walking, keep—*

"Hey, Jada! I was hoping I would run into you."

"Good morning, David. You're pretty casual today," she said, noting his jeans and crewneck sweater. David was a man who struggled to look pulled together even when wearing a suit, so this definitely was not the best look for him.

"It's a light day for me, a well-needed office day—no client meetings and no internal meetings, either. I'm taking it easy today."

You take it easy every day. What makes this day different from any other?

"Lucky you. How are you doing otherwise?"

"I'm great. *Really* good, in fact."

"That's good," Jada said. She had several inches on David, and she was hoping she could outpace him or at least discourage him from trying to continue the conversation. If they kept talking, she knew that he would either start comparing her success with projects to his own, or bring up something at which he was having better success at than she; that was how he kept score. Her tactic didn't work.

"Hey, did you know that last week I had four new client briefings? How many did you have?"

"I had two last week and one the week before."

"Oh. Those client briefings are hard to come by, aren't they?"

"They sure are." Jada was nearly at her office door now, and he had not gone away.

"How much potential business is that?" he persisted.

"Hmmm. I don't remember. Maybe a few million."

"Oh? If all of mine come in, it's almost five million in potential billings."

"Good for you, David. Congratulations." Jada was trying to sound her collegial, back-slapping best, but was sure she was falling short. What with two and a half hours sleep, her concentration was on not twisting her ankle as she walked in her serious pumps. "I hope all of your potential clients turn into billable ones; we need the business!"

David lifted his head triumphantly. "You know, I have one of the best client-conversion rates in the agency. Almost everyone who briefs with me ends up signing on."

"Well, good luck. As I said, we can sure use the business. That will be great."

"Yes, let me know what happens with your three potential clients. I'll be curious to hear."

Yeah, I'm sure you will be curious. "Sure, will do. Have a good day," Jada said, quickly ducking into her office.

About an hour later, the phone rang and Annie picked up. Jada had actually wanted to grab the call, thinking that it might be Luca calling her again, but Annie routinely screened her calls.

"Jada, it's Vince Jordan, your contact at the restaurant you presented to last week."

"Thanks, Annie. Vince, it's good to hear from you! What can I do for you?"

"Well, Jada, I wanted to get back to you after your agency presented to us last week. We've thought about it and we've decided to go in another direction with our agency support."

"I'm really sorry to hear that, Vince. May I ask you where you think Honoraria fell short?"

"Well, we were looking for an agency that would be a little more prescriptive."

"Prescriptive?"

"Yes. Your presentation focused on your creativity and the strength of your team. We're not advertising honchos and we kind of felt that we'd be a little overwhelmed by it all . . . you know, too many choices that we'd have to work through."

"I see. So you thought we were too creative?"

"Yeah. Sort of."

"Well, Vince, that's where I and the other account executives on the team come in. It's our job to help you sort through those creative ideas. You get the choice of the most creative concepts that we can give you and if you need our help, we can work through which one is the best one with you. On top of that, we're not going to present you with anything that is off-strategy, so you're going to be safe no matter which idea you choose."

"That's interesting. I guess we hadn't thought of it that way."

"Vince, I hope you won't mind me saying this, but I'd like to help clarify any of your concerns about Honoraria if there's still an opportunity to do so. Have you told the agency you were planning to select that it has won your business?"

"No."

"Then, please, I'll be happy to come over to your office and address any concerns you may have about us. I'd like you to at least have all your questions answered before you make a final decision. Of course, there's no obligation to choose us, but I believe the best decisions are informed ones."

"That makes a lot of sense . . . Can you come here later on today?"

"Absolutely. Is two o'clock a good time?"

"Yes, two would be great."

"Well, I'll see you then, Vince. Thanks for giving me the chance to clarify things a little more for you."

"Thank *you* for being willing to do it."

Jada hung up the phone, now pretty confident that she would be able to win them over. While she had known they had not worked with an advertising agency before, she hadn't picked up on how unfamiliar Vince's team was with the advertising process. Like many, they feigned more knowledge than they actually had during their presentation.

The phone rang and Annie again picked up and passed the call through to her.

"It's Luca Alessandri from Allegro."

Jada was so nervous she could barely speak. She didn't know why she was so keyed up. She had expected the call, and there was no way that Annie would suspect anything out of the ordinary.

"Thanks, Annie."

"Luca?"

"*Amore mio.* You made it to the office. Are you okay?"

"I'm exhausted but I'm hanging in there. It's going to be a long day." Jada was trying to talk softly. She didn't want Annie to overhear her conversation, but she did not want to close her door and cause Annie to wonder why she was having a closed-door conversation with a potential client. "How are you?"

"The same. I have a busy day, so that will keep me from remembering how sleepy I am. Tonight, I think I'll go to bed very early. Thank God I don't have any business meetings tonight."

"You're lucky! I'm supposed to be meeting up with my friends tonight."

"Oh, no, *amore!* Can't you cancel? You need to get some sleep."

"No, we never cancel on each other, no matter what. I won't hang out too long, and maybe I'll get my second wind."

"I hope so."

"What kinds of things do you have to do today?"

"Well, we're trying to decide on where our office will be located. We've been working with an agency here for several months, and now we've narrowed it down to a few options. One is not far from your office, one is in the South End and the other is in the Back Bay. That is sort of in order of price from low to high. So much of it depends on the message that the location sends about your company, doesn't it? Based on what you know, where would you locate the office?"

"The South End."

"That was a pretty quick answer."

"Well, for me the South End says international, creative, cutting edge, boutique. I associate all of those things with Allegro. Downtown, where my office is, also has an area that is a little like that, but it doesn't feel like the right place for a company like yours. And the Back Bay is very exclusive, which you may want, but it's certainly not cutting edge or creative. Instead, it's pretty traditional and even snobbish. Aren't you sorry you asked?"

"No, it's interesting you feel that way; I have had many of those same impressions. So have Fiorella and Hugh. We'll see. There are some other factors that we have to consider—like the square feet available in each location—but if I can work things out, we will indeed be in the South End. What do you have on your schedule today?"

"Well, I have to visit a potential client who called me this morning to tell me that he was going to choose another agency."

"Oh, I am sorry. Why would he do that?"

"Well, he decided he was going to pick another agency because we are too creative and basically he wants someone to tell them what to do. He felt we offered the potential for too much choice."

"That is a really strange perspective. I think that choice is good. I would hate for an agency, to give me one idea and tell me that I must do it."

"You know, I think this client would actually hate it, too. But they've never worked with an agency, so this meeting is my last-ditch effort to win them over."

"You'll do it."

"Thanks for your vote of confidence."

"Jada . . . I know that I am not exactly objective, but your presentation was fantastic. You sell your agency hard, but you also listen and you're good at addressing concerns. If he's given you the opportunity to talk to him again, you'll get the business. I would put money on it."

"Do you want to be my agent?"

"Any time. But right now, I must go, Jada. We will talk again soon, all right?"

"Okay. Luca?"

"Yes?"

"Thank you. My day was off to a rotten start. You've turned it around."

"I'm glad. *Ciao, amore mio.*"

"*Ciao.*" Annie came to the door just as she was hanging up. She heard Jada say goodbye to Luca in Italian and looked at her curiously, but didn't make any comment.

"What's up?" Jada tried to act as cool as possible.

"I'm going to the coffee shop. Do you want anything?"

"Can you get me a cappuccino?" Jada cringed as soon as she'd asked for an Italian breakfast coffee. She always drank them, but it made her feel as if she was fixated on all things—and people—Italian.

Annie took it all in stride and stored it in her memory bank for later reflection.

"Sure. You can pay me when I get back."

CHAPTER 7

"Papà?"

"Luca! *Come stai?* How is everything going?"

"Everything is fine, Papà. We've got a lot going on at the moment, but it is all going well. We'll have a decision on a location soon, and I'm meeting with attorneys and accountants and interviewing potential support staff for the office."

"That's fantastic. It seems that things are staying on schedule."

"They are, and they will continue to stay on schedule if I can help it."

"So tell me, did you meet the beautiful Jada for dinner?"

"I met her last night, yes; we had drinks."

"*Allore?* What was your evening like?"

"We had a wonderful time. I really enjoyed getting to know her a little better. She is witty and smart, ambitious and creative. She's a lot like me."

Lorenzo couldn't help laughing. "Is that so?"

"We talked for hours at the bar. We kissed. We talked some more after she went home last night. I just talked to her again a little while ago."

Lorenzo was happy to hear his son sound so animated. "Tell me, son, with all this talking on the phone, when did you actually sleep?"

"Sleep?"

"Ah, I thought so."

"I walked back to my hotel hoping the air would make me tired, but it just made me more energized. I'll sleep later. I don't have any plans tonight, so I will catch up then."

"Luca, now I'm talking as your father. Take care of yourself. Should I remind you that you're not some young man in his twenties anymore?"

"I will be okay, Papà. Last night was special, an exceptional circumstance. I'm not going to make a habit of it, believe me. I've got too much I need to get done."

"You're certainly your own man, but every now and then we need someone to put us back in line. Isn't today the day you decide on the agencies that will pitch to you?"

"Yes, and I've made my choices. We'll see if Hugh and Fiorella agree. We're meeting later on today to talk about it."

"Even if they don't . . ."

"I know. I'm the president. Still, I want to hear the opinion of my team. That's what I pay them for."

"True. So did Jada's agency make your list?"

"Yes, absolutely. Her agency is really a very good one. But the truth is if things continue as they are between Jada and me, I don't think I can hire them. It would be an impossible situation for her, even if she weren't in charge of the account. I know her boss has put a lot of pressure on her to land our business, and I don't want to be the cause of problems for her. She has already warned me that, because of all this, she's not sure there's any future for us no matter what I do. I really don't know which option would make things worse."

"Hmmm. That *is* a problem."

"Yes, but over the next several weeks the agencies will all be working on their pitches. At Honoraria, most of the work of pulling it together is done by the creative team, based on strategic guidance from Jada. Then she will lead the pitch presentation and do the introduction and the wrap-up."

Bit by bit, Lorenzo's understanding of Jada Green was becoming more clear. He had already received an initial report about her from his high-priced but thorough detective agency. It was amazing how much one could learn about someone in a matter of hours with just a phone call; all that was required was money and the right sources.

Lorenzo enjoyed learning as much as possible about friends and foes alike. It was a little bit of a hobby, and one that drove his wife, Olivia, crazy. Lorenzo had been suspicious about Jada's motives, but from what he had learned, it was clear this woman was not after Luca for his money; in fact, she hadn't been after him at all. Turns out it had been Luca who had made initial contact with Honoraria, and Jada's assignment to the business had been completely random. Destiny. Lorenzo believed in it. If Luca had read things right, Jada had fallen for Luca just as he had for her. Lorenzo liked that she took her job seriously. She was black, and he was still coming to terms with how he felt about *that*. But, more than anything,

Lorenzo wanted to see his son happy. He had some good friends and connections in the Boston area through professional organizations. It was one of the reasons Boston had ranked high on their list when they decided to branch out to the States. Maybe he could make something happen.

"Papà? You keep going quiet on me . . ."

"Sorry, Luca. I was just thinking . . . I have to go now. Something has come up."

"What is it? Can I help?"

"No, son, I need to handle this myself . . . *A presto.*"

"Yes, I'll talk to you later, Papà."

CHAPTER 8

Jada was so tired she didn't know how long she'd be able to last. Still, she hadn't for a moment considered cancelling her monthly get-together with the girls; it was sacrosanct. They were all there when she arrived: her best friend, Renie; Carmen, a lawyer who was a relatively new friend; Liz, whom she'd met in college; and India, whom she'd known almost as long as Renie. They were all single, all relatively successful and only one of them—Liz—had ever been married. Jada thought about the last forty-eight hours and didn't know how to explain it to her friends. She wasn't even sure she wanted to give Renie an update. The connection she'd made with Luca was intense. She just wasn't sure she was ready to share it with anyone. But a part of her felt as if she was betraying their sisterhood; they had often talked about finding a man with whom things just clicked as they had with Luca. Another wasn't sure if her friends would be truly happy for her, and she felt guilty for even feeling that way. Moreover, she didn't know how things would end up with Luca. Jada finally decided that it would be best to keep her mouth shut about this development in her personal life.

They were, as always, at Oscar's, one of their favorite places: prices reasonable, drinks delicious, service excellent. They got their first round and settled in for an evening of catching up. Many a month Jada had lived for these get-togethers. Her friends had kept her grounded, had kept her sane, often helping her to hold on when she doubted whether she could survive swimming with the sharks at Honoraria.

"What's up with the St. John suit, Jada?" Liz asked. She managed a boutique and recognized the designer's style immediately.

"Well, I knew it was going to be a rough day, so I thought a power suit might help me through it."

"Did it work?"

"Actually, it was a pretty good day."

"So, what's up, you all?" Renie asked.

"People need to be cool," Carmen said. "I have never had to juggle so many cases at once. I mean, I work in a small practice, but we are hopping with all kinds of criminal and civil cases. I don't even have time to pee some days!"

"Oh, no!" they all exclaimed at once.

"What do you think is going on, Carmen?" Jada asked.

"I don't know. It just seems that with the economy and all, people are going a little bit crazy. It's kind of scary. Some of my clients are just such a mess. It seems like it's something in the air. It wasn't this bad even a year ago."

"Hmmm. Maybe this is the worst of it, and things are going to get better now," Jada said.

Liz shook her head, saying, "I wish I could be so optimistic. If we have twenty customers in a day, I'm ready to do a happy dance. We've had special sales, big discounts; we've tried fidelity programs. People just aren't shopping like the good old days. Right now, people aren't even *looking*."

"What else can you do?" Renie asked.

"Not much. Just ride it out and hope the owner doesn't decide to cut costs by cutting me."

Then everyone became quiet, realizing that they were all fortunate to have pretty great jobs despite the economic crisis.

India, who was a bank VP, said, "Things are looking somewhat better in the banking sector."

"Spoken like a banker," Carmen said wryly.

"No, seriously, money is freeing up. More loans are being made—good ones, not the toxic stuff that fucked us up before. And sales of large hard goods are getting better. People buy big stuff like refrigerators, TVs and cars when they're feeling better about the economy."

"Well, I hope you're right," Jada said.

"What about *you,* Jada?" Renie asked. Jada flashed her a don't-go-there look, which registered right away with Renie.

"Well, we've got a bunch of new business prospects. I'm waiting to get word on a couple of pitches later this week." Jada let it go at that, hoping no one would ask for details.

"What kind of companies?" Renie asked, a smug smile on her face.

Jada sighed. *I'm going to kill her.* "Well, I've got a credit union, a design firm and a restaurant on my docket that could pan out. I met with the restaurant earlier today. They had chosen another agency, but I think I was able to convince them to reconsider. They will make a decision in the next twenty-four hours. The design firm is due to give us a thumbs up or down on whether we'll get to move on to the next round and pitch to them in a day or two. It's a lot of good business, so I hope I get them all."

"Good luck," India said.

"Thanks, India," Jada mumbled, hoping they would move on, but at the same time wondering what Luca was doing right then.

"Don't be mad at me, girlfriend," Renie whispered. "We're all your friends. You should say something. Everyone will be happy for you!"

"What are you two whispering about?" Liz asked.

"Nothing important," Renie answered.

Jada loved that about her old friend; she would never blurt out her news. Renie respected the fact that it was Jada's story to tell. Now she had a choice: she could just nod in agreement that they weren't discussing anything important or she could 'fess up.

"Ummm. I sort of went on a date the other day."

"What? And you didn't say anything until now? What's wrong with you, girl? You know that we live for hearing one of us say, 'I went on a date.' Spill the beans!" Liz said.

"Well, I . . ."

"Details! Who is he? Where'd you meet him? Are you going to see him again? We want to hear it all!" Carmen chimed in.

Jada really *did* want to share her excitement, so their enthusiasm and curiosity helped her get over her earlier reluctance.

"His name is Luca Alessandri . . ."

"Luca Alessandri . . . What is he, Italian or something?" Carmen asked.

"Yeah, he is. Luca is from Torino, or Turin. He's over here because the company he owns is setting up a US office. It's kind of weird because I met him when he came in for an agency overview presentation. I broke my cardinal rule by going out with him in the first place, and since we're going to pitch to his company, I can't go out with him again, anyway. I told him we can talk on the phone."

"That's too bad. I mean, he must be pretty special for you to have gone out with him in the first place." Liz felt genuinely sorry that her friend had gone on what she would call a hopeless date.

"Yeah. It *is* too bad. I don't know what happened when I met him. It was kind of like one of those lightning bolts you hear people talk about; it was kind of nice." Jada smiled.

"Well, I can understand why you don't want to date him right now, anyway," India said. "It sounds like you feel guilty you told him you'd be willing to talk to him on the phone. You shouldn't. There's nothing wrong with continuing to talk to him! I mean, if you had that kind of a connection, why can't you at least develop a friendship? Keep talking to him. Life takes funny twists and turns; you never know what can happen in the future."

Jada considered what India was saying. Maybe she was right; she really did need to lighten up a little. There was nothing wrong with building a friendship with Luca. Lots of account people ended up becoming good friends with their clients. That was not so unusual . . .

"I can't believe you'd even consider that!" Carmen exclaimed, her indignant voice interrupting her reverie.

"Why not?" Renie asked. "What's wrong with keeping her options open?"

Carmen could sense that no one else saw the situation as she did, so she became defiant. "It's such a cliché: rich white foreign guy comes over here to do some business. He's looking for fun and 'an American experience' so he tries to pick up the pretty single sister he meets while he's doing his job. The man probably has a wife and six kids at home, and you'll never be the wiser. No, the best thing to do is *stay away.*"

"Carmen!" India scolded her friend. "That's kind of cold. Give Jada a little credit for her ability to judge the man's character."

"Luca isn't like that. He laid it all out there for me. He's been divorced for the last ten years . . ."

"How do you *know*? Really?" Carmen asked, refusing to back down.

"You could Google him. Did you Google him yet?" India asked.

Jada didn't know how to answer. She had believed what he'd told her, but he *could* have been lying. "No, I didn't even think of Googling him. But why would he lie?"

"Jada, I know it's been a while, but he'd lie to you to get you in bed!"

Jada didn't want to believe Carmen, but what she said made some sense. Nevertheless, she felt compelled to defend Luca's honor.

"Carmen, for heaven's sake, we didn't sleep together; there was no question that we would. He told me that he wanted to, but he was a perfect gentleman."

"I rest my case," Carmen said with finality.

"Rest your case for what? What man's ultimate goal *isn't* to get a woman in bed? I give him points for not trying to hide it," Liz retorted. "Jada, here's my advice: be friendly with the man if you like him and see what happens. Life is too short."

India added, "Yeah. If he's nice to you and you like him, don't compromise your professional ethics, but don't give him the cold shoulder, either. I know you are sensitive about being Miss Perfect in that job of yours, and you *do* have to be careful not to do anything stupid. But I know you: you won't. Even if he picks your agency and you guys start dating, I'd bet $100 that no one at the agency would ever know it because you're that much of a professional. He sounds like a nice guy, and I think even though you don't go out much, you've dated enough turkeys in your lifetime to know when you're dealing with the real thing. You need to trust your intuition. Give things a chance to evolve. Evolution is a good thing, girl!"

Jada nodded silently, taking in what everyone had said. She was sorry she'd brought it up in the first place. Why had she listened to Renie? She was dead tired, her head was spinning, and the evening seemed to go from being one about fun and laughter to being a group project on her social life.

It wasn't long before the group decided to leave. Carmen resorted to sulking quietly at the corner of the table when no one agreed with her cautionary advice. The others all seemed lost in their own thoughts of how nice it would be to have a "problem" like Jada's to deal with. As for Jada, she was happy that the day was officially coming to an end. She couldn't drive home fast enough and, within minutes of getting in bed, she was sound asleep. Luca, Honoraria and all the other problems of the world would have to wait.

CHAPTER 9

It was D-Day, Friday, April 16. The pitch to Allegro was scheduled for late afternoon. Jada had not seen Luca in the few weeks since he had formally advised her that Honoraria was in the running. He continued to try to convince her to meet him for drinks, a movie, anything, but she steadfastly refused all his invitations, so they continued to talk to each other on the phone. They had talked every night—about what happened during the day, about their dreams and their fears.

"Luca, may I ask you a question?"

"Of course. Ask me anything. I will always tell you the truth."

"Okay, what scares you most?"

"Failure. I don't like making mistakes and feeling that I've done everything wrong. I learn from my mistakes, but I don't like making them. What about you?"

"I'm the same; failure scares me, too. Maybe that's why I work so hard to make sure it doesn't happen. Whether it's work or fun, I like to be successful."

"And what about relationships? Do you feel you've failed because you're single? Does it bother you that you don't have children?"

Jada considered her answer. "I think I've decided to measure personal happiness in a different way. It's possible to be happy and to be alone, even if you want to have a relationship. There are a lot of miserable people who are part of a couple."

"That's certainly true," Luca said.

"And children . . . It's not that I wouldn't like to have a child, but I wanted to have a husband first. So it's useless to regret the second step if you've not done the first." Jada paused. "Since you said I can ask you anything, I was curious . . . how did you meet your ex-wife?"

"We met at university. She was studying business and I was an architecture and design student, but I decided to take business courses, too. There weren't many girls in the class, and it was hard not to notice her."

"Is she very attractive?"

"Yes, she is quite beautiful. After university she worked for a short time as a model."

"Did you have a lot in common?"

"It seemed like we did. On the surface, we were a lot alike. Both of us were from Torino, though my family and hers weren't friendly; we were both only children, and we had many of the same interests. Everyone was very excited when we started dating. She was my first serious girlfriend."

"Really?"

"Does that surprise you?"

"Yes, sort of."

"Why?"

"Well, in case you didn't notice, Luca, you're a pretty attractive guy. I'm sure there were women chasing after you all the time."

Luca laughed softly. "There were at times, but I've never been a man to fall that easily for a woman. I'm actually pretty cautious."

"How long did you date each other before you got married?"

"A long time. Six years."

"Six years? I guess you really *are* cautious!"

"I don't know . . . at some point during that time, being with her just became part of the routine. We were an attractive couple. We traveled together. I started working with my father, and after she decided to stop modeling she started working in her family's business, too. They own a chain of gift shops in Torino and in Milan. Everyone kept asking us when we were going to get married, and it occurred to me that I was supposed to ask. So I did. I never really stopped to think about why I had been content to have us go on as we had for so long. That's how I know now that I was never in love with her. I couldn't have been. If you're really in love, it is unacceptable to stay in limbo as we had been." Luca wanted to tell her that's why he knew that he was falling in love with her, because he was anxious for their relationship to move to the next phase, but he remained silent. He had promised not to pressure her . . .

"So is that why you got divorced? Because your relationship was in limbo?"

Luca thought about the question before he answered. "I think that I divorced Mirella because I was finally able to admit that we shouldn't have married in the first place.

Being good at keeping up appearances for family and friends isn't the same as having a good marriage. We were fantastic actors for a long, long time. But when the two of us were alone, we really didn't have very much to say to one another. I made up excuses not to be around her. Can you imagine? I used to look at my parents some-times—they are always laughing, talking, touching. They cannot help it. They are just so in tune with one another. Mirella and I never had that. I never longed to kiss her or to hold her hand. When I was away on business, I didn't think about how nice it would be to make love to her when I got home. I finally realized the reason why: there was no real love there to sustain us. I fought it for a while. I was very ashamed that things had gone on for as long as they had and that it had taken me so long to actually do something.

"Mirella and I hurt each other a lot. It was my parents who persuaded me to find the courage to ask for a divorce, and it was one of the best things I've ever done for myself. I made so many mistakes, throwing myself into work and conveniently ignoring Mirella's needs, hearing but refusing to listen. There's no doubt my marriage has been my biggest failure in life, but I hope I came out of it a better man." He was silent for a moment as he chased away regrets. "And what about you? You told me you wanted a husband, but did you ever come close to marriage?"

"No. Some time ago, there was a man I was pretty serious about, but it never got that far. No one has ever even asked."

"I find that amazing. You are such an incredible woman! I'm not complaining, though, because I've managed to meet you now and I wouldn't have otherwise."

"You're very nice."

"I'm not trying to be nice. I'm being honest."

Luca had returned to Italy for almost a week, but he still called her every day during the wee hours of the morning in Italy just so that they could maintain their schedule.

"Isn't it really late there? Why are you calling me now?"

"I *need* to talk to you, Jada. It helps me to get through the day. Besides, I don't want you to get out of the habit of talking to me. This pitch has meant the only contact I can have with you is over the phone, so I'm going to make sure that I talk with you as much as possible every day. It's important to me."

Jada had to admit it: she had grown accustomed to their daily chats. In fact, she needed to talk to him, too. Without her really realizing it, Luca had become a part of her life—an important part. She didn't know how it happened, but she was falling in love.

They had talked about what Honoraria winning the pitch might mean for them.

"Jada, we're getting near the time that we have a decision to make. It is clear to me that I want to have a relationship with you. I think we have to find some way to make this work. I can't go a day without talking with you, and we cannot build a relationship by just talking on the phone. My question is: do you want to pursue this? Am

I wrong to think that we could have some kind of future together?"

Jada's response was solemn. "No, you're not wrong. I want us to have a future together, too."

"Then what can we do?"

"If you choose Honoraria, I'll have to hand your account over to a colleague. I don't see any other way. No feather in my cap for bringing in new business; no big bonus. I won't be able to have it all."

"Jada . . . I'm sorry."

"It's not your fault. Getting to spend more time with you will be worth it."

"I'm glad you feel that way. Well, I'm going to continue to think about other alternatives. Maybe there's another solution. I'll talk to you later, *amore mio*."

"Bye, Luca."

Allegro was due in the office in thirty minutes. Jada was in her office going through the presentation when Annie stuck her head in the door. She found that practicing a presentation as often as possible helped to keep the jitters away.

"What's up?" Jada asked, mildly irritated that she'd been interrupted.

"Gene wants to see you."

"Can't it wait until *after* the pitch? Why does it have to be now?"

"Says it's urgent."

Jada took a deep breath and made her way to her boss' office. *Ugh. Just what I need before this pitch—a whiff of that awful cologne.* Jada stood by the door.

"Gene, Annie said it's urgent . . ."

"Yeah, uh, come in for a minute. Well, there's not a subtle way of saying this, so I'll just fire away: We're withdrawing from the pitch for the Allegro business."

"What? Gene, we're due to present in less than a half hour! What happened?"

"We've got a bigger account that's come in— Burrows, the big commercial design house. They want us *without* a pitch, and they're willing to pay big to have us. I hate doing this to Allegro at the last minute, but this is just too large a piece of business to turn down. But, Jada, this is still good news for you."

"How do you figure that, Gene?"

"Burrows wants you on the team, overseeing the account services. They said that the word on the street is you're one of the best, and they want the best on their team." He looked somewhat awed that an account like Burrows would even know her name.

"Wow, that's . . . great. I don't know what to say."

"It's a great opportunity for you and a big coup for Honoraria."

"So does Allegro know what's happened?"

"How could they? You're their key contact."

"Right. So they're coming here for a pitch, and I have to tell them that for reasons I wasn't aware of until thirty minutes before the scheduled start of the pitch we're withdrawing. Talk about the eleventh hour! Gene, why wasn't I at least given a heads-up on this? "

Gene looked down at the floor and cleared his throat. "We, ah, probably should have given you a heads-up, but we weren't sure it was all going to come together; when it did, it happened pretty quickly."

Jada waited for the magic words—*I'm sorry*—but it was clear that she had received as much of an apology as she was going to get.

"Maybe they're just leaving the Ritz now . . . Let me try and get Luca on the phone."

"Great work, Jada," Gene said. He wasn't sure what for, but it seemed like the right thing to say.

"Thanks," Jada said, only because her mother had told her it was polite to say 'thank you' when given a compliment.

Luca saw Jada's number on his telephone and smiled. He was in a taxi with Fiorella and Hugh, so he assumed a casual tone.

"Hi, Jada. Is everything okay? We're almost there."

"Luca, something has come up. Can I see you in my office when you get here?"

"Of course. Is there a problem?"

"I'll explain when you get here," she replied, her voice sounding strange.

Something was definitely wrong, Luca thought, now worried for Jada. Unable to imagine what was going on, he stopped the taxi and told Hugh and Fiorella to go back to the Ritz. He then continued on to Honoraria on his own. He was afraid that someone had seen them together on their one fateful date and Jada's position at the agency had been compromised. Or maybe someone had found out about their phone friendship and misconstrued what was going on. But who? His head was pounding by the time he got to Honoraria. Annie had been alerted that he was on the way and was to see Jada immediately upon his arrival. She brought him straight into Jada's office. He closed the door.

"Jada, are you okay? What's going on?" He was excited to be in her presence again and wanted to touch her, but he kept his distance.

"Honoraria is withdrawing from the pitch."

"What?"

"Luca, I'm sorry. I just found out myself. I don't know what really happened, but the upshot is that we got an offer of bigger business in the same category as yours—an offer too good to refuse."

"Out of the blue? That seems so strange."

"Even more strange . . . the account we got has insisted that I lead the account relations team."

"Really? May I ask what's the account?"

"Sure. It's Burrows. They're a direct competitor of yours."

Luca froze. It was all a little too tidy. He knew only one person who could pull this off . . . his father, Lorenzo.

"Well, that's great news. I'm happy for you, Jada." The need to restrain himself having instantly vanished, Luca drew her into his arms, transmitting all that he was feeling and breathing in the faint scent of her perfume. He felt a great sense of relief that their budding romance hadn't put her reputation at risk.

"Luca?"

"Yes, *amore mio.*"

"Gene wanted to meet you."

"I'll meet him on one condition."

"What is it?"

"Well, Signorina Green, there is a silver lining, as you say, in this situation: I am no longer your client; you are no longer my potential account person. We are free. It's Friday, so I want you to leave the office right after we see Gene, go home and put on something beautiful and let me take you to dinner to celebrate your new account. You don't have any excuse now."

"Okay!" Jada said happily.

"Oh? Really? Good. I had expected some kind of resistance. I'm very happy."

"No, I'm not going to fight this anymore, Luca," Jada said. "I feel so connected to you just from talking on the phone. But dating you and dealing with issues that might come up because we're an interracial *and* international couple is very different from having nice conversations every night. I want to see if we've really got what it takes to be a couple. So I'm happy, too." She looked up and kissed him, which surprised Luca, but he couldn't have been more pleased. After more than a month of phone calls, he was finally going to have a relationship with Jada without any restrictions.

"We'd better go now," Jada said, reluctantly leaving his embrace. "It would be very easy for me to lose track of time with you, and people will start wondering what we're doing in here."

Annie watched them closely as they walked out of Jada's office. She'd had a strong feeling that something was going on between them, her first hint having been the way Luca had walked into her office and closed the door. The familiarity of the gesture had signaled a connection beyond that of potential client and account executive. Their faces were flushed, and in spite of the sudden turn of events, they looked relieved, content—not upset. In fact, they were smiling, and their faces told her more than they might have imagined. *I would not have put them together, but they make a lot of sense as a couple. Luca Alessandri is stunningly handsome, polite, and it doesn't hurt that he's incredibly rich, too. She could do a whole lot worse.*

"Come in, please have a seat," Gene said and gestured toward the le Corbusier-style black leather sofa in the corner of his office. The view of Boston Commons was spectacular from there and, when all else failed, a great view worked wonders. He sat opposite them in a firm, but comfortable, leather chair.

Gene laid on the charm thicker than usual with Luca. After all, it wasn't every day that a reputable agency like Honoraria dropped one potential client for another just before a pitch. Luca, in turn, played his role as the ditched client to the hilt and ate up all the platitudes.

"It is wonderful to finally meet you, Mr. Alessandri."

"Please, call me Luca."

"Okay, Luca. You have a really impressive business. I'm sure you'll have a lot of success here in the US."

Luca smiled warmly. "Thank you, Gene. We're certainly hoping for great success, and I'm sure Boston is the right place for us to establish our headquarters. I must tell you, I am very impressed with your agency. Jada gave one of the most engaging and thorough agency overviews I've ever sat in on. It doesn't surprise me to hear that Burrows asked for her specifically. You should give her a promotion *and* a raise."

Gene looked at Jada and shifted uncomfortably in his chair. Initially he was a little angry with her for having mentioned that she would head the Burrows team, but then he realized that Luca may have asked her and that it was probably best to give him all the details rather than having him find things out piecemeal.

"Well, we're glad to have her at Honoraria; Jada is one of the best. Again, please accept my apologies for having let things go down to the eleventh hour. It is not the way we like to operate. But this was an exceptional circumstance and an incredible business opportunity, and I don't think either of us would want a situation where we were working on two competing businesses."

"Certainly not. I do understand the difficulty of the situation for Honoraria, and you are right: It would have been unacceptable for us to share you with Burrows. I'll follow up with Jada to get her point of view on what we might expect from the other agencies on our list."

"Good idea . . ."

Luca rose and extended his hand. "Gene, it was nice to meet you. I have some plans that I need to make since this presentation was cancelled, so I must go." Jada looked away because she could feel Luca's eyes looking in her direction.

Shaking Luca's hand warmly, Gene said, "I appreciate your stopping by, and I hope there are no hard feelings. Glad to meet you, too,"

"No hard feelings whatsoever. I hope we can do business in the future."

"I'll walk you to the elevator," Jada said, her tone businesslike.

On the way, Luca whispered, "I want to pick you up later on."

"No, it's coming out of town to go back in. It doesn't make sense. I'll meet you."

"Well, meet me at the Ritz. We're going to go to the restaurant together and leave together. We have no reason to hide."

"Okay. I'll meet you there. What time?"

"Come as soon as you can, *amore mio*."

Jada squeezed his hand. "See you soon."

On his way back to the Ritz, Luca called Hugh and Fiorella and filled them in on what had happened. "So it's good news for you: you're both free for the weekend. We'll have the rest of our pitches next week as planned. Have fun."

He didn't want to see them or speak to them for the entire weekend. This was the moment he'd been waiting for with Jada, and he wasn't going to blow it. There would be no distractions. He stopped at the concierge to get suggestions for dinner, but passed on all of them and decided to make other plans. But first, he had one other thing he had to do. Back in his room, he dialed the familiar numbers.

"Papà."

"Okay. By now, I know you know. I had to do it, Luca . . . I was trying to be helpful. Ambrose Burrows and I have been friendly competitors for years, and I happened to know that he was looking for a new agency—a big one like Honoraria. You did the research; we know there are several agencies in Boston that can handle our campaign; that's why we decided to meet with so many before deciding who would pitch to us. Please don't be too angry."

"Papà, your meddling has reached epic proportions now! How will I explain this to Jada?"

"Luca, business contacts recommend good people to work on accounts all the time. All Jada has done is be good at her job. I'm not even sure how I feel about your interest in her; I don't know why you decided to pursue a black woman, but I care enough about you to want you to be able to find out if she is really everything you seem to think she is. No one loses here; if things don't work out between the two of you, at least she's got a big, new account out of it. There's not much else I can say."

Luca pressed his fingers to his temples. He had conflicted feelings about the whole mess, but there was not much to be done about it now. He would just have to be honest with Jada and see what happened next.

"Papà, Jada is a wonderful woman; one day you will agree. You frustrate me to no end when you interfere like this, and I should be furious now, but in your own twisted way, I know you were trying to help. Thank you, Papà."

With that reaction, Lorenzo knew things with Jada were becoming more serious than even he had imagined. That was the only explanation for Luca *thanking* him for meddling not only in Allegro's affairs but in his personal relationship; he had blasted him for less in the past. How *did* he feel about the prospect of a black daughter-in-law and, quite possibly, no grandchildren? He wasn't really sure. At least on paper, Jada was everything he and Olivia would want in a wife for their treasured son; except that she was older than they'd like and the wrong color. What was it about her that made Luca fall so head over heels, anyway? He had no clue. Regardless, she was a refreshing change from some of his most recent girlfriends with their bottle-blonde hair and overly generous implants. Indeed, Luca seemed to date them only because they got him—and more specifically, Allegro—a lot of attention when they were on his arm. Olivia had found one more distasteful than the next, and eventually Luca took pains to limit any interaction between his parents and the women he dated. Clearly, he was not the least bit serious about of them. But Luca talked about Jada with the expectation that they had a future. He wanted them to meet her, which drove Olivia to look through the dossier. The investigation thing was Lorenzo's obsession, not hers, but since he had the dossier, she read it painstakingly. Olivia was impressed, and that carried a lot of weight with Lorenzo.

"Papà! You're doing it again."

"Sorry. Sorry, Luca. I was just—"

"I know, you were just thinking . . ."

"Yes. So what will you do now?"

"I've invited Jada to dinner tonight."

"Ah." Lorenzo laughed. His son must think men lost common sense with age. Luca was going to begin his seduction offensive in earnest now. If he knew his son, his courtship of Jada was about to go into overdrive, and he wouldn't be surprised to be meeting Jada Green in Torino very soon. "Well, son, have a wonderful evening."

"I'll call you this weekend and we can talk some more."

"Well, just in case you don't get the chance to call, have a good weekend. You deserve it."

CHAPTER 10

Jada handed her car keys to the valet and headed for the lobby. Readying herself for her date had taken longer than she'd expected. Everything she tried on seemed to make her look fat, and her red dress looked too vampy, the yellow one, too girlish. In the end, she wore her navy blue wrap dress—plain, but it hit her curves in all the right places. She wore her favorite drop earrings, but left her neck bare. Feeling really nervous, Jada called Luca's room from the house phone.

"Can you come up to my suite? Number 4250?"

Jada hesitated a moment and then said, "Sure."

Luca opened the door with a big smile as soon as he heard her knock, exclaiming, "Welcome!"

"Thanks . . . What's this?" Jada asked, glancing around the living area of his suite. It had been transformed into a restaurant for two, complete with a spectacular view of Boston Commons, the Public Garden and the city. The lights in the suite were romantically dimmed and candlelight gave it a warm glow. She walked further into the room. In the center, there was a small, draped table for two with a centerpiece of delicate fuchsia French tulips. Off to the side was a bar trolley with a bottle of champagne on ice and two fine crystal flutes. And at the far end, nearest the small hallway that led to

the other room, there was an inviting sofa, perfectly positioned to enjoy the twinkling city lights from the comfort
of the suite. Jada took it all in; it was truly breathtaking.

"I considered several restaurants but decided we
didn't need any distractions. We can order what we like
and take as long as we like without interruptions. Jada,
just to be clear, I don't want to hide what's going on
between us, but I really do want us to have the chance to
spend some time together without having waiters, colleagues, or anyone else bothering us. We had to wait long
enough for this date. I hope you don't mind waiting a
while longer before we go public."

Jada noted the closed bedroom door. She wasn't
naïve; she knew there was a strong possibility that they
would end up there before the night ended, even if they
had gone out to dinner. But considering the lengths he'd
gone to make his suite feel like a private dining room, it
seemed unlikely he had set this up to ensure a shortcut to
his bed.

"Thanks for saying that, Luca. No, this is great," she
said, smiling. "I've never had an elegant dinner in a suite
at the Ritz."

"Please forgive me; I was so excited to see you I forgot
to tell you as soon as you walked in the door . . . you look
beautiful." Now that they were completely alone, Luca
felt strangely shy; he was nervous, too. If things went
wrong now, he'd have no one to blame but himself. And
he did not want to blow it.

"Thank you." Jada felt a little self-conscious as he
stood wordlessly staring at her. But then she caught him-

self and walked over to the bar trolley, opening the bottle with an animated "pop."

He kissed her lightly and said, "Here, have some champagne."

"Thanks. Cheers." They touched glasses.

"To your new account."

"Thank you!"

Looking uncertain, Luca cleared his throat and said, "Jada . . . I have a confession to make."

Oh, no. Here it comes. He's going to say something like "I'm not really divorced" or "I've decided this really isn't for me." That's what usually happens when I start to imagine possibilities. Jada braced herself for bad news, the look on her face mirroring her thoughts.

Sensing her concern, Luca said, "Jada, it is not what you might think. I have been completely honest with you about everything, and I always will be. What it is, is my father . . ."

"Your father?"

"Yes. I had told him about our dilemma—what might happen if Honoraria won our business . . . or lost it. *On his own*—I did not know—he talked to Ambrose Burrows, who is a friend of his, and suggested that he take his business to Honoraria, which would almost certainly force you to pull out of the pitch for our business."

"You're kidding!"

"No, I'm not kidding. Jada, I didn't know. I began to suspect only after you told me that, out of the blue, Burrows was moving its business to Honoraria without a pitch and had specifically asked for you to be on the business. My father sometimes meddles in things. It was all too tidy, so I just suspected that he was somehow involved. When I called him after I left you, he admitted he had done it."

"Wow! Why would he do that?"

"He knew I was worried for you and he wanted to help . . ."

My goodness, what did he say to his father about me? "Your father doesn't even know me. Why would he do that?" Jada repeated. "People get accounts through personal contacts all the time, but *this* is something different."

"I know it's not the way you want to get new business, but you are above reproach in all this. Believe it or not, he was really trying to be helpful."

Jada looked out the balcony window. She felt uneasy to learn how she had really won the account, but Luca was right; stuff like this happened a lot. Jada might have liked to win the Burrows account strictly on her merit, but now the best thing she could do was take the opportunity and run with it. "So your parents know . . . ?"

Luca put his arms around her waist. "About what's happening between us? Yes, they do."

"Do they know I'm black?"

"Yes."

"What did they say?"

He smoothed her hair. "They wanted to know why I chose you."

"What did you tell them?"

"The truth. We've known each other for a little over a month, but from the moment we met, I've felt connected to you." He laughed. "I really didn't like the idea of only talking on the phone after our first date, but it forced us to talk, and to *listen*. I know what scares you and what fills you with joy. I've learned about your childhood wishes and your grown-up dreams. Do you realize how long it takes many couples to learn those things? It's crazy and it's fast, but I've fallen in love with you. Where your being black fits in, I do not know."

"You're in love with me?"

"That is what I was trying to tell you the other day when I said it's unacceptable to keep a relationship in limbo if you're really in love."

Jada folded her arms protectively. "It's been a long time since I was in a relationship."

"I know."

"But I think I've fallen in love with you, too. Still, I have to admit something, Luca: I'm scared."

"Why, Jada?"

Moving away, Jada shook her head. "There's plenty to be afraid of."

Luca pulled her back into his arms and held her tight. He decided not to probe, already suspecting what some of her concerns were. He hoped his just being there would ease her mind. There was plenty of time to talk.

"I promise it will be okay. Come on, are you hungry? Let's order dinner."

Holding hands and chatting, they enjoyed the spectacular view from Luca's balcony while waiting for their dinner to arrive. In short time the waiter came in, quickly set everything up efficiently and silently and left them alone to enjoy their meal in peace.

Dinner was a superb feast that they savored slowly. They shared an appetizer of pâté with crusty, rustic bread and a leafy green salad, and enjoyed delectable salmon and halibut entrées. Jada decided it was the most romantic evening she had ever spent with a man.

"Luca, this was a fantastic idea. It is so special. Thank you."

"I would do anything to make you happy. Jada, I'm not trying to rush you, really I am not, but please stay with me tonight. I will not lie to you; I want nothing more than to make love to you. We don't have to if you're not ready, but please stay, anyway. Just be with me. At the very least, I can finally hold you until you fall asleep. Of course, I will respect whatever you want to do."

Jada got up and went to the window. Luca followed and gently turned her to face him. "Tell me what you're thinking, Jada."

"Luca, it's been a long time since I've been with anyone."

Luca had known this was one of her fears, and it made him sad that making love scared her so much. "Jada, it doesn't matter; it will be our first time together."

"That's not the same . . ."

"Sure it is. I promise you it will be okay." Still, he was not sure if he should hear out all her anxieties. He didn't want to rush her, didn't want to seem insensitive, but he felt the only way he could prove her fears unfounded was to make love to her. So he took her hand and led her to the bedroom.

Luca opened the door to reveal a space almost as large as the living area. Surprisingly, the room had only a few functional furnishings—all black and accented with chrome—a desk, two cube night tables, two leather chairs, a bed and a sleek desk where Luca's laptop was open and papers stacked as if he had been hard at work until shortly before Jada arrived. The bed was covered with a fluffy white duvet and several oversized down pillows. The lighting, like that in the living room, was mellow and pleasing. Jada turned to Luca and looked at him nervously.

Luca's heart was racing; he wanted her badly. But he realized this first time had to be all about her. And so he proceeded slowly, first helping her out of her slinky dress and then pushing the straps of her bra off her shoulders. He kissed her deeply, letting his tongue explore every corner of her mouth, and feeling her slowly relax. He unhooked her bra, releasing her softly rounded breasts and caressing them, pausing when he was suddenly struck by the stark contrast of his paleness against the richness of her coffee-colored skin. Until that moment, it really hadn't been all that remarkable to him. It was simply another dimension of his love for her, like her beauty, her integrity and her determined spirit.

"You are so beautiful," Luca whispered huskily.

"No, I'm not," Jada quickly disagreed.

"Oh, but you are; believe me, you are," he said, pulling her onto the edge of the bed. "Jada, don't be nervous or afraid; making love is natural. For you, it may seem like you've been sleeping for a while, but you will wake up," he assured her, covering her quivering lips with his own while pushing her back further onto the bed.

He stripped away their remaining garments. Her bare skin felt so amazing against his own that he felt he would be happy just to hold her forever. He kissed her breasts, sucking her nipples to hardened points and then going back to enjoy the taste of her lips. As he worked his way lower, Jada was pliant and trembling, shivering uncontrollably when his tongue touched the essence of her sex. He kissed and explored slowly and lovingly. Her fingers entwined in his hair, she implored him to stay there. When she came she shouted his name, and the force of her release made her spring almost upright for a moment. Still, Luca did not stop. He kissed her inner thighs and languidly worked his way back up to her mouth. Jada tasted herself in his kiss.

"Luca . . ."

He smiled and caressed her face. "Are you waking up yet?" he asked, his face glistening in the dim light.

"Yes, I think so."

"Good. Excellent news," he murmured, kissing her again.

Jada felt him hard against her leg. She bent to kiss him, but he stopped her.

"Jada, I plan to make love with you all night, but if you touch me there right now, it will be all over. I need to be inside you."

"Luca, I feel like a teenager asking this, but do you—"

Immediately understanding what she was trying to ask, he said, "Don't worry, *amore mio;* I have protection for us."

Luca reached for a condom, put it on quickly and entered her as slowly as he could. He felt an unsettling mix of strength and emotion and strained to control himself. He wanted to focus only on her, but scenes from his life—happy and sad; triumphant and despairing—all flashed in his mind. He thought of his marriage and how he had tried and failed to create a loving relationship, or to even really feel love. Now he was here with this woman whom he had known only a little more than a month and he had fallen in love. He could not explain how it had all happened so quickly. Perhaps it was the magic of love, the mystery of destiny. He finally lost control, moving against her faster and faster, shouting her name again and again.

"Look at me, Jada . . ." Jada's eyes closed and opened and finally locked with his. No more words were spoken. They were in perfect synch, and like a flawless symphony, reached their crescendo together.

Luca collapsed by Jada's side. Stillness and silence ensued, and then he kissed her moist neck.

"Are you okay? I hope I didn't hurt you."

"No, I'm fine."

"Tell me, Jada, are you awake now?"

Jada looked over at him and smiled. "Yes, I think so."

"Good."

They remained quiet, each understanding what it meant for them to be lovers. Luca spooned her in his arms and silent contemplation eventually morphed into sleep. After a few hours, Jada finally stirred.

"Where are you going?" Luca whispered, becoming wide awake the moment he felt her move from his side.

"Just to the bathroom."

"Okay. I just wanted to make sure you weren't going to sneak away without saying anything."

"No, I wouldn't do that."

She walked naked to the bathroom, at the far end of the room, turned on the lights and closed the door. She looked in the mirror and scrutinized her body, which somehow looked different to her—softer, slimmer. It was silly, but she felt beautiful, really beautiful for the first time in her life. After finishing whatever she needed to do, she rejoined Luca in bed. He sighed with relief.

"You're sure you're okay?" Lying there without her had made him feel vulnerable and uncertain.

"I'm sure." She kissed him softly and snuggled in his arms.

The kiss was all Luca needed to become completely aroused again.

Without hesitation, Jada proceeded to do what she had started to do the first time they'd made love. She took him gently in her hands, feeling Luca shiver with her touch. She kissed him softly, tentatively, with Luca encouraging her and enjoying every sensation and feeling overjoyed that she wanted to love him this way despite her insecurity about making love. It made his feelings for her even deeper. But he did not want it to end—not yet, so he pulled her up and kissed her hungrily.

"I love you so much," Luca said hoarsely, holding her gaze as he entered her again. This time he was more able to focus exclusively on how happy he was to be with her. Making love had brought them both great pleasure, and her earlier fears about her lack of recent experience had proven unfounded. Taking their time, they studied each others' faces, sometimes stopping almost entirely to savor the intimacy of the moment. When the time came for them to be carried away, they clung to each other tightly, neither wanting to let go.

Jada stared straight ahead, quietly thinking about her love life. It had been so . . . unremarkable. In her forty-five years, she'd had five lovers, and if she were completely honest, sex had never been all that exciting . . . until now. Her last and most serious boyfriend was Ken, a lawyer she'd met through her friend, Carmen. That was ten years ago. They had a healthy sex life, but because their primary concern was making it in the corporate world, it felt like they were on a timer whenever they were together. Eventually they drifted apart; their relationship had fallen victim to their ambitions. She heard from Ken every now and then, most recently when he called to tell her that he was engaged to a thirty-year-old at his law firm.

With Luca, everything seemed different; it all seemed to make sense. It all felt *good*. She had had sensations that she hadn't even known existed. He had emboldened her to touch, talk and respond as never before. It was a little scary. But it was nice.

"What are you thinking about?" he asked, kissing her softly. "You're a million miles away."

"I was thinking about a lot of things, but I want to ask you something."

"What is it?"

"Why me? You told me that you had never dated a black woman, so what was it about me that, well, drew you to me?"

Propping up on a few of the Ritz's extra-fluffy pillows, Luca turned and looked at her. "I knew you might ask me this one day, and I have thought about how I would answer. The truth is, I don't know. I'd met black women before—mostly in business situations. Birmingham, where we have our UK office, is one of the most diverse cities in Europe. But I never dated any of the black women I met. No particular reason that I know of; I just didn't. Perhaps convention kept me from even thinking about it. I don't know. Socially, I've met very few black people; my circle is pretty closed. In my circle of friends, many of us have known each other since we were children, and our parents have known each other since they were children.

"Anyway, I saw you and something just happened. You are so beautiful, who couldn't notice that? But there was so much more. I was captivated by your passion for your work; you had great ideas and it was clear that you had taken the time to really consider our needs even though we were meeting for the first time. I admire your determination and your integrity. I've thought a lot about our conversation when you told me that as a black vice president you have to be extra-careful about who you associate with and what you do. Jada, I will never know what it's like to endure the things you do, but I can appreciate the effort it takes to be successful. Your determination shows through in everything you say and do.

"But that's not all. I love everything about you. I love your color. It looks so extraordinary—even now in the dim light. I love your skin, which feels different to me than any other woman I've been with." He ran his hand along her body outline, from her shoulder to her waist, pushing the covers down to her hips. "I love your shape. You have an amazingly sexy body. I love those things because you are you. And you are black. I cannot separate one from the other . . ."

"I don't know what to say . . ."

"You don't have to say anything; it is simply how it is. What about you? Am I the first Torinese man you've ever dated?" They both laughed.

"I told you. There really haven't been a whole lot of dates. I had a relationship that ended about ten years ago. Since then, there have been a few casual dates, but not much."

"I know I asked you before, but why?"

"Because men don't seem to ask me out. Maybe I scare them away without even trying."

"I can't believe that. I find it hard to imagine that you could scare men away. Are men here blind? How can that be?"

"Well, it's hard to meet men, and when I do, some find what I do intimidating. You say you admire my determination, but that can also be a turnoff. Also, I'm looking for a man with whom I can share my interests.

One of the nicest things you've ever said to me is that you want to go to a dance performance with me so you can experience something that I enjoy. That's really special, and no matter what happens, I will always remember your saying that. I've never been like some of my friends who swear they would never date outside of their race, but no one outside my race has ever asked me out. Maybe I'm too exotic or just too risky. Who knows? I never was a nightclub person and the idea of online dating kind of freaks me out. With all that, I guess I never figured out where to go from there, so I ended up alone."

He was sorry that she had been alone, but then he realized that had she not led as solitary a life, he might not now be with her. "I'm sorry you were alone for so long, *amore mio,* but I'm happy we're together now."

"You know, I never imagined that I'd be forty-five and unmarried. But I've also learned to appreciate the things that I've got. I'm a successful businesswoman and I've been to Asia; I've seen the pyramids in Egypt. I've had experiences no one else in my family has ever had. I'm not some coldhearted woman who feels she doesn't need anyone. I've always wanted to have love, but the right love. I just don't want to sacrifice my soul so that I can say I have a man in my life."

She traced a fingertip along his lips. "I suppose you could ask me 'why you?' and the answer would be like yours. I told my friends that when I met you, it was like the lightning bolt you see in the movies. You left me flustered and a little breathless. The moment I met you, I wanted to know more about you; I thought you were so handsome. And those eyes of yours! It was as if you were looking into my soul. I loved your passion for what you do. You intrigued me, but you scared me a little, too. Then I scolded myself for even allowing myself to believe that you might be interested in me."

"Why wouldn't I be interested in you?"

"Because in my world, men like you don't fall for women like me."

"Well, I did."

"I guess that's because you are exceptional." She smiled.

"Jada, I understand why you asked the question, but I hope that we can just *be*. I don't want to overanalyze what we have. We met, something incredible happened and we fell in love. We may not have planned it, but we are right for each other. I believe that everything doesn't have to make perfect sense, or be logical or unfold the way we think that it should. Sometimes things just happen, and they are magically the way they are supposed to be. That's the way it is with us. Perhaps if we could step outside of ourselves, even we would not have predicted that we would be together. But we just are. It's that simple."

"Hmm. I know you're right," Jada said, moving into his warm embrace. Once again, they were overcome by sleep, but even in sleep, they breathed in and out as one.

They didn't leave the hotel suite the entire weekend. Going to the front door to hang up the "Do Not Disturb" sign was the farthest Luca went. They ordered room service, watched TV, bathed together, lay in bed talking or thinking their own private thoughts. And they made love, never seeming to tire of one another.

Watching Jada sleep peacefully, Luca asked himself, *How will I ever go back to Italy and leave you?* He decided that working out how he would manage that question must be his top priority. The weekend was almost over and he had not called his father. The thought made him laugh.

CHAPTER 11

Fiorella kissed Hugh's shoulder and tried to encourage him to hang up the phone.

"Still no answer," Hugh said softly. "He still has a fucking 'do not disturb' on his hotel phone."

Fiorella loved Hugh, but his romantic-hero looks were in stark contrast to his brash, rough perspective on life. "I told you, he is with a woman. If I had to guess, I would say it's Jada Green, the woman from Honoraria."

"The black woman?"

"Why not? She is beautiful. Did you notice how Luca behaved after he met her?"

"No," he said, smoothing his brown hair back twice, a nervous habit of his when he was thinking things through.

"Really, Hugh! How could you miss it? He was speechless. Did you notice how he spoke to her on the phone yesterday? It sounded like she was his lover, not a business contact. He recognized the phone number before he even answered the phone. Did you wonder why he explicitly told us to take the weekend off, as if to say, 'Don't even call me if someone in your family dies and you have to fly back to Europe'?"

Hugh thought about it, smoothing his hair again. "Yeah, I suppose. I guess he wouldn't want to hear my inside track on this agency then, would he?"

"Monday, Hugh. *Late* Monday. Our first appointment isn't until eleven."

"Okay, darling. I can take a hint . . . If it is this Jada Green, what do you think it means?"

"Maybe that he's found a woman he likes to sleep with . . . Nothing."

Smiling deviously, Hugh twirled a strand of Fiorella's wavy blonde hair. "Now you're not seeing the big picture. When was the last time you knew Luca Alessandri to be away from this business for more than twenty-four hours? When was the last time he spent a weekend locked in a hotel room fucking his brains out?"

"Hugh, your language! Okay. I do see what you mean."

"What if he's serious about her?"

"Hugh, they met no more than a month ago. How serious could they possibly be?"

Hugh scratched his head. "Yeah, I suppose. Still, I can't help thinking about how he answered Jada Green's question 'Why Boston?' He said, 'Because I like it.' I don't want to be crossed. He gave me his word that I'd get to head the US office. If he's involved with someone here, he'll be here all the time or, worse still, he'll decide that *he* wants to run it."

"Then you'll run Europe."

"With the old man breathing down my back? No fucking thank you!"

"Hugh! One day you're going to slip up and swear in front of someone at the wrong moment! For now, I think you should just wait and see. Even if Luca is having a fun weekend, it's probably not serious. Luca has flings."

"You should know, right?"

Fiorella blushed with a combination of anger and embarrassment. "I wish I'd never told you. It was only once, a long time ago—just after he divorced and long before I joined Allegro."

"Sorry. That was not fair. I suppose you're right about waiting to see what happens. I just want my chance to run an office. He'd better not let me down."

Fiorella reached under the sheet and rubbed his thigh. "Can't we concentrate on more interesting things now?"

Hugh smiled. "Fuck, yeah."

CHAPTER 12

"Luca, I have to go."

"Just a little longer."

Jada did not want to leave, but it was 6 a.m. Monday morning, and she knew she needed to go home to shower and change for work.

As much as he wanted to prolong their time together, Luca realized he had business matters to attend to and Jada had to go to her office. They had shared so much, yet there were still so many things to talk about, many things still to discover. He wanted to bring her to Torino. Would she come? When could he meet her parents and friends? What was her favorite color? He wanted to know more about this man from her past who she had mentioned. What was he like? He had no answer for any of the questions popping into his head. For now, he just had to know when they would see each other again.

"What time tonight can we meet?"

"Who said I'm free tonight?"

Luca's heart was in his mouth; this had not been a weekend fling for him. He could feel rising panic. Could it be they wouldn't be able to see each other again soon?

"You're not free?"

Jada giggled. "I'm joking."

"Jada, you scared me. I thought I was going to lose my mind if we couldn't see each other."

"Sorry. It wasn't even a good joke. I'll make sure I'm done by 6:30, no matter what."

"Me, too. What should we do?"

"Do you want to come to my house?"

"I would love that."

"Great. I'll pick you up here at 6:45, okay?"

Luca fixed his deep blue eyes on Jada. "I will be ready. Remember, *amore mio*, I love you. Thank you for this weekend and for loving me."

"I do love you, Luca. I don't know how this all happened, but I'm really happy."

Jada picked up her bag and walked to the door.

"See you soon."

Fiorella walked into the lobby after her morning workout and was ready to conquer the day. Out of the corner of her eye, she saw a woman who looked an awful lot like Jada Green getting into her car. She knew it! She watched the car drive off. Goodness, they had spent the *entire* weekend together! Maybe Hugh *was* right. This might be serious.

CHAPTER 13

Jada didn't have much time to revel in her extraordinary weekend; the real world was calling. She quickly showered and changed into a navy blue suit with a richly colored green-and-blue silk blouse and a longer, tapered jacket.

Monday was the weekly directors' meeting, and by 8:15 Jada was in her office about to review facts and figures about her accounts. She wanted to be well prepared because she was sure that the virtual gift of the Burrows account would raise the professional jealousy to a fever pitch.

Annie had followed her into her office and was giving her the lowdown on what to expect the day to be like. Also, she had pulled together a file containing pertinent information about all of her key accounts.

"Thanks, Annie. Did you have a good weekend?"

"It was good. Both of the boys had playoff games this weekend, so it was all about them. Still, I enjoyed myself. How about you?"

Jada couldn't keep from smiling. "It was great."

"What did you do?"

Jada hadn't planned an answer to the question; social chitchat usually didn't go further than it already had. She had to think fast.

"Oh, I got together with a good friend. We hadn't seen each other in ages, and we got to spend a lot of quality time together this weekend. It was just . . . nice."

Annie looked at Jada. *Now I am 100 percent positive. Jada is involved with someone, and I would bet a hundred dollars it's Luca Alessandri.* She was sure she'd find out the details in due time. But for now, she kept her response simple: "That's nice."

The meeting was going as it usually did: The twelve directors and six VPs took turns reporting on the state of their respective responsibilities, highlighting the triumphs and downplaying the problems. If nothing exciting was happening, it was permissible to pass, but no one was allowed more than ten minutes. The dynamic of the meeting changed from week to week, depending on whether any of the partners showed up. This week two of the five partners were there: Gene, whose presence wasn't a surprise since there had been so much activity on the accounts under his direction, along with Alison Samson, the only female partner.

Including Alison, there were five women in the room: two directors, another VP, Sheila Kent, and Jada. Over the years, Jada and Sheila had been fascinated by the gender difference in the level of preparation for the meeting. It was unusual for any of the women to show up unprepared or without backup notes and specific figures, while most of the men seemed to be much more blasé about it. They noted that where men opted for humor to bridge an awkward moment, women usually promised to provide more detailed follow-up.

"We've got to be more like the boys," Sheila said one day over lunch.

"I know what you mean, but it's easier said than done. Jokes and sports analogies just don't roll that easily off our tongues. Women want to answer everyone's questions and wrap up loose ends."

"That's true, but I'm sick of it. Any of the men walk out of the meeting and that's the end of it. You or I walk out with hours of extra work for us or our team because we attempted to answer someone's obscure question. Let's make a pledge to give each other a high sign if we're on the verge of offering to dig up data for something that no one will care about when we leave the room. Deal?"

"Deal."

From then on, if either of them saw the other twirl their pen, they knew they were on the verge of making work for themselves. It worked so well, they brought the female directors in on it, too. But this meeting was going smoothly. Jada was feeling pretty good that no daggers had been thrown her way. And then:

"Can we talk about the Burrows account?" David Heath asked, pushing his thick glasses up the bridge of his nose.

Uh-oh, here it comes. Jada knew that if anyone were to cause trouble, it would have to be David.

She had to give David his due: there were few who were better at landing accounts than he. He got some accounts through his network of personal contacts, but David also knew what to say to get clients on board, with minimal effort on his part. It was an invaluable skill honed over his years at Honoraria.

But unlike Jada, David had little time or interest in the process of creating advertising. Until now, he had enjoyed the prestige of having the largest value portfolio among the vice presidents; Jada's acquisition of the Burrows account would take that prized distinction away. Undoubtedly her appointment to the Burrows account had put him on a slow burn, and she was sure he wondered how she had done it. If he ever found out how the account *really* came to be hers, his bloated face would surely explode.

"What about it, David? It's a great piece of business and the client requested that Jada manage their client relations," Gene said.

"Why?"

"They requested it, David," Gene repeated sharply.

Oh, my Lord! That almost sounded like a rebuke! When Gene admonished one of his favorite sons, things were really bad.

"Okay, then, what account is Jada giving up?"

"Why should I relinquish an account, David?" Jada jumped in. She hated people talking about her as if she weren't there. All eyes fell on David. His straggly beard served to hide his rather prominent Adam's apple, but Jada could see it moving up and down quickly as he tried to keep his mouth from going dry.

"Well, with all due respect, you're not the most senior VP. The Burrows account alone is worth almost five million, and if you keep it you'll be responsible for more business than anyone else."

"And your point is?" Jada's heart was pounding. *Please, Lord, don't let me lose my cool now!*

"Well, it's not fair."

"Well, David, as a wise person once said, 'The world ain't flat.' You only recently told me that you had four client pitches to my three. None of yours came through and all of mine did. That's not my fault; that's just the way it is. The client *specifically* requested me. My other accounts, I might add, are all happy and thriving. So unless that situation changes, I will not be relinquishing any accounts unless senior management directs me to do so." She finished by looking directly at Gene and Alison.

Alison looked at Gene, waiting for him to say something first, since Jada reported to him. When he remained silent, she said, "I don't see why we would need to move any accounts right now."

Gene shuffled his papers, closed his notebook and stood up. "I think that says it all. Let's go build the business."

Jada hated Gene's wrap-up line, which he said whenever he attended a Monday meeting. It was more than time for a change. His little battle cry sounded more cheesy and lame each time he uttered it. But there was no point fixating on it. More importantly, she was once again leaving a directors' meeting feeling only slightly supported by her boss. That pissed her off. A lot.

Sheila caught up with Jada on her way out of the meeting. "Well done, Jada. I didn't even have to pick up my pen, let alone twirl it. You put an end to *that* discussion."

"Thanks, Sheila. It had to be said." A thought of Luca flashed through her mind and made her smile. Could it possibly be that only a few hours ago she had been lying happily in his arms?

Annie was waiting for her in front of her office. "Jada, you've got to call Katrina right away."

"Is something wrong?"

"That was her question to me."

"Huh?"

"She said that she hadn't been able to reach you all weekend and she's a little worried about you."

Jada nodded knowingly.

"I'll call her right away." She went into her office and dialed Katrina's cell phone.

"Girl, don't do that to me again!" Renie yelled into the phone.

"I'm sorry, Renie. I just spaced out on calling you."

"Where *were* you? I tried you at home all weekend and the phone just rang . . ."

"I—"

"Oh, my goodness! You were with him, weren't you? Luca? I thought you guys were playing it cool until after the pitch and his final decision. I was dying to hear how it all went."

"The pitch was cancelled."

"What? No shit? When? We spoke to each other about an hour before you were going to present your stuff!"

"And half an hour before, Gene called me in and told me we were withdrawing because we'd just won a bigger competitor's business without having to pitch for it."

"Wow! How often does that happen?"

"Hardly ever. What's more, the client—Burrows—asked that I lead the account team."

"No shit! You go, girl! That's fantastic!"

"Apparently, that's Lorenzo."

"Lorenzo? Who's he?"

Jada laughed. "It's a little bit of a story; I'll explain it later. It is good news for me, though."

"And this also means you and Luca are free to be who you want to be. So what happened?"

"Hold on." Jada got up and closed her door. "So, Luca came here and I told him what happened. He took it pretty well. I mean, he had every reason in the world to be furious. I've reviewed what he should expect from the other agencies—"

"Jada, *I don't care!* I want to know what happened between you two."

"Sorry. Okay . . . He invited me to dinner, you know, to celebrate."

"Cool. Where'd you go?"

"The Ritz."

"The Ritz? Nice. Very nice. What's the restaurant like?"

"I don't know."

"What do you mean you don't know? You just said—"

"We ate in his suite."

"Oh. I get it."

"No, you don't get it. It wasn't like that. It was really beautiful. He had the hotel set up a dinner table with candles and flowers in his suite. We had champagne and we ordered off the restaurant menu. He has an amazing view from his balcony. It was just really nice . . ." Jada's thoughts drifted back to how special the evening had been.

"Well, so far, I'm liking this guy. He's got class and style and he's romantic. So I still haven't heard why I didn't get you when I called you at home at 2 a.m., 10 a.m. or 4 p.m. on Saturday or Sunday."

"Let's just say it was a long dinner."

"Jada!"

"I had a wonderful weekend."

"Well, I guess so!"

"He is . . . I really love him."

"Whoa. This is kind of serious, isn't it? So what was it like making love to an Italian guy?"

"He was wonderful. He made me feel so many things—happy, beautiful, treasured, loved."

"Hey, are you okay?"

"Yeah, I'm fine. I guess it all makes me emotional. This all came out of nowhere . . ."

"I know, girl, but you deserve it. You're a wonderful person. You're going to become our new symbol of hope! So when do we get to meet this man? I've got to check him out and give him the Katrina seal of approval!"

"I want you to meet him, too. He's coming over tonight, so we'll talk about it. We've got a lot to talk about . . ."

"Like what?"

"Like the fact that he doesn't live here. Like what this all really means, like—"

"All right, I get it! Well, I understand why you want to talk about some of that stuff, but just remember that the most important thing—always—is what you think of each other. If this guy is anything like you, I know you'll work through all the other stuff."

"You're right. Thanks for saying that."

"You know no matter how much I give you grief, I've got your back. I've got to run. I'm glad nothing was really wrong."

"Thanks, Renie. Talk to you later."

Jada had just a few meetings scheduled for the day, so she spent a good portion of it researching the Burrows business; it was a design firm, almost twice the size of Allegro. She wanted to get a better understanding of what her new client would expect from Honoraria, and she wanted to have concrete recommendations to offer in time for their first meeting.

Later on, she passed some colleagues in the hall and a couple congratulated her on snagging the Burrows account; others just looked on in silent envy. But nothing could bring her down. She was in love.

CHAPTER 14

Jada pulled into an illegal spot in front of the hotel and Luca hopped in. His heart was racing.

"I missed you, *amore mio*," he said, covering her face with kisses. He didn't think he'd get enough of kissing her.

"I missed you, too. How was your day?"

"I'm fine now. It was a stressful day, but I can barely remember what the problems were now. It's so good to see you."

"Let's go."

Jada was pointing out various points of interest along the way, but Luca was scarcely listening; not because he didn't care, but because earlier in the day he'd had a conversation with Hugh that had made him realize that finding a way to be with Jada was going to be more complex than he had thought. Hugh was good at what he did, but he had his weaknesses, too, which were minimized when he worked side by side with Luca. But right now those weaknesses were a problem, and Luca wasn't sure what to do about it. He wanted to talk to his father, but he was pretty sure what his father would say wouldn't be helpful. In a few weeks, he would be back in Italy full time, and he honestly didn't think he could do it if he hadn't worked out a plan for how he and Jada could be together.

"Luca?"

"Huh? Sorry. I was just thinking . . ." He laughed. "Oh, God, I sound just like my father . . . What were you saying?"

"I was saying that my neighborhood is a little different from the neighborhood around the Ritz."

"It doesn't matter to me. I want to know where you live. I want to know your family and friends, and I want them to know me."

"I think they'll all like you. My friend Katrina—I call her Renie—she's dying to meet you."

"Really?"

"Yes. She's the only person I told after that day when we first met. I gave her a scare this weekend because she'd been trying to reach me to find out how the pitch went."

"Oh, and I didn't let you out of my sight—or my bed—all weekend."

"I wouldn't have changed it for anything."

"Me, either."

Luca looked out the window as Jada drove on in silence. She was right. Streets that had been filled with expensively dressed people were now streets with people of more humble means. He saw people of various shades of brown, but very few who looked like him. Jada slowed down and drove into a sleek, modern garage attached to a colonial-style house that stood out among the others on the short street. She pushed a button and the door closed silently behind them.

"How long have you lived here?"

"In this neighborhood, all my life; in this house, about ten years. When I was looking for a house to buy, everything else was slightly out of reach. I was never offended by this neighborhood the way some of my successful friends are, so I'm happy living here. I know my neighbors and they look out for me. Not everyone can be rich and live in the Back Bay . . ."

"You're right," he agreed, helping her with her bags.

"I'm going to cook us dinner."

"Yes? Do you like to cook?"

"I do. And I'm pretty good at it. I'm keeping it simple tonight, though."

"Simple is good," Luca said.

Jada eyed him suspiciously. "All right, Mr. Alessandri, let me change, and then you're going to tell me what's bothering you."

"I—"

"Luca, I may not have known you for long, but I *know* something is bothering you. I can feel it, so think about how you're going to tell me what's on your mind. I'll give you a grand tour after I change. Meanwhile, the bar is over there; make yourself at home."

"Okay. Come back quick." Luca looked around the spacious living room and dining area which was a carefree mix of contemporary and classic; he was impressed, and for a fleeting moment, he wondered if she'd used a designer to set it up. Different textures and shades of grey were used as the base color throughout. A large, grey-on-grey, floral-pattern rug extended across the two rooms. In the dining room there was a large oval-shaped table surrounded by classic art-deco chairs covered with bold graphic designs. The focal point of the living room was an oversized dark-grey sofa positioned between a window and a small fireplace with a traditional mantle. Elegant, overstuffed wingback chairs completed the formal seating, and bright fuchsia leather hassocks and pillows accented the muted shades, giving it all a personal touch.

She had a wall of amazing works of art—all small pieces—some pen and ink, some watercolors, some photography. The color scheme was different, but some things reminded him of his own apartment in Torino. He immediately felt at home.

"Do you like it?" Jada asked. He turned and saw that she'd changed into a velvety sky-blue track suit. The top had a bejeweled zipper closing and the bottom clung to her hips in all the right places. On anyone else, it would have looked nice but ordinary. On Jada, it looked spectacular.

"I like it a lot."

"I'm talking about my place," Jada said, chiding him gently.

"I'm talking about you. I like your house a lot, too. The way you've used colors reminds me of what I've done in my home." Luca smiled.

"Really?"

"Yes, it's really nice."

"Thanks. I have three bedrooms and an office upstairs. It's probably way too much space for a single person, but I like it a lot. You don't want anything to drink? Water, wine, beer? A soft drink?"

"Wine, please."

"Not a hard sell," Jada said, pouring two glasses of red wine. "Okay, Luca, time is up. What's wrong?"

He took her in his arms. "Really, nothing is wrong. I . . . I am supposed to go back to Italy soon."

"I know," Jada murmured.

"I've been trying to work out things at the company so that I can stay, but it's not going the way I want it to. I don't want to leave you."

Jada tensed. "Why do you have to go?"

"*Amore mio*, I don't want to, but I had set everything up under the assumption that Hugh would run the business here and I would run the European operations from Torino. I never imagined that I'd want to live here full time . . . even though I like it."

"Switching assignments isn't that easy, is it?"

"No, not at all. Hugh really isn't up to leading the projects that are about to kick off in Italy, so I'm thinking, would you ever consider moving there?"

Jada pulled away and looked down.

"Move to Italy? Maybe one day, but right now I couldn't consider it."

"Why not?"

"We've got these feelings for each other, but it's all so new. Besides, I'm not that adventurous. I don't speak Italian, and I don't know anything about life or business there. I could never do something like that so fast."

"I'll help you. I'll be there."

"Honey, you just said you have big projects to manage there. Even if I were game, it wouldn't be fair to

113

you for me to move there, needing all the time you haven't got. I've already started to look into Italian classes; I want to know your native tongue. But it's going to take time; *we* need time."

Luca sighed deeply. He knew she was right, but he wasn't happy.

"Luca, we're going to work it out . . ." Jada could feel herself getting a little upset, so she needed to do something to keep busy. Like her dilemma over managing the Allegro account, figuring out how they could be together didn't have any easy solutions.

"I'd better get started on dinner. Come talk to me." She walked into her large, eat-in kitchen. The décor carried through the color scheme from the other rooms with slate-grey walls accented with colorful tiles, striking silvery granite countertops and stainless steel appliances. A small bistro table completed the space.

"I can even help. I'm a horrible cook, but I take directions well."

Jada laughed. "I can't believe you don't know how to cook!"

"Yes, it's a bit of a problem being single. I eat out a lot, and I am one person who is happy that the concept of takeout has finally caught on in Torino."

Luca wasn't lying. As promised, he took directions well, but it was clear he had two left hands in the kitchen. Jada had decided to make a chicken soufflé. The recipe was simple but the dish was unusual and elegant. It also required a fair amount of chopping, cracking of eggs and stirring of ingredients—perfect assignments for a non-cook.

"Have you always enjoyed cooking?"

"Always. I think it's relaxing, and fun. I like taking a recipe and putting my own twist on it; sometimes it works out well, sometimes it's a disaster. You're safe tonight, though. This one is tried and true."

Luca carefully continued chopping the chicken into perfect cubes.

"So when will I be able to meet your friends?" he asked.

"I've been thinking a lot about that ever since Renie mentioned it earlier today. There's not much time left before you go."

"I know."

"Scheduling things with people is such a pain, and we're both pretty busy over the next couple weeks, so I think we'll have to get creative."

"What do you mean?"

"I'm hosting a party for my parents two weeks from Saturday; it will be their fifty-second anniversary. They didn't want to make a big deal about it, so it's going to be pretty casual. But everyone will be there: my brothers, Renie, all my other friends, and you, I hope."

"I wouldn't miss it."

"It's a little unfair; you'll have to meet everyone at once. But it's very efficient."

"It sounds like the perfect plan."

Luca helped Jada load the last few glasses in the dishwasher after they finished their meal.

"So tell me more about your friends."

"They're great people. I call them 'The Fabulous Four.' As I've gotten older, I appreciate them more than ever. Family is important, too, but it's friends who know more of the ins and outs of what you're going through."

"That's true."

"Let's see, I've mentioned Renie. We've been friends since we were babies. Our parents are friends, too. I don't think there's anything about me that Renie doesn't know and vice versa. If she thinks I'm going off track, she'll let me know in an instant."

"That's good, I guess."

"Well, some people might think she takes the evil twin thing a bit too far sometimes, but I understand where she's coming from. What's more, I'd do the same thing for her if the tables were turned."

"Uh-oh. What does she think of me, then? Of us?"

"Aside from being furious with me for disappearing without a word this past weekend, she's happy for me. She knows I'm not one to say I'm in love with every guy I meet, so she knows you must be a special person."

"Good! I've got one fan."

"You're not off the hook yet; she's got to meet you first."

Jada poured them both another glass of wine and led them to the living room, where they sat on the sofa. "Then there's India and Liz. India and I became friends when her family moved next door to my parents' house. It was so much fun to have a friend nearby who was my age. Renie lived a few miles away, so we had to arrange our get-togethers, but India and I used to do things at the drop of a hat. We had a lot of fun growing up."

"She's got an unusual name."

"Yeah, her parents named her India because it's a country they dreamed of visiting one day. It's kind of corny, but cute, and somehow, the name suits her.

"Liz and I have been friends ever since meeting at college, when we were the only two black girls on our floor in the dorm. I was a bridesmaid at Liz's wedding, but she got divorced a few years ago."

"I'm sorry."

"Marvin turned out to be a pretty unpleasant guy. She's better off . . ."

"So who's the fourth one?"

"Carmen. Based on the one chat I've had with all of them about you right after we met, I think that you could walk on fire and part the seas, and she would still think you're too good to be true."

"How so?"

"She thinks you're only out for a good time, and then you're going to go back to Italy and I'll never hear from you again."

"You don't believe that, do you?"

"Well, no. But men do that kind of stuff all the time, especially to older women who have been single for a long time."

Luca lifted her chin so they were eye to eye. "I am *not* that kind of man, Jada. You don't have to worry."

"I believe you."

"So it seems I'll have my work cut out for me with at least one of your friends."

"Yes, you will."

"Well," he sighed, "that's another problem for another day."

He unzipped her top, revealing her delicate blue lace bra. "Why do they make things like this? It's so unbelievably sexy," he murmured.

"They make them so that some lucky woman like me will get to hear the man in her life say that he's turned on by what she's wearing." She looked up into his eyes, smiling.

"God, you are so beautiful . . ." His hands traced along the top and around to the hooks in the back. The bra drifted to the ground as he kissed her breasts with a voracious hunger.

"I've been dreaming all day about making love with you. I don't think I can wait a moment longer." Jada took his hand and led him upstairs to her bedroom.

Sometime later, Luca was holding Jada close and stroking her arm absently.

"Luca?"

"Hmm, *amore mio*?"

"I have an idea. Can you . . . can you come here for a week a month while you work on your projects? At the same time, I can take my language classes and learn more about Italy. By the time your projects are done, maybe I'd be ready to consider something as major as a move to Italy."

Luca didn't answer.

"So what are you thinking?"

"It's probably the best we'll be able to do right now, but it doesn't feel like enough . . . I had a crazy thought . . . maybe I should close Allegro. I could just start over."

Jada sat up and stared at him. "Luca, no! That *is* a crazy thought. First of all, it's not your decision alone to make. You have a partnership with your father. On top of that, you and your dad have worked too hard to build Allegro into the company it is today. You shouldn't give that up for anything!" she said, stroking his face.

"I know you're really trying hard to find a way for us to be together right now. But commuting is a good short-term solution. We'll make it work. We just have to be a little patient, that's all. Thank you for being willing to do that for us, though."

Luca pulled her closer. "I have to ask you a favor."

"Sure, what is it?"

"Will you come back to Italy with me? I want you to meet my parents, my friends. I'm going to leave for good in three weeks. By then, I will have finalized all the leases on the office and the equipment and worked out the contract with your competitor and my new advertising agency, Cornerstone."

Jada shoved his shoulder. "You love rubbing it in, don't you? You know that my competitive nature makes it hard for me to hear you say their name."

Luca laughed. "Yes, I do enjoy teasing you."

"Are you happy with them so far?"

"So far, yes. They have been helpful, and I really like the creative team that they've put together."

"Rize is a great agency, too, they're just a little bit larger than the others. My hope is that since Cornerstone is small and hungry, they'll give you that little bit extra for your money."

"Well, I hope they do. But it's nice to know that we have another viable option. If I'm disappointed at some point, I can remind them of that fact."

"Luca Alessandri, you are a tough businessman."

"I know that I can be, but I like to think that I am demanding but reasonable."

"Do you think that you are too hands-on?"

"Hmmm. Sometimes maybe I am. Why do you ask?"

"All those contracts that you have to get completed . . . couldn't you delegate at least some of them to Hugh? I mean, he's your deputy, isn't he?"

"Yes, he is, and he probably could take care of all of them for me without a problem. But my father always had this thing about negotiating and signing all of Allegro's contracts and not leaving things like that to a deputy. If they're really complicated, he'll work with a lawyer, but he never lets the lawyer negotiate anything without him being present. It's one of the many lessons I learned from him, and it has proved to be a good practice on more than one occasion."

"You don't like Hugh very much, do you?"

"He's a smart man, but like him? No, not really."

"Do you trust him?"

"I used to. Now, I'm not so sure."

They were quiet for a while. "I'll work on getting time off so that I can come with you."

"I would be so happy if you could do it. It would make all the difference if we could fly over together. That will at least delay the time before we will have to be apart."

"I'll do what I can."

CHAPTER 15

"Well, Papà, that's about all that's been happening . . ."

"You've been busy, Luca. It is very exciting to see all our plans become reality."

"Yes, I'll be glad when all of these contracts are finalized. That will truly mark the end of the first phase of all of this."

"And the rest of life? How is your beautiful Jada?"

"She is fantastic, Papà . . ." Just the mention of her name took him back to the night they had just spent together. As he'd promised when they first met, he took her to a dance performance—a modern dance premiere. Jada was thrilled to explain the moves and technique to Luca. And because he shared the experience with her, he enjoyed it immensely. Afterwards, they had a late dinner at one of the new restaurants in town and ended the night with a long walk around the Back Bay, window shopping and enjoying the sights and sounds of the city. They hadn't slept much; they were still very much at the stage in their relationship where everything about the other person was a mystery and a wonder, so it was much more interesting to make love, hold each other close and talk in the darkness than it was to sleep. Still, when Jada had dropped him off at the Ritz in the morning, he felt rested and energized. "I'm hoping to bring her with me to Torino when I come home, so you'll finally be able to meet her."

"Things seem to be moving fast with you two. What's the rush, Luca?"

"Because I know this is what I want. She's the one."

"Well, I'm happy for you, son. I just hope that you and Jada know what you're getting into. Different races, different cultures; you'll have more than your fair share of challenges."

"We will work it out, Papà. Trust me; I know what I'm doing."

"Luca, I *do* trust you, even if I have concerns. So tell me, are you planning to stay in the US and send Hugh back?"

"I considered it, but I had promised Hugh—" Luca could have kicked himself for starting his explanation with that argument.

"Luca, you're the president. You can do—"

"I know, I can do whatever I want. But it's not just that I told him he could run the US; I had set up things assuming that I would be in Torino. I have projects—"

"Luca, I hope you know that I can manage them for you. I don't want you to be there full time, but that is not a problem if staying in Boston is what you want to do."

"No, Papà, you just said, I'm the president. I want to manage the projects I conceived and developed."

Lorenzo couldn't argue with that.

"So what *are* you going to do?"

"I'm going to spend a week a month here in Boston. Meanwhile, Jada wants to start studying Italian. We'll get to spend more time together so we can figure out what's next for us. If it were just up to me, things would move a little faster, but Jada is thoughtful and meticulous in everything she does. "

"Hmmm. I know . . ." Lorenzo cringed. He had not meant to say that out loud. He didn't want to let on that he knew more about Jada Green than Luca could ever imagine.

"What do you mean you know?"

"I just meant, based on what you've told me, I know that Jada is her own woman."

"She is."

"Have you met her family yet? Her parents and her two brothers?" Lorenzo hit his head. What was he doing? Again, he gave away more information than he was supposed to know.

"How did you know she has two brothers?"

"You told me."

"I am pretty sure I didn't, Papà."

"No? Luca, you must have. What other explanation could there be? Unless it's just your father's psychic intuition."

Luca didn't know if he believed him, but he decided to let it go. If he thought too much about all the things his father was up to at any given time, he might not like him as much as he did.

"Anyway, Papà, I'm meeting them all next week at her parents' anniversary party. Jada is going to tell them about me soon. She thinks they'll be happy because she's happy, but wary about what my intentions really are."

"That's not really a surprise; things between you *are* moving quickly. At the same time, I have to tell you, your mother's parents were very suspicious of me, too. Even after I married Olivia, they were still uncertain if I was really sincere. But you don't need to worry, Luca. You are a wonderful person; they can't help but like you."

"Thank you, Papà. I have to go now. I have a meeting scheduled with Hugh."

"Luca, I have to tell you, I'm not very fond of that man; he might have been educated in Italy, but he's still a pompous Englishman. And he's sleeping with Fiorella."

"What?!"

"Just a little information to keep in your pocket. Watch your back."

"I will, Papà. Thank you, *ciao*."

"*Ciao*, my son."

Luca hung up and shook his head. "Fiorella and Hugh?"

CHAPTER 16

As she walked toward Honoraria's reception area, Jada took several small breaths, simultaneously flexing her fingers. She was about to have her first meeting with the team from Burrows, the commercial interior design company that had asked for her sight unseen. Much was riding on her making a good first impression, given Luca's father's role in getting the account. If things got off to a rough start, it would make what was already a somewhat awkward situation even dicier. Phone conversations with the principals—Ambrose Burrows, Holly King and Matt Sanders—had gone well enough, so she told herself her worrying was probably her usual first-meeting jitters.

Jada was wearing a grey Calvin Klein suit—simple, understated, comfortable—for this initial meeting. "Good morning," she said, striding confidently toward the Burrows executives. "I'm Jada Green."

"Jada!" Ambrose Burrows said, smiling broadly. "It's good to see you again. I haven't seen you since the big advertising conference in San Francisco."

"That's right. Little did I know that our chat about online rates would result in my working with you here at Honoraria."

"Indeed, indeed." Ambrose, a tall, impeccably dressed, patrician man with a jolly smile, gestured to his colleagues. "Meet Holly King and Matt Sanders, the rest of the team."

Jada shook hands with the group. "It's great to meet everyone, and I'm really looking forward to working with all of you."

"We've heard nothing but the most wonderful things about you from your clients around town, and also from Lorenzo Alessandri."

Jada was momentarily thrown off of her stride. She knew that Luca's father had spoken to Ambrose about her, but she had assumed their conversation would not be public knowledge.

"Well, I appreciate Mr. Alessandri's confidence in me," she said. She realized her reply sounded somewhat unsure, but it was all she could think to say.

They went to the conference room, where Jada's prospective team of writers, art directors, media planners and her account services director, who would handle the day-to-day activities, were waiting. Everyone in New England knew the Burrows name when it came to commercial design. This account was a big deal for the agency, and perfection was the only option. To avoid unwanted distractions, Jada had devised a way to keep Gene from attending this meeting. Lately, he had been more irritating than usual in questioning her ability to effectively manage the Allegro negotiation and then wanting to sit in on her kickoff meeting with Burrows. Was she the VP of client services or not? She never heard him or any other member of the steering committee asking to sit in on new client meetings with David or any of her other peers. It seemed that no matter how much she achieved, there remained some question as to whether she could really handle the responsibility that came with success. Why did he want to babysit her kickoff meeting? It bugged her to distraction. She and Luca had talked about it at length, and his perspective was insightful, though Jada at first had resisted it.

"*Amore mio*, I know it makes you angry when Gene doubts you or questions your decisions, but I wonder if sometimes you don't give his words and actions more weight than they deserve."

"What do you mean?"

"Well, why do you feel that everything that he says and does is a threat to your career?"

"Luca, he's my boss. What he thinks about me plays a major role in whether I move ahead or not."

"I know. Look, Jada, I'm an outsider looking in. I am not you, and I cannot even imagine some of the things you deal with in the work environment every day, so understand the spirit in which I'm saying this . . ."

"Okay." Jada said, feeling herself becoming defensive before he had even started. She'd tried hard to suppress the feeling.

"Yes, he is your boss, and of course that is very important, but every opinion he has is not necessarily something you have to react to, and all his motives may not be sinister. Some things he says may seem totally ridiculous, but when we talk, it seems you give the same weight to his stupid comments as you do to his more constructive criticisms. Also, you think that he is determined to see you fail or to trip you up, but you could be wrong. I am sure he has his own insecurities and feelings of inadequacy. It's possible that some of his requests to sit in on meetings or to talk about some project are not hovering, but his awkward attempt to be more collaborative with you, because in spite of everything you are more likely to help him than some of your peers. I guess I'm trying to say that his ultimate goal may indeed be to keep you in your place, and you should trust your instincts on that, but don't completely alienate him if there's some potential for him to at least be a passive ally. You need to consider his motivation before you instantly react negatively to his comments and actions."

"But—" Jada had caught herself. She was about to do exactly what Luca had been talking about—ready to defend her position before thinking through the points he'd made. So she'd taken a breath and considered his words. One thing she knew for sure: Luca had talked to her from a place of love and support, and it had not been his intent to be critical of her in any way; he had simply tried to show her a different point of view. Besides, there was truth in what he'd said: Gene could be a big help to her by simply not blocking her advancement. Even his passive support could go a long way. After all, serious opposition from him could have derailed her upward climb at any point.

"I guess I see what you're saying."

"The end result might be the same—you may still want to tell him to go to hell—but the route you take to telling him what you think will be different."

"I understand what you're saying, Luca. Thanks for your perceptive insights."

"Jada, you know I think you're fantastic, and I want you to have all the success in the world."

So when Gene asked to sit in on her first meeting with Burrows, Jada had put what Luca had said into practice and had handled it very differently from the way she would have just a few months ago. Sounding perfectly reasonable, she said:

"Gene, I know that Burrows is going to be one of our biggest accounts, and of course you need to get to know the key players. But I don't think this kickoff meeting is the best time to begin building that important relationship. So why don't I arrange a lunch for all of us? It will be an opportunity to have a conversation that goes beyond the projects they want us to work on. And who knows? There may be some other aspects of their business in which we can play a role."

To Jada's surprise, Gene's entire demeanor changed. "That's a great idea, Jada! Let me check my calendar . . . yes, I'm free for lunch every day next week except Tuesday."

"Okay. I will make it happen."

Gene smiled. "Great thinking. Please be sure to tell me how the kickoff meeting goes."

In that brief exchange Jada seemingly had managed to make more inroads with him than she had since becoming a VP. They were still virtual strangers, but apparently her offer to arrange a lunch and include him had made Gene see her in a slightly different light.

After Jada introduced the Burrows people to her assembled team, Jada kicked off the meeting. "Ambrose, I think we'd all benefit from hearing what your expectations are from the agency."

"Certainly. We're a big commercial design firm; we've been around for over thirty years now, so we have strong points of view on everything. But we need to be challenged. Times are changing, and our advertising and the way we reach our customers has to change, too. It's very easy for us to say, 'We've always done it this way.' But the tried and true approach is no longer the best way forward. We expect your team to come to us with fresh ideas and measurable results. A team of yes men—and women—won't work for us."

"Well, Ambrose, you have before you some of Honoraria's most talented and forward-thinking people. I can guarantee you that you'll be challenged and inspired by their work. We've got some preliminary ideas to share with you today."

With a nod from Jada, her team began laying out their thoughts. There was lots of bantering back and forth, and it was clear that the relationship was off to a good start. Before going into advertising, Jada had imagined that all agency/client meetings were like this. In fact, very few were. So she was happy with the goodwill evident at this meeting and excited about working with her new client. She may have come by the opportunity through a personal connection she hadn't even known existed, but she was determined to work hard to make sure this account thrived under her leadership.

"Jada, this was just fantastic," Ambrose Burrows enthused as he and his team were leaving the meeting room. "Lorenzo and I have known each other for years. We're competitors, but I respect his advice, which is why I'm here. I'm going to call Lorenzo and thank him for telling us about you."

Jada looked around to see if anyone at the agency was within earshot of his comment. To her horror, she saw David Heath walking down the hall. But he was a distance away. *He couldn't have heard anything. If he had, he would have surely reacted in some way.*

But he had heard. *"Who the hell is Lorenzo?"* David wondered. Turns out he was having a busy day, so he just filed the overheard comment away for later investigation.

After walking Ambrose and his team to the elevator, Jada retreated to her office. She was excited about the way the meeting had gone and couldn't wait to tell Luca all about it.

"Jada, I have been waiting to hear from you. How was the meeting?"

"It went really well. I couldn't have asked for a better result."

"That's fantastic! From what my father told me about Ambrose Burrows, I am not surprised that the two of you hit it off right away."

"He doesn't pull any punches; his team is excellent, too. I think it's going to be a great account to work on; I'm really excited."

"Why do I hear some hesitation in your voice, then?"

"Well, Ambrose mentioned your father's first name when we were walking out of the meeting. He said that he was going to thank him for telling him about me. I think one of the VPs may have overheard . . ."

"Oh." Luca thought for a moment. "But does it really matter? Even if this person knows who Lorenzo is, it's not unusual for people in the same industry to share information about agencies."

"I suppose so," Jada said. She wasn't entirely convinced, but what could she do?

"Did your colleague say anything to you?"

"No, he didn't. You're right; it's probably nothing. Maybe I just need something to worry about since the meeting went so well."

"I'm a little worried about another meeting coming up soon . . ."

"Who are you meeting?"

"How could you forget? Your parents, family and friends. Talk about jumping in at the deep end!"

"I know it's a lot, but I'm sure it will be fine."

"Have you told your parents that you've invited me yet?"

"I'm taking care of that later today; I've been so busy dealing with other stuff for the party, I just haven't—"

"Jada, don't procrastinate. That will only make it worse. My father has told me that he's worried we're moving too fast, so I expect your parents will feel the same way. It's already Thursday. Promise me you'll call and tell them today."

"I promise."

"Good. Well, I've got to go now. We'll talk later." Luca hesitated before adding, "I love you."

"Me, too."

CHAPTER 17

Jada took a deep breath before dialing the familiar number. *Why am I so nervous?* She knew why.

"Hi, Mom. How are you?"

"Jada, at last! I was just saying to your father that we were going to have to put out an APB on our daughter. We usually hear from you every week, and, suddenly, silence."

"I'm sorry, Mom. Things have just been crazy lately . . ."

"That job! I've told you before: no job is worth being stressed out all the time. You are so bound and determined to make it to the top of that agency; I hope you're still healthy when you get there. Let me get your father on the other line. Horace . . . phone!" Horace Green picked up the other extension.

"Work has been busy, but there's been other stuff going on."

"Oh?"

"I met someone, Mom . . . almost two months ago."

"Well, that explains it. So, who is this man? Why didn't you mention him when you called the last couple times?"

"I just wasn't ready to talk about it yet."

"So tell us about him, baby." Horace Green's booming voice made Jada jump.

"His name is Luca Alessandri. He's president of a commercial design firm." There was an uneasy silence as her parents took it all in. "He's a wonderful man. He's Italian."

"I think we gathered that, Jada. How did you meet him?" Ida asked.

"We met at Honoraria. He was a prospective client." Silence.

"Ummm. Things are going well between us. They're getting serious. I want you to meet him before he goes back to Italy."

"Goes back to Italy? He doesn't live here?" Ida Green asked, with worry in her voice.

"No. He lives in Torino, Italy. He has been here for the past few months finalizing things for his US office, which will be based in Boston."

Horace cleared his throat, "So how do you plan on having a relationship with someone who lives in another country?"

"He's going to be here one week a month. We'll see how things go from there. I'm hoping to visit him for a couple of weeks when he leaves."

"I see. What about his family? Who are they? What do they think of all this?"

"His father is a businessman and his mother is at home. Luca is an only child. He has told his parents about me. I know his father thinks we're moving too fast."

"Well, I would agree," Horace said.

"Dad, I'm forty-five years old, and—"

"That's right. So you should know better!"

"Dad—"

"Please, you two!" Ida pleaded. "Arguing over the phone isn't going to change anything. When will we get to meet this Luca?"

"I've invited him to the party on Saturday. It will be the perfect chance for Luca to meet everyone before he leaves. You know, I don't expect either of you to embrace this with open arms, but just meet him. I know you'll like him if you give him a chance."

"Jada, we know this man must be pretty special, because I don't think you've had a steady boyfriend since Ken . . ."

Jada laughed. "Mom, I haven't even had an unsteady boyfriend since Ken."

"That's what worries me. You're rushing headfirst into this relationship with a white man who doesn't even live here. Things have changed, but not that much. You're a smart girl, but I think you're being naïve."

"Dad, I'm just asking you both to trust me and be open-minded."

"We'll do our best," Ida responded quickly.

"That's all I can ask for. Someone's on the other line. I'll see you Saturday." Jada hung up before anyone had a chance to prolong the conversation.

∽◦∾

Jada's cell phone rang, giving her a start. It was Luca. "Hi, what's up?"

"I'm right around the corner from your office. Do you have a few minutes? Let's take a walk."

"I do; I'll be right down."

It was Friday and the streets were bustling since it was just after lunchtime. She ran into his arms and he caressed her face affectionately. "How is your day?"

"It's moving along. T.G.I.F.!"

Laughing, Luca took her hand. "I agree. What did your parents say when you told them about me?"

"Some of the same things your dad said. They're concerned that I'm being naïve, they're worried you might be using me, that we're too different . . ."

"I hope you weren't surprised by their reaction. You're their daughter, and no matter how old you are, they're going to worry."

"I know. Still, I'd hoped they would trust my judgment."

"*Amore mio*, I'm sure they do. But they're your parents. I'm a different race and I live in a different country. They have reason to express concern. We'll be okay, but this next step is important. I can't wait to meet them."

"I'll be busy tonight, putting the finishing touches on everything."

"I had intended to leave you in peace tonight; that's another reason why I wanted to see you now."

They had walked around the block and were back in front of the Honoraria building.

"Come around six tomorrow? Things should be in full swing by then."

"Okay. Six it is." He lifted her chin and brushed her lips. "Until then."

CHAPTER 18

The large, open space comprising Jada's living and dining rooms made it the perfect place to have a party. Ida and Horace Green had been reluctant to have any sort of celebration for their anniversary, so Jada's offer to have a small party at her home was an excellent compromise. It was a nice excuse to get their children and grandchildren together and a nice reason to have friends drop by.

Jada silenced the cheerful and boisterous crowd and said, "I'd like to raise a toast to my parents, Ida and Horace. To fifty-two years of togetherness. Cheers." Everyone touched glasses. Ida looked content as Horace pecked her cheek.

Carmen, India, Liz and Katrina chatted with Jada. "You've outdone yourself, girlfriend."

"Thanks, Renie. I had it all catered, so I can't take much credit for it."

"It's good to see your parents. I know they're not the lovey-doviest, but *fifty-two years*; that's something special," India said.

Nodding agreement, Liz said, "We should all be so lucky."

"You look nervous, Jada. What's wrong?" Carmen asked.

"It's almost six. Luca will be here soon."

The friends looked at her, stunned.

"He's coming here? Why didn't you say something?" Renie asked.

"After my talk with my parents, I decided to keep it to myself." The bell rang, and Jada took a deep breath. "That's probably him now."

Jada opened the door to Luca's smiling face. "Hi." They kissed affectionately.

Luca looked over her shoulder and saw people milling around. "How are things going?"

"Good. Everyone seems to be having a nice time. Are you ready?"

"As ready as I'll ever be."

Jada took his hand. "Let's go."

Katrina, India, Liz and Carmen were waiting in the room, determined to meet Luca before anyone else.

"Luca, meet my good friends."

He smiled, "The Fabulous Four I've heard so much about."

Jada made the introductions. "Katrina, India, Liz and Carmen."

He shook hands warmly with each of them.

"It's nice to finally meet you."

Renie said, "I think I speak for all of us when I say we've been looking forward to meeting you."

Jada tugged at his hand, saying, "We'll be back. I want to introduce Luca to my parents and my brothers."

She could feel the eyes of family and friends as they made their way to her parents, who were sitting on the sofa. They looked up as they approached.

"Mom, Dad . . . I'd like you to meet Luca Alessandri."

Horace extended his hand to Luca, while Ida Green brushed away the proffered hand and gave him a hug.

"It's nice to meet you, Luca. I know that Jada is very fond of you," she said.

Glancing at Jada, he replied, "I'm very fond of Jada, too."

"Please, sit down." They sat and talked for about ten minutes, with the Greens grilling him about his family and Allegro. Eventually, Jada got restless. "I'm going to introduce Luca to Darren and Craig now."

"Hold on," Horace said, raising his hand. "Luca, I can't say this relationship thrills me. You two just met and things seem to be racing ahead and I wonder why. Still, my daughter has asked us to give you a chance, and we're willing to do that. I hope you're worth it."

Horace's concern for his daughter was palpable. Luca nodded. "I understand, sir. Thank you for giving me a chance. You won't regret it. Excuse us." Jada led him to the center of the room.

"Well, that wasn't as bad as I thought," Jada whispered as she watched family and friends watching them with interest. "Do you want a drink?"

"Sure. I think I've earned one."

"I'll be right back."

Katrina approached Luca as he stood collecting his thoughts. Peering at him over the rim of her glass, she said, "Well, you look pretty calm, but some part of you must be sweating bullets. There's a whole lot of personality in this room."

"It's not too bad. I expect people to be tough. They should be."

"Hey, my friend, if you can survive a grilling from Horace and Ida, you'll be fine. Keep the faith. I've got to mingle." And with that, she flitted off to talk to Carmen.

Jada returned with his drink and gestured to the other room. "Darren and Craig are over there with Craig's wife, Helen. Let's go meet them."

As they approached Luca noticed Darren's body language change instantly, but Jada seemed oblivious. "Craig, Darren, Helen, I want you to meet someone special in my life, Luca Alessandri."

Craig extended his hand right away. "Nice to meet you, Luca," he said sincerely. Helen shook hands politely; Darren made no attempt to shake his hand. They stood in awkward silence until Helen asked, "How long have you been an item?"

"It's been a couple of months now."

"That's all?" Darren asked.

Jada nodded. "We met when Luca was looking for an advertising agency for his business."

"I own a commercial interior design firm," Luca added.

"You're Italian?" Darren asked, continuing his interrogation.

"Yes, I am from Torino. I've been here on business for the last few months."

"I see. So what, you're here for a while and you find some woman to pass the time with and then you take off? Why are you messing with my sister's head?"

"Darren!" Jada raised her voice. "No one ever questioned you when you were dating a white woman. Where do you get off?" The room got quiet as people began to sense the tension.

Luca put his arm out to keep Jada behind him and he took a step toward Darren so they were nearly eye to eye.

"I am not messing with your sister's head. What Jada and I have is very special—unlike any relationship I've ever had. I love her and I would never hurt her."

Luca's protectiveness of Jada surprised Darren, but he wasn't done. He looked at Jada. "What's wrong with black men? You've become a big shot at some downtown agency and now your own people aren't good enough for you?"

Craig piped up. "Darren, man, why don't you calm down?"

"Darren, how can you say that?" Stunned, Jada was could feel the sting of tears on her cheeks.

"Darren Green!" He whipped around at the sound of his father's booming voice. "You come with me." Horace Green led his son out into the hallway. Katrina and India rushed over to comfort Jada, and Luca stood there feeling embarrassed and upset—more so for Jada than himself. The silence in the house was overwhelming.

Horace started in on his oldest child. "Son, you are out of line. Your sister has a relationship with this man, and it's serious enough that she wants us all to meet him. You can approve or not approve—hell, I'll admit to you I've got mixed emotions about it—but you don't have a right to come in here and act a fool."

"That's my sister, Dad!"

"And that's *my* daughter. But she's a grown woman—she's forty-five, not some sixteen-year-old dewy-eyed girl. Darren, you know you can call Jada a lot of things, but stupid isn't one of them. Give her the benefit of the doubt. Be supportive. From what I've seen, the guy has handled himself pretty well tonight. I'm willing to give him a chance. I want you to go back in there and apologize. And for your sister's sake, look beyond his color and see how he treats her."

"Okay, Dad. I'm sorry."

"I accept your apology, but you've got to apologize to Jada and Luca." Horace tried to lighten the mood a little and said jokingly, "Don't go ruining my party, man."

Darren nodded sullenly and went to join the others. Jada, Luca and Katrina were talking quietly together. He went over to them. "Jada, Luca . . . I owe you an apology."

"Darren, I've fallen in love. Be happy for me," Jada pleaded.

"I'll try."

"Darren . . . I am an only child, but I imagine that I would be protective like you if I had a sister—especially one as amazing as Jada. You don't know me and I understand why you are suspicious. I appeared out of nowhere, and now I'm leaving. But I'll tell you what I told Jada when I first met her: I am an honorable man. I hope you give me the chance to prove that to you."

Darren nodded. *This sure isn't your run-of-the-mill white guy out for a good time on the other side of the tracks.*

I see what Dad was talking about. I came down hard on him, but he responded with guts and class.

He extended his hand to Luca. "You got it, man."

"Thanks."

India, Liz and Carmen stood on the sidelines with Mrs. Green, watching Luca and Darren.

"Score another one for the good guys!" India said.

"Here's hoping," Carmen muttered.

"You don't think he seems nice?" Mrs. Green asked.

"I kind of agree with Darren. He just appears out of nowhere and sweeps her off her feet? What's up with that? What does he really want?"

India scowled at Carmen. "You're not back on that again, are you? From everything Jada's told us, he's only been nice to her."

"He's too good to be true, that's all I can say. He's got to be hiding something."

Ida Green shook her head warily. "I feel bad that you girls have all had such bad experiences with men. It's not hearts and flowers all the time, but I hope you all don't stop believing that love happens and could happen to you."

Carmen rolled her eyes and walked away.

"She's not a very happy woman, is she?" Mrs. Green asked. India and Liz looked at each other and decided not to respond.

Darren spent the rest of the evening watching Luca and his sister. When Jada spoke, he hung on her every word; sometimes he'd put his arm protectively around her. When they were on opposite sides of the room, he'd glance at her with intense affection. He left with a changed view of his sister's relationship. He still wished she'd found herself a brother, but as his father had said, she was a grown woman.

"It was good to see you, Darren," Jada said as he was leaving.

Darren laughed. "Are you sure you really mean that?"

"I do. You're my brother, and I am always happy to see you . . . even when you piss me off."

They both chuckled.

"I'll talk to you later."

Before heading out, Renie, her last guest, had helped her clean up and was now at the door about to leave.

"Well, girl, I think your parents enjoyed their anniversary, in spite of the little bit of drama courtesy of your dumb-head brother. Darren is certainly consistent—consistently putting his big-ass foot in his mouth. He's been that way as long as I can remember."

"I think he actually meant well, but his approach was all wrong," Luca offered.

Renie looked at him and shook her head sadly. "Luca, you're giving Darren *waaay* too much credit. He acted like an idiot."

"If you say so." He laughed.

"Well, I'm gone. Take care, you two."

"You do the same!" Jada said, sighing deeply as she closed the door. "Thank God it's over."

"It wasn't so bad," Luca said, taking her in his arms and holding her tightly.

"Are you kidding?" Jada asked. "I thought I was going to die of embarrassment when Darren started causing a scene. Renie was right; he acted like a dumb-head."

"As I said, he loves you; he was being a protective big brother. But, Signorina Green, there *is* one good thing about people doubting my feelings for you . . ."

"There is?"

"Yes. That means I get to prove to you how wrong they all are." He began his ribbon of kisses on her hair and continued it from her forehead to her ears, the tip of her nose and then her lips. He pulled her into the darkened living room and they began shedding their clothes. For a long while, they just stood in the middle of the room naked, holding each other and enjoying the feel of each other's skin and the heightened sensation brought on by the darkness. After a time, Luca led her to the sofa, tossed the pillows onto the floor and guided Jada on top of him.

Thus their slow journey began. Luca was able to appreciate the full beauty of her body, and he filled her completely, all the while watching her breasts move in tempo with their rhythm. Watching Jada and looking into her eyes as they made love left him awash in emotions that threatened to overwhelm him. They were getting close, so he turned on the light by the sofa.

"Jada—"As they moved, Luca guided her further down on the sofa, watching as her face contorted slightly and the energy in her body intensified. He believed she enjoyed making love with him, but Luca sometimes felt that before her release she waged a war within herself.

There was complete surrender in the end, but he wondered what forces were at play within her.

Stroking her breasts, he sought to reassure her. "*Amore mio*, everything is all right . . . let go. It's okay to let go." Almost as soon as he said the words, her release came with a force that they had never experienced. As soon as Jada started, Luca slipped over the edge, too. Breathless and covered with a fine layer of moisture, they lay silently, wide awake. Luca held her close and wondered what had just happened. Was it the extra assurance he'd offered, or was he just making too much of a spectacular moment?

Jada trembled uncontrollably even though she was warm, enveloped in Luca's arms. *This man never ceases to amaze me. From the moment we met, he has told me what I needed to hear, encouraged me, comforted me and done sweet things for me that have touched my heart.* Jada tried to stop her tears, but they flowed anyway. Luca felt them as they hit his chest.

"Jada, what's wrong? What's happened?"

She shook her head. "I'm really happy."

He held her even closer, trying to comfort her.

"Jada, don't cry. Shhh. It's okay. I love you and I'm not going to go away."

CHAPTER 19

Hugh sat in his office at the newly established Allegro USA. For months before they got to Boston, their agent sent them specs of high-rise buildings, buildings at the city limits and buildings in neighborhoods with a little more character and charm, such as the loft building in the South End they'd ended up renting. It was in an up-and-coming part of the neighborhood and had a creative energy that felt like a good fit for a European company trying to make it big in a city that was somewhat closed to outsiders.

He was feeling pretty good, despite having some misgivings about whether Luca would keep his word and let him retain the title of US president, especially after Fiorella had told him she'd seen Jada Green leaving the Ritz at 6 a.m. the Monday after the pitch that never was. But everything had moved ahead according to plan. He didn't know what was going on with Luca and that woman, and he didn't really care as long as it didn't interfere with his aspirations. On top of all the other good things that had happened, Luca had agreed to Fiorella staying on in Boston as creative director to help establish Allegro. They had all agreed to wait and see whether it made more sense to have Fiorella relocate to Boston and to hire a new creative director for the European operation or to do it the other way around. Luca had decided that he could manage the creative director role in Italy in the near term, and he and his father would start a search for someone there. That solution was very pleasing to Hugh, because it meant that he and Fiorella could continue their rather wonderful dalliance. He wasn't in love with her or she with him, but they thought alike and sex with her was pretty fucking amazing. Now that they would be able to come out into the open, who knew what could happen? Yeah, his life was fucking good at the moment.

Hugh was waiting for Luca, who was coming by for a wrap-up meeting before taking off for good, leaving the management of the US office to him and him alone. He'd be glad to see the back of him. Family-owned businesses were a pain in the ass, and both Luca and his old man had a tendency to micromanage when they were around. He had his own way of doing things, and seven thousand miles would ensure that he had a chance to establish his own style without interference from the Alessandris.

But Luca was late, which was out of character for him. Where was he? With his black girlfriend? No, that was doubtful, since the buzz he'd heard about Jada from other agency people was that she was as wrapped up in her job as Luca was in his. No wonder they ended up together! Still, it was unlike him to be late. Just as he picked up his phone to try to reach him, Luca appeared at the door.

"Luca, I was just beginning to wonder. Come in . . ." But Luca had already walked in and put his briefcase down at the conference table.

God, I fucking hate *that. While he never says anything, his body language always reminds me that it's his company and his office, not mine. It's this smug sense of entitlement that rich people have that makes me want to punch his fucking lights out. Calm down, Hugh,* he cautioned himself. *Remember, you're in control.*

"I just wanted to just go over a few key points before I leave."

"Sure. When are you taking off?"

"The day after tomorrow," Luca replied, pretending to look through some files. The thought of leaving Jada still bothered him, and even though she was flying over with him, he knew that the easy, carefree days of their romance were quickly nearing an end. And so it was an effort to stay focused on Hugh's report on new projects—the reception area of a dental practice, the new offices for an engineering firm, and the crown jewel: three floors in a skyscraper for a law firm.

Hugh, on the other hand, was happy. Everything was going fine—better than he'd expected. He answered questions and shared his ideas and Luca seemed to accept them. And then came the unexpected:

"Hugh, I need to tell you there is a possibility that I will relocate here to Boston in six months to a year; should that happen, you would go back to Torino to run the office there."

"No fucking way!" Hugh blurted before he could stop himself. *Fiorella had warned me . . .*

"*Excuse* me, Hugh?" Luca couldn't believe that Hugh had spoken to him that way.

Hugh realized right away that he had overstepped the boundary with his boss. Luca was a pretty even-tempered man, but it was clear he was furious and trying hard to control his anger.

"Luca, I apologize . . . It's just . . . I think my talents would be best served here in the States. I have great ideas for how to grow the business."

"The Torino office, in case you didn't know, oversees all the European operations and is twice as large as what we're forecasting for the US. If you're not interested . . ."

"Torino would be a great opportunity; it's just not the one that suits me best."

Luca considered his options. He could not afford for Hugh to get frustrated and quit now, no matter what misgivings he might have about him. He needed him to feel motivated, engaged and unthreatened.

"Well, it's just a possibility right now. There are a lot of things that would need to happen first. Your talents are indeed well-suited to the US. Still, you know I like being up-front with my team about my thoughts."

"I know; I appreciate that a lot. Again, I apologize for my outburst. You won't regret making me president here."

Luca smiled. *Mission accomplished.*

"No apology required," he said, gathering his papers and shaking Hugh's hand. He looked at his employee's chiseled features and jewel-like green eyes and thought of him with Fiorella. They were both good-looking people, but it was hard to imagine them together. Still, his father's sources were pretty solid; he hardly ever got these things wrong.

CHAPTER 20

Holding hands, Jada and Luca boarded the Milan-bound plane and settled into their first-class seats. Luca had worked a full day at the office and was an exhausted bundle of nerves. On one hand, he was happy to be taking Jada to his home to discover his city with her and to meet his family and friends; it was a big step forward in their relationship. On the other, this trip marked an ending. He would no longer wake up next to her almost every day. They would become slaves to the telephone: cursing every just-missed call, forgetting to share funny stories. He hated the idea, but the past few days had crystallized the realization that the situation was temporary. He vowed that by this time next year, they would be married and they would be living together—in one place or another. Now it was all about making his dream happen.

Jada finally let herself relax. The past couple of weeks had been more than a little stressful—between the party and then dealing with Luca's scheduled departure and the drama surrounding her asking for vacation time. It shouldn't have been as hard as it had been, of that she was sure. Looking out the window at the infinity of clouds, she revisited her conversation with Gene.

"Gene, I'd like to take two weeks off."

"*Two* weeks? That's pretty extravagant, isn't it?"

"I have to go out of town to take care of some personal things."

"Going anywhere special?"

Since it was clear that he wasn't even trying to be friendly, just nosy, she demurred.

"I'm going to a few places. I'll have to do some back and forth." *All technically true.*

"Rumor has it you started seeing Luca Alessandri a while ago. What, you lost the business and won the man?"

Jada was not going to answer that question! Had someone put Gene up to asking? In all her years at Honoraria, they had never had a conversation as personal as this. She was a little unsure of how to answer him, so she went with her first impulse.

"Gene, what I want to know is where do people get this stuff?" she said, laughing dismissively. "Considering the fact that I don't talk about my personal life with *anyone* around here, the things people say are almost comical!" Jada had said a lot without confirming or denying anything.

"Look, I've already lined up things with my team, so everything should run smoothly. I'll have my cell and my PDA with me. Relatively speaking, this is a quiet time. Besides, I haven't taken more than a few days off in over a year."

Gene nodded. "Gee, is there any way you could make it a little less than two weeks . . . maybe arrange things so you can come in on the Friday so that you're on top of everything by the directors' meeting the following Monday?"

What a ball-buster. I bet he wouldn't do this if one of the guys were asking—like David. But given how unusual two-week vacations were in the world of advertising, she relented.

"Sure, I can do that. Thanks, Gene." She might need the goodwill of that compromise later. Jada stood up, ending it quickly before he could make any more requests she didn't want to fulfill.

"What an asshole," Jada mumbled. Luca stirred, but didn't wake up. Jada watched him as he slept. *My poor baby; I know he's tired.* Suddenly filled with affection, she moved a stray strand of hair away from his eyes. *He looks so cute when he's sleeping.*

Again, her thoughts went back to work: After leaving Gene, Jada went to Annie, having decided to tell her about Luca, despite suspecting that she already knew. But she didn't believe Annie had said anything to anyone. She and Luca never hid; they went out to dinner, for walks and to the movies. No doubt they were seen around town, and she imagined that after having nothing but speculation to feed off, actual facts about Jada Green were fodder for fresh gossip.

"Annie, I'm taking a couple of weeks—well, almost a couple of weeks off."

"Good for you! If anyone deserves a vacation, you do."

"Thanks." Not sure how to broach the topic, she hesitated. Sensing she needed help, Annie obliged.

"Are you going anywhere special?"

"Yes, I'm going to Italy. Annie, I want you to know—"

"You're seeing Luca Alessandri."

"So you *did* know?"

"Well, to be honest, I've suspected from the day he came here when the pitch was cancelled. I don't know, but the way he looked at you . . . and this is going to sound strange . . . the way he closed the door when he came to the office. I thought that if you two weren't seeing one another, you would be soon if he had anything to say about it! I also noticed that he called you a few times on your personal line even after Allegro pulled out of the pitch. He has a pretty distinctive voice. I'm happy for you, Jada. He seems like a nice man."

"He is a really wonderful man. Annie—"

"You don't need to say it; this is between you and me. But you should know that there's been talk about the two of you."

"I know. Let them all keep guessing. But I want you to know the real deal in case anything comes up. I'll leave you all of Luca's numbers in Italy just in case."

"Jada, thanks for trusting me."

"Thank *you* for being someone I can trust."

"Hey . . ." Luca said softly, as his just-awakened voice interrupted her thoughts. "What are you thinking about?"

"Work."

"Oh, no. I'm putting an end to that now. You are on vacation. I know this is a strange concept for an American, but it's a great thing. You're supposed to let it all go now. I'm going to do everything I can to make you forget about Honoraria. After some of the things you've told me, and hearing about how Gene wouldn't even give you two full weeks' vacation, I don't think it's that nice a place after all." He took her hand and kissed it gently. "Let me tell you some of the things that I've planned for us to do in Torino. It will be morning when we land, so we'll go to my house and rest; then we're having a late lunch with my parents. Tomorrow, we'll see some of the sights of Torino and have dinner at my favorite restaurants. I'm going to arrange a dinner with my own Fabulous Four friends at some point, but I haven't arranged it yet. We'll play the rest by ear."

"It all sounds great. I'm excited!"

Before Jada knew it, they were landing in Milan. The flight seemed to have gone by in the blink of an eye. Passport control was fairly routine, and when the customs officer told her *benevento nel' Italia*, he seemed sincere. She felt pretty welcome, too.

Luca had arranged for a car to take them from the airport to Torino. "It's not the most interesting one-hour drive, but you'll get some feel for the landscape and crazy Italian drivers!" Luca laughed.

As soon as they'd landed, Luca seemed like he became a different person—a little less intense, more animated and lighthearted. Jada wondered if she went through a similar transformation when she returned home after a vacation or business trip. She didn't think so.

Luca stopped talking after a while and let her take in the passing scenery. At first, just as he'd warned, there was nothing that interesting to see—fields and lots of cars much smaller than American ones sped by. But as they approached Torino, the snowcapped Alps provided a magical backdrop. Renaissance buildings with majestic arches and elongated columns were everywhere. But she also saw ultra-modern buildings, all glass and sharp angles. While the winding streets and the mix of old and new architecture reminded her of home, she knew she was definitely *not* in Boston.

"I hope you don't mind having lunch with my parents today; they are anxious to meet you."

"Well, I'm looking forward to meeting them, too. Is it horrible for me to say that I'll be glad when all this meeting-of-the-parents stuff is behind us?"

"No, that's not horrible. It's normal to want your family to like the person in your life, no matter how old you are, but that doesn't mean it's not stressful. I'll be happy when it's over, too."

Jada sighed. "I still can't get over Darren. He's had more than a couple girlfriends who were not black, so his reaction to us took me by surprise."

"Well, you're his sister. What he does is one thing, but what he wishes for you may be entirely different."

The car stopped in front of a large Renaissance-style building. It was quite imposing and had an enormous door and ornate roman columns at the entrance. The driver retrieved their bags and put them in front of the door. And while Luca paid him, Jada stood there thinking.

If someone had told me three months ago, I'd be here in Italy with a man I'd fallen in love with, I'd have called them a liar. Life takes some amazing turns.

Luca looked back at her. "Is everything okay?" he asked.

"Yes, everything is fine," Jada said in her perkiest voice. She didn't want him to mistake her pensive mood for anxiety.

Luca punched in a code and pushed the door, which opened into a cobbled courtyard surrounded by an array of hydrangea, and lush, evergreens. "Just go straight across and through those doors. I will catch up with the bags."

Jada walked through the heavy glass doors and into a polished marble lobby with a multi-tiered crystal chandelier that seemed almost too nice for an entrance. Luca led the way to the elevators and pushed five, the top floor.

"Oh, the penthouse. Why am I not surprised?" Jada teased. Luca looked down and smiled. His excitement that she was actually there with him made him tongue-tied. His nervousness showed as he fumbled with the keys as he opened the door.

"This is my home," Luca said proudly as he revealed his apartment to the most special visitor he had ever had in his house.

Jada marveled as she walked through the spacious entrance, adorned with his own elegant chandelier. However, his was a modern sculpture of lights, positioned over an antique mahogany end table. "Luca, you didn't do your apartment justice when you described it."

When Luca first visited Jada's house, he'd mentioned that her house reminded him of his own. She immediately saw what he meant. It was almost uncanny—where she'd used accents of fuchsia, Luca had used red. She could see a wall of small, framed works of art—just like hers—in another room. As she glanced at the furnishings and accessories, it was clear they both enjoyed mixing classic and modern in their décor.

"So you like it?"

"How could I not? It's gorgeous."

She walked down the glossy, parquet-floored hallway. To her left was a living room, seemingly twice the size of her own, dominated by an enormous fireplace and two overstuffed and inviting burgundy sofas. She passed the dining room next, a whimsical play on modern and traditional décor, with a magnificent sculptured glass table surrounded by sixteenth century Venetian chairs. Both contemporary and Renaissance-style candelabras accented the room, and Jada imagined it must be a romantic space in which to dine. The kitchen was ultra-modern and, in Jada's opinion, way too well equipped for a man professing to not being able to cook. Jada teased him about it as she walked through the kitchen.

"Well, I kept saying that one day I would teach myself to cook or that I'd meet a woman named Jada who would appreciate all of these incredible gadgets."

"You're very funny."

There were two guest rooms on the other side of the hallway, each with its own bath and decorated in warm earth tones.

"This is a fantastic place. I love your house, Luca."

"I'm glad. I hoped you would."

At the very end of the hallway, set apart from the other rooms, was the master suite. "This is our room," he said, liking the sound of that. "There's space in the closet for your things. When you're unpacked, I can put the suitcase in the storage room downstairs or in one of the guest rooms—whichever you prefer."

"Okay." She stood motionless, trying to decide what to do first. Her brain felt like mush.

"You're tired, aren't you?"

"A little, but I don't want to sleep. I'll be all right."

"Here, leave the suitcase. Sometimes it helps to sleep for a few hours—but not too long. You will have enough energy for the rest of the day, then you can go to sleep at night and you'll be right on schedule the next day. I promised that I would let you get some sleep, and I will keep my word. So why don't you lie down?"

Even though Jada had been determined to stay awake all day, the mere suggestion of taking a nap made her even sleepier. She was so tired, she felt as if she could just curl up on the floor and be instantly asleep.

"Luca?"

"Yes, *amore mio*?"

"Will you hold me? Just until I fall asleep?"

He touched her lips with his own. "Well, you're asking a lot of me. I'm not sure." Jada looked at him questioningly.

He pulled down the duvet. "You *are* tired. I was only joking; lie down."

She slipped under the cozy covers. Luca pulled the heavy drapes and the room became almost pitch black. He then slipped in the bed on the other side and set the alarm clock. "Three hours should do it." He pulled her into his arms. Happiness coursed through his entire body. Within minutes, they were both fast asleep.

CHAPTER 21

Reenergized after a short nap, a quick shower and change of clothes, Jada and Luca set off for the Alessandri home.

"It's not a long drive, but you will at least be able to see some of the highlights of the city from a distance, like the Mole Antonelliana, which is the tallest spire in the city. I've been many places in the world, but I love coming back home. When I come back and see the snow-capped Alps and the beautiful city, I fall in love with it all over again," Luca said.

Before long, they were there. Luca's parents lived in an elegant home in the hills just outside the city limits, but there was little around to suggest they were anywhere near a city. As they pulled into the driveway, Jada thought about how close Luca was to his parents. He was their only child, the star of their lives. Even though he had assured her everything would be fine, she couldn't help thinking back to her brother, Darren's, initially hostile reaction to Luca. Were they in for another surprise? *Please, Lord, let this go smoothly.*

Luca looked at her, and as if he could read her thoughts, said, "It will be okay, Jada. I promise." With that he got out the car, opened her door and took her hand. As they neared the entrance to the house, Olivia opened the door and rushed out.

"*Luca! Figlio mio . . . come stai?*"

"*Bene grazie, Mamma. Sto molto bene,*" he replied, drawing his mother into a huge hug.

Watching the warm exchange between mother and son, Jada took quick inventory of the mother: Olivia Alessandri was a tall woman—as tall as she. She had brown eyes, and her salt-and-pepper hair was cut short to frame her face. She looked and moved like a woman much younger than her seventy years.

"Mamma, this is Jada."

"Jada! We finally get to meet! Luca has told us so much about you. Welcome to Torino." Olivia hugged Jada and kissed her on either cheek.

"Thank you, Mrs. Alessandri. I'm happy to finally meet you, too."

Luca stood to one side, smiling. In truth he had been a little nervous about their meeting. His mother had always been the tougher judge of the women in his life. With Olivia's warm greeting, any worries about his parents liking Jada flew out the window. Whatever misgivings his father might have about his relationship with Jada, he knew that if his mother liked her, eventually his father would, too.

"I almost feel like I know you," Olivia said, taking Jada's arm and leading her inside. Olivia laughed to herself because there was more truth in that statement than either Jada or Luca could ever imagine. "And you have excellent taste in clothes!" she continued, noticing that they both wore similarly styled loose-cut navy-blue trousers and blue-and-white striped nautical tops.

They both laughed, and Jada felt herself relaxing a bit.

Lorenzo was waiting for them in the living room. He was excited to see his son and to meet Jada, but he had not run to the door to greet them. He felt such an act was perhaps expected of mothers, but not of fathers. Luca was the mirror image of the senior Alessandri: Luca had a couple of inches on Lorenzo, but they had the same facial features, the same wavy hair (though Lorenzo's was nearly all white) and the same arresting blue eyes.

"Ah! Luca," Lorenzo exclaimed, pulling his son into a hug. The bond between them was undeniable. "You look pretty good for an old man! It's good to see you, my son."

Jada and Olivia stood in the background, allowing Lorenzo and Luca to have their special moment together.

"Papà, I want you to meet—"

"Jada, I am so happy to meet you! I don't know why Luca kept you from visiting for so long," Lorenzo said, kissing her on either cheek. "He has told us so much about you, except he failed to convey how absolutely beautiful you are."

"Thank you, Mr. Alessandri."

Lorenzo was being completely honest. Neither Luca's description of Jada nor the photos provided by the detective agency had done her justice. Her flawless skin and attractive shape made her traffic-stopping beautiful. If he hadn't known for a fact that she was forty-five, he would have never believed it. She didn't look much over thirty. On top of that, she had style! No one had more style than his Olivia, and they had coincidentally worn almost the same outfit. *That* was a good sign.

"Please . . . let's go in the garden. We're having lovely weather for May. It's warm enough today for us to have lunch outside." Olivia and Lorenzo led the way.

"You see, I told you it would be okay," Luca murmured, taking her hand and kissing it as they walked outside.

They had a wonderful time together. Jada was struck by the formality of the meal—there were four courses, and each one started with Olivia serving everyone. And the flatware was not touched by anyone until Olivia had picked up hers. First, there was the antipasto, a traditional tomato and mozzarella caprese salad that was delicious simplicity at its best, bursting with flavor. Next came the pasta, a mouthwatering linguine with a spicy sauce, all homemade by Olivia. She said it was Luca's favorite. Though Jada was already feeling full, there was more, a delectable veal dish and to finish off the meal, a light, pleasing panna cotta topped with strawberries, a stiff espresso and delightful Italian chocolate, made in Torino. It was different from the routine of meals at her parents' house, or at the house of anyone she'd visited in the US. Still, she felt welcomed and accepted.

Olivia couldn't help peppering the conversation with stories about how kind and intelligent Luca was as a child. She told them how he used to bring a coffee to his father's office at home and then ask him all kinds of questions. "He wanted to know all about business, fashion, architecture, design, how Allegro started, who worked there, how much they were paid." Olivia chuckled. "It made Lorenzo crazy; every day, he had more questions.

But Luca was just trying to figure out life. When he finally came to work at Allegro, he had more answers than questions. It was Luca's idea to expand the company outside of Italy," Olivia said proudly. Luca was flushed with embarrassment at the parental adoration.

It was all amusing and insightful, but suddenly, Jada was finding it hard to keep from yawning. She felt really rude because her eyes kept closing in the middle of the conversation. But Lorenzo came to the rescue.

"Luca, you are not being very sensitive. Jada is tired. Look at her! Take her home now. And let her sleep." Lorenzo couldn't resist teasing his son a little. An afternoon watching him look at his girlfriend had provided visual evidence of what he had heard in Luca's voice over the phone; he was besotted.

"Jada, I'm sorry. My father is right. I'm so used to flying back and forth that it doesn't bother me too much. We should go."

"Please, Luca, what are you apologizing for? I've been having such a wonderful time. Thank you so much, Mr. and Mrs. Alessandri."

Olivia patted Jada's arm. "You are most welcome, Jada. I hope that Luca won't keep you all to himself while you're here. I would love to see you again."

"I'll make sure we see each other often, Mrs. Alessandri. Don't worry," Jada said, glancing at Luca. To Luca, the day couldn't have gone better. His father had expressed misgivings when he was in Boston, but he could not have hoped for his parents to be more accepting of Jada.

"Well, Jada, I think it's safe to say that my parents liked you——a lot."

"I'm glad. I really liked them, too. It was really interesting. Your parents are so different from mine—a lot more formal."

"Formal?"

"It was fine. I don't mean that in a bad way . . . it was just different. How can I explain it? My parents are kind of all over the place. They laugh loud, they mumble, they raise their voices. Your parents are sort of always at the same pitch. It was . . . refreshing."

"Refreshing. That's an interesting way to put it. Well, I'm glad that you liked them. My friends will be a piece of cake after meeting them!"

CHAPTER 22

The next morning, Luca brought Jada breakfast in bed; it was almost 10 a.m.

"Good morning, *amore mio*. Breakfast. Did you sleep well?"

"Well, when I finally got to sleep, yes. Thanks for your concern, Mr. Alessandri."

Luca laughed, happy that Jada had gotten a second wind when they got home. Making love with her in his home in Italy seemed, in some ways, even more special than their first time together.

He had moved into the apartment after his divorce, and for several years it was little more than a hollow shell. None of the rooms had been decorated, and the furnishings had comprised the bare necessities—a bed and a sofa. At times, he had questioned the wisdom of having bought such a large apartment. Eventually, his friends urged him either to make it a place he actually enjoyed living in or to sell it. He agreed with them and had thrown himself into making it a place he wanted to come back to at the end of each day. His efforts had made a big difference, but the apartment was still a place he associated with being alone.

Over the years, Luca had brought women to his home, but such liaisons had always been temporary. This was different. Walking Jada through the house, showing her "their bedroom" and making space in the closet for her clothes, had all made her presence seem more permanent. With its dark drapes, imposing fireplace and touches of Venetian gold, his bedroom had always seemed quintessentially masculine. Jada's presence made the room seem brighter, more feminine. He could easily see them living there together; she seemed to fit perfectly.

"Luca, this is delicious! And the coffee, it's *so* good!"

"I'm glad you like it. Lavazza is a famous Italian coffee, and it is based here," Luca said, watching Jada devour the breakfast his housekeeper had left for him in the kitchen. There were flaky croissants, pastries and a homemade berry jam.

"Sorry, honey. I *will* leave some for you."

"Have what you like; there's more. I'm glad you like the coffee. Like I told you, my culinary skills aren't the greatest, but I do make a good coffee."

"Well, this is excellent coffee," Jada said again. "All right, my dear, now that I'm rested and fed, tell me, what's the plan for today?"

Luca rubbed his hands together eagerly, "Today, my love, I'm going to show you Torino. My Torino."

CHAPTER 23

The Beanies, the most coveted advertising awards in Boston, were coming up. Taking home the most Golden Beanpots was the aim of the best agencies in town. Derived from Boston's nickname, Beantown, the beanpot was a popular icon for a number of local awards, but none of them as prestigious as the ad industry's Golden Beanpot.

David Heath was elated. Stuck-up smart-ass Jada Green was out of town and, consequently, would miss the deadline for Beanie nomination submissions. Each account team was responsible for gathering all the data required for their respective nominations. David had checked with the people on Jada's various accounts; none of them had been asked to prepare nominations for Beanie awards.

"Gene is going to be furious!" David said out loud, his glee ill-disguised. Honoraria didn't limit the agency's nomination submissions, even though each one was costly, especially if the ads were not selected for awards. But the agency's management believed each team should have the chance to showcase its work on the city stage. In the competitive world of advertising, agencies in New York and as far away as San Francisco paid close attention to the awardees at the Beanies; winning one was great career PR.

Most of the six Honoraria VPs selected the work they deemed worthy of consideration. But David and some others preferred to have their entire team meet together to justify their top picks. This approach also ensured that David need not have a handle on every piece of creative work generated by his team. In fact, his role at the meeting was more like that of a facilitator than anything else.

"I make career-building opportunities for the people on my team!" he said triumphantly. *Boy, I've got to stop talking to myself out loud. People might think I'm crazy.*

David's team came up with submissions in four categories for the Beanies. He assigned leaders for each submission and told them they had to have all the required information turned in two days before the deadline. He considered his approach brilliant—the team got to feel as if they were getting the opportunity to lead the charge, and he basically just let them do it and got the credit. It was a win-win strategy, he thought.

"Thanks to all of you for your hard work over the past year. We're going to be *big* winners for Honoraria at this year's Beanies. I can feel it." His team left the conference room feeling energized and excited.

"What's going on?" Annie asked one of the junior copywriters leaving the meeting.

"Beanies. David is just having us get our submissions in."

"Oh? Where did I get the idea that the deadline was a while ago?" Annie loved playing dumb sometimes.

"No, the deadline is next Thursday and David wants us to have everything in by Tuesday. So it's a top priority from this moment on."

"Do you have lots to do?"

"Yes, but David is pretty excited about our chances. He said that some teams at Honoraria didn't even bother to submit work this year."

"Is that so? Did he say who didn't?"

"No, but David said our team is probably a shoo-in for at least three of the four categories we're going for!"

"That's great. Well, good luck!"

"Thanks."

Annie never ceased to be amazed at how easy it was to get information out of people, since everyone—especially the young guns—believed that a secretary was too clueless to totally understand what was being talked about. The arrogance was unbelievable at times, but she used it to her advantage. Ashley, whom she'd just pumped for information, was a pretty nice girl, but even she had a demeanor that sometimes bordered on the unbearable.

Ashley's comments had told Annie that David thought Jada had not done her nomination submissions before going on vacation. Little did he know that Annie had completed the paperwork on the five nominations days ago and had hand-carried them to the Beanie award office just to be certain that nothing slipped through the cracks.

No doubt about it, Jada was on top of her game and was a full step ahead of David. She had Annie keep files on all the work done by her team for her various accounts. Jada made the decisions about nominations, because she knew every piece of work developed by her team, and when the Beanies or other awards came up, she could make decisions quickly on what should be nominated without having to interrupt everyone's ongoing work. David thought that bringing his team together to decide things for him was team-building, but in truth, the ongoing process of stopping work on billable projects to gather data for award nominations was frustrating, no matter how prestigious the award. But his head was too high up in the clouds to notice.

David's sophomoric games of one-up with Jada were sometimes amusing, sometimes irritating. Jada usually took the high road when they clashed, but Annie had to admit she felt perverse pleasure when David Heath came out on the losing end. Imagining his reaction when he realized he'd drawn the wrong conclusion about Jada's Beanie submissions, she smiled broadly. "This is going to be a fun one to watch unfold!"

CHAPTER 24

Hugh was settling into his new life in Boston. He *loved* being president; he loved the title and the perks. It was silly, but he still got a charge out of introducing himself as "president of Allegro, USA." He liked being in charge, and it showed in everything he said and did. He had promised Luca he would prove he was the right man for the job, and he was completely focused on doing just that. He'd heard that Jada Green had flown back to Italy with him to meet his family. *Good. Maybe she'll decide to stay there, and Luca could fuck off out of my space indefinitely.*

Hugh had found a nice duplex condo in a brownstone on Marlborough Street in the Back Bay that seemed to fit with his image of how a company president should live. The Back Bay was the most expensive area in the city, and living there represented the ultimate in success to him. He decided to ask Fiorella to live with him, too. He wasn't sure what would happen to them in the future, but for now, he didn't have to worry about an escort as he made the rounds of social functions to drum up business. She could chip in for a share of the living expenses and the sex was fucking fantastic. Who could ask for more?

Yeah, he and Fiorella made a great team—in the office and out. Life was pretty damned good. Together they had made inroads at some impressive companies, and if even only one of them came through, he was sure that both Luca and the old man would see him in a different light.

Fiorella walked into his office unannounced, interrupting his thoughts. He *hated* it when she did that!

"Great news!" she said, flopping down onto one of the sleek, Italian-design, cocoa-colored leather sofas in Hugh's office.

"What's happened?"

"I just got a call from that accounting firm—Case & Battle. They're in!"

"You're joking?"

"I never joke about success, Hugh, you know that."

"This is excellent news, and it calls for a celebration."

A fridge and a small space that concealed a minibar were behind one of the cabinets near his desk. The fridge always had a bottle or two of prosecco, an Italian sparkling wine that Hugh offered to clients upon introduction or to close a deal. It was a nice touch, reminding clients that when they worked with Allegro, they got the *real* European aesthetic, not the fabricated one in the minds of Americans. Otherwise, Hugh and Fiorella celebrated the end of the week (or the day) with a toast or two after everyone else in the small office had gone.

The sun was setting and Hugh had the lights in his office on dim, so the room took on an almost ethereal quality as they sat on the sofa sipping their drinks.

"Shall we call Luca and tell him the news?"

"It's late. Luca has gotten into the habit of turning off his mobile phone when he's left the office. Jada is there with him, one of our mutual friends told me. He has not met her yet, but expects to in a few days."

"Do you think this is serious?"

"I don't know, but I've known Luca for a long time, and I've never seen him like this with a woman before."

"I don't get it. All this from meeting some woman at an agency review . . . fucking ridiculous."

"Really, Hugh, you may *look* like a romantic hero, but you have absolutely no sense of romance!"

"What? I'm romantic. I buy you flowers sometimes. I take you out for romantic dinners. I'd just call myself . . . practical."

"Practical?"

"Yeah. I mean, how much do you want to bet that this thing with Jada Green doesn't work out at all? I mean, she's from here; he's from there. She's black; he's white. They've got too many opposites—too much going against them. It's not practical."

"Hugh, I don't think love works that way . . ."

"Rubbish. Now look at us. We're different. I'm from the greatest country on earth—the UK—and you're from one of the countries of former glory. But we're in the same place—none of this to-ing and fro-ing. We're building an empire. It *works*."

"We are building an empire, aren't we? This Case & Battle job is big. It's the first we've gotten without any support from Luca."

"I'm telling you, Fee, I am determined to kick ass here so much that there's no way he'd ever *consider* having me take over Europe. It would be easier to guarantee if Jada Green weren't in the picture. I'd love her to just go away so his fixation with being here could end, but that's just a minor obstacle. They can stay together or not. We're going for greater glory!"

They raised their glasses in a toast.

CHAPTER 25

"I thought I'd drive you all around the city and then we can get out and walk. We Italians love our cars, so it's a nice excuse for me to drive," Luca said, opening the passenger-side door to his Alfa Romeo Spider.

"And may I say you have a really nice car in which to do so, Mr. Alessandri," Jada said, slipping into a black leather seat that was almost sinfully soft.

"Thank you. I do like my car a lot; I enjoy driving. I have another car, but it's from that other country."

"What kind is it?

"A Porsche 911. I keep it at my parents' house. It's a very fast car, and I would be too tempted driving around the city with it, so I don't get to drive it that often."

Jada looked at him with mock pity. "My heart bleeds for you, honey."

Luca laughed. "I know, I know. But I'm not complaining. I don't have many vices, but cars and women named Jada are at the top of my list," he said, earning a smile from her.

"Now the tour begins. I bet you didn't know that, for a short while, Torino was the capital of Italy?"

"Really?"

"Yes, it wasn't for long, but in the late 1800s this was the capital. It was moved to Rome around 1865."

"I didn't know that."

"I know all kinds of fun facts. That spire you see there is the Mole Antonelliana. It has become one of Torino's most iconic structures. It's even on the Italian two-euro coin! The building was originally meant to be a Jewish temple, but it is now a museum."

"That sounds like a good story. What happened?"

"Oh, it's the familiar story of many buildings in Italy that were conceived and took forever to be completed. Antonelli was hired to build the temple, but his vision kept changing, and the spire got taller and taller, the cost higher and higher. Eventually, the Jewish community said, '*Basta!*' and the city of Torino took over the construction. In the end, it was 167 meters tall, almost 550 feet, significantly taller than the original design."

"What kind of museum is it?"

"It's the National Museum of Cinema—a very popular place. We'll drive by for a closer look later."

"How many people live here?"

"Close to a million. It used to be a bit bigger; people moved away in the eighties, but it's growing again."

"The same thing is happening in Boston."

"Yes, but Boston has an enormous metropolitan area; Torino is a bit more self-contained. This park is Parco Mario Carrara—a lovely place. As industrial cities go, Torino is very green. Maybe it's because we have the Alps around us to remind us of nature."

"It is absolutely spectacular." Jada had been to many cities in the US and she'd visited Paris and London, but to her Torino, all awash in Renaissance elegance and pic-ture-postcard Alpine charm, was unlike any city she'd seen before. *I could easily imagine myself living here.* She quickly banished the thought, not wanting her dreams to get too far ahead of her reality.

Luca had known she would be bowled over by the charm of his city. But in a split second, she'd gone from admiring to pensive. "Hey!" He touched her knee. "What's wrong?"

"Nothing; it's just really beautiful."

Luca wasn't convinced, but he decided to let it be.

"That's the Palazzo Reale di Torino—the royal palace of the House of Savoy. Much of it was done or modern-ized in the seventeenth century, but the House of Savoy has existed since the 1500s."

The façade of the palace stretched over a very large city block. Situated in front was an enormous piazza. People were milling about, taking pictures and enjoying the midday sunshine. Two majestic horseman statues stood on either side of the palace entrance, which was lined with deep-green sculpted trees. "It is extraordinary. I'm beginning to sound like a broken record!"

"It *is* amazing. On the other side of the Palazzo is the cathedral of St. John the Baptist."

"That's where the Shroud of Turin is, right?"

"Yes! I suppose that's the thing most people know about Torino."

"I had expected it to be a more elaborate place," Jada said as they drove past the rather plain stone cathedral.

Luca was momentarily distracted as he maneuvered through the increasingly busy streets, occasionally uttering a few choice curse words under his breath.

"I'm back. Yes, I suppose it's not surprising to hear you say that. That's the Museo Egizio over there, the Egyptian Museum. There are more Egyptian antiquities there than anywhere in the world, except Egypt, of course. Now I'm going to drive closer to the Mole Antonelliana so that you can actually see it. Then we'll walk, I promise!"

He took her to the bustling pedestrian zone, via Garibaldi, and they strolled, looking in shop windows at buttery-soft leather goods, all kinds of jewelry—from delicate gold chains to chunky, contemporary designs— the latest fashions, and typical tourist shops filled with any kind of trinket one might want to bring home for a friend or loved one. Jada bought gifts for her parents, her brothers and Renie. Luca bought Jada perfume by a local designer, a scarf and a beautifully designed pair of gloves. "You have to have them, *amore mio*," he said. He took note of a delicate Byzantine necklace that she had admired. In need of a break, Luca took her to Caffé Platti for coffee. "One of my favorite places in the entire world," Luca enthused. "Excellent coffee, even better hot chocolate. Incidentally, did you know that chocolate bars were invented in Torino?"

They took a romantic stroll along the River Po. "This is a beautiful spot," Luca said, stopping to take in the view of the bridge over the river, the city and the hillside in the distance. Rowers glided by effortlessly along the river. "When I was a teenager, my mother used to bring me here for inspiration."

"Really?"

He sighed. "Yes, I was smart, but pretty lazy. Even though Allegro is a family company, she didn't want me to mindlessly accept my role as company heir. She wanted me to choose Allegro and not have it choose me. 'Everyone needs a dream,' she would say. 'Find what inspires you and work to get it. That's what life is about.' She brought me here *a lot*, and somehow I did find inspiration. That's why I went to university and studied design and architecture and didn't just go to work for my father. Papà wasn't thrilled, but he knew my mother was right. It had to be my choice to work with him, not his."

Jada listened thoughtfully. "What a wonderful gift your mom gave you. I could tell from her story yesterday that she has always wanted you to be your own person. No one can live someone else's dream."

"What about you? I imagine you had lots of dreams."

"I had plenty. The problem was figuring out how I could make them happen. Sometimes, the gap between what I imagined and where I was—*who* I was—seemed insurmountable. My parents are hardworking people. Dad is a retired postal worker and Mom is a nurse. They always encouraged me to aim high, but I didn't have access to internships and jobs, and they didn't know how to help, so I was on my own. It's not an unusual story, but a whole lot of people get fed up and forget about their dreams. I never could do that; I couldn't give up."

"That doesn't surprise me. Your focus and determination shows through in everything you do; it's one of the things I love most about you." Glancing over his shoulder once again at the view, he took her hand and said quietly, "Let's go home."

For Jada, it was an extraordinary day. Torino, a city she'd never set foot in three days ago, felt so comfortable and familiar. For his part, Luca was just happy to be with her in this place he loved so much. Any lingering doubts he might have had about their being together for the long term were quickly dissipating.

"Tonight I'm taking you to my favorite restaurant in all of Torino."

"Really?"

"Yes. It's owned by an amazing man who was quite an adventurer. His son is the chef, and the menu is always original and delicious. And the wine is fantastic. They get much of their wine from some of the smaller vineyards in the area. I think you'll like it very much."

"I'm sure I will." Jada was exhausted after touring Torino all day, but she was looking forward to dinner, since Luca wanted to share yet another one of his special things with her.

And the meal was everything Luca had described and more. They shared the entire meal—a seafood soup overflowing with tender shrimp and juicy mussels, followed by a chicken piccata, exploding with citrus and salty flavors in each bite, homemade fettuccine and a tart lemon sorbet to complete the meal. Luca was drinking an espresso when the owner came over to say hello. Jada complimented the chef, saying, "Luca promised me an unforgettable meal tonight, and this was. Thank you."

"Everything is homemade and comes from the region or close by. Where are you from?"

"Boston."

"Ah, a delightful city. I've been there and traveled all throughout the northeast, trying out Italian restaurants along the way. You have some nice ones."

"Yes, we do."

"Well, I hope you enjoy your visit to Torino, Jada, and I know that if Luca has anything to say about it, we will see you again soon."

"I hope so. Thanks again for such a wonderful meal."

In the car on the way home, Luca said, "*Amore mio*, I'm afraid I will have to leave you tomorrow. I have some things at the office that I have to take care of."

"Luca, I never expected you to be with me every minute of every day while I'm here. I'm the one on vacation, not you."

"I know. Still, I would like to spend another day taking you around town."

"We have time. Tomorrow I can do some sightseeing on my own, or I'll call your mother and visit with her."

Luca groaned. "I don't want her telling you any more 'when Luca was a little boy' stories. I nearly died of embarrassment yesterday."

Jada chuckled. "Luca, the stories were so cute. It's clear that you're the light of your mom's life."

"Still, I don't want you holding these things over my head one day."

"I think you can count on that!" Jada joked.

Still thinking about what to do while Luca was at the office, she said, "Actually, I may just stay home and read and relax tomorrow . . . maybe check e-mail."

"That's fine, too, as long as you promise not to do work. Remember, you're the one who just reminded me that you are on vacation!"

Luca returned to work with renewed vigor the next morning. Rising early, he showered, shaved and was on the phone by 8 a.m. Jada got to observe him in his work routine, his tone by turn exasperated, joking, conciliatory. And even though she couldn't understand what he was saying, she could tell when he was closing a deal or making casual conversation. Listening to him deepened her respect for him as a businessman and offered a glimpse into why he was so successful managing Allegro.

Eventually he left for his office, leaving Jada with every possible means short of a smoke signal for getting in touch with him. What to do in his absence was solved when his mother called and invited her to lunch, arriving promptly at noon.

On the drive to into town, Olivia said, "I chose a nice little restaurant Lorenzo and I enjoy when we come to town. I hope you'll like it."

"I'm sure I will."

The restaurant, with its dark wooden walls, heavy, burgundy drapes and crisp white tablecloths, was tucked away on a quiet side street. Jada imagined it was a place frequented by the ladies who lunch (and at times, their husbands).

"Jada, I am so glad you were able to meet me for lunch today," Olivia said as they took their seats.

"I meant it when I said I was going to make sure we got the chance to spend more time together. Luca was feeling badly about having to go to work today, but I reminded him that I'm the one on vacation, not him. Anyway, now it's given us the chance to meet again! But I have to tell you, Mrs. Alessandri, Luca is petrified."

"Why is that?"

"He's afraid that you're going to tell me a lot of stories about him when he was a little boy, and that I will in turn use them to embarrass him at inopportune moments." They both laughed at the notion.

Olivia considered herself a good judge of character and she was pretty sure Jada was sincere, but she would be even surer by the end of lunch. A woman who was not sincere almost always showed her true colors when her man was not around.

"Luca is happier than he's been in a long while, and it seems that it's all because of you."

"He has completely changed my life, too. I love him very much, Mrs. Alessandri."

"Have you talked about the future?"

It hadn't worried Jada that she and Luca hadn't had "the talk" about marriage, but when Mrs. Alessandri asked about it, she immediately felt that something must be wrong. Maybe they should have had that discussion by now? On the other hand, they hadn't known each other that long. Still, she felt a little insecure as she replied.

"About getting married? No, not specifically. But we've discussed how much we want to be together and the pros and cons of living in one place or another. Your husband and Luca have worked hard to build Allegro, and as much as I love him, I don't want anything to jeopardize that. Right now, it seems Allegro would be best served by Luca being here in Torino. It's too soon for me to consider moving here; our relationship is still so new. Besides, I couldn't move here and just be idle. I want to work; I want to be productive. I'll start Italian classes when I go back. In the near term we won't be together all the time, but maybe this is a good way to test our feelings for each other, to see if what we believe we have is strong enough to survive being separated."

Olivia liked what she was hearing. "Why have you never married, Jada?"

"Quite frankly, Mrs. Alessandri, no one ever asked me. When I was in school, I was focused on getting the best grades I could to ensure getting a good job; when I got out of school, it seemed no one was really interested."

"That doesn't seem possible. You're an extraordinary girl! Are you sure you weren't just focused on your career?"

"I was focused on my career, but I have always been open to dating. I am a true believer in balance, so even at my most work-obsessed, I've always made it a point to fit in friends and things unrelated to work. It's hard to find men to date these days. I told Luca I'd seen statistics indicating that seventy percent of professional black women are single. I'm just one of them."

"Seventy percent? That number seems too high to be true."

"I thought so, too, when I first came across it, but I actually made a random list of twenty friends and acquaintances, and, to my surprise, the percentage actually holds true. I guess, at some point, you stop believing it's meant to be. I'm not desperate; I'm good at being alone."

"But you're not alone now. Luca is very much in love with you."

"I know. But the last thing I want to do is smother him because he's my boyfriend now. I think the best way for us to stay happy as a couple is to continue to be who we are. That's why I didn't want Luca to stay in Boston just for us. We'll work something out, but it will take time."

Squeezing Jada's hands, Olivia said, "Luca is very lucky to have found you. I told Lorenzo I thought you were by far the nicest woman he's ever had in his life."

"Thank you. I have to ask you, Mrs. Alessandri, does my race bother you?"

"I will be honest, at first it did, but your age did, too. Lorenzo and I had dreamed of having lots of grandchildren. But that is our problem, not yours. We could have had more children of our own, but we were a little selfish ourselves, and I realize that we have been wrong to then pass our selfish wishes to our son. More than anything, we want Luca to be happy. He is my son, and I know I am a little biased, but he is a wonderful person. Very sensitive. His marriage wasn't a happy one. I think he married Mirella because he felt it was what his father and I expected. And it was, to a certain extent. He tried so hard for a long time to make it better, but he was miserable from the start, and Mirella was not very supportive of him at all. After seeing what that unhappy marriage did to him . . . Jada, nothing is more important than my son's happiness. You make him very happy. When I first heard about you, I asked, 'Why did he choose a black woman? Why did he choose an American? Why didn't he choose someone younger?' Now that I have met you, I ask, 'How could he choose anyone but you?' "

Quickly brushing away her tears, Jada said, "Thank you for saying that, Mrs. Alessandri; it really means a lot. Luca means the world to me."

"And you, dear Jada, mean the world to him, too."

CHAPTER 26

"Did you enjoy lunch with my mother?"

"Yes, a lot, and not one when-Luca-was-a-little-boy story, so you can breathe easy."

"Thank God."

"She made me cry, though."

"What?"

"Oh, nothing bad. She said such nice things about me. That was the reason for the tears."

"Of course, she would, *amore mio*; you are wonderful."

"Thanks."

"I hope you're not too tired; we're going out tonight. You will finally meet a few of my closest friends—my Fabulous Four. They have been complaining that you've been here for three days and they have yet to meet you. So tonight you'll meet Antonio and his wife, Natalia, and Daniele and his girlfriend, Elena. Antonio and Natalia were childhood sweethearts. I've known them both since we were babies. They have been married for almost twenty-five years. I met Daniele in grade school. Elena and I met at university thirty years ago."

"You weren't kidding when you said you had a pretty closed social circle, were you?"

"No, I wasn't. It should be interesting for you because Natalia is a stay-at-home wife and Elena is a vice president like you, only she works for a high-tech firm. I don't want to say much more. When you meet them, you'll make up your own mind about everyone."

"All right. I'll go get ready."

Luca had told her that it was one of the restaurants frequented by the most elite Turinese, and she could see it from the moment they walked into the long, narrow restaurant. The walls were all mirrored and draped with sheer curtain panels. A sleek onyx bar dominated the entrance, and round and curved tables were situated toward the back. Everyone seemed to know everyone; it was the kind of place that would have made Jada intensely nervous in her twenties or thirties, but age had endowed her with a higher level of self-confidence. A protective arm around her waist, Luca headed straight for the table where his friends were seated without looking left or right.

He greeted them warmly and began the introductions. Daniele and Antonio both rose to greet her. Daniele and Luca had a similar coloring, but Daniele had a more portly build. Antonio was tall like Luca but almost bald. His face was weathered and tanned like he'd been at sea. They introduced their respective partners. Elena was a petite brunette with a high-energy demeanor. Natalia was tall and reed thin with an extraordinary mane of wavy blonde hair that she had casually pulled to one side. Jada recalled Luca saying she and Antoino had been married for twenty-five years, but she didn't look much over thirty.

"It's nice to finally meet you, Jada," Daniele said. "Welcome to Torino."

"Thank you, Daniele. I'm really glad to be here."

They settled into friendly conversation about what Jada had done since arriving, and they asked her about her impressions of Torino and how it differed from Boston. Elena was animated and engaging; Natalia seemed bored, or perhaps a little cold. Jada caught Luca's eye, and he winked at her as if to signal he understood how she was feeling. Fortunately, Natalia's less-than-warm vibes had not ruined the evening; she was having a delightful time. And so were Luca's friends, all of whom spoke fluent English.

Jada especially enjoyed the wine and the prosecco and, for the first time in a long time, she felt a pleasant little buzz. Then, out of nowhere, a woman—tall, blonde and beautiful—appeared. Speaking rapid-fire Italian, she aimed her ire exclusively at Luca. Some in the group looked down, others looked away. Luca waited out her tirade and then responded in a loud and angry voice that was entirely new to Jada. The woman spun around and walked away quickly.

"Who was that?" Jada asked, already suspecting the identity of the enraged intruder.

"Unbelievable," Antonio said. "That was Luca's ex-wife, Mirella."

"Oh." Jada didn't quite know what to say, especially since she did not know what the two had said to each other. No one was talking at all; the jovial mood of the group had changed in an instant. Luca quickly asked for the bill and everyone left immediately.

The ride back to Luca's apartment was quiet and awkward, but it was clear he was inwardly seething.

"Do you want to talk about it?"

"Jada, Mirella has some emotional issues. I don't know how we lasted for ten years."

"You probably thought staying married was the right thing, so you hung on."

"That sounds like my mother's assessment of things. Did you two talk about my marriage today?"

Jada didn't want to upset Luca any more than he already was, but she wasn't going to lie to him, either.

"A little. She told me how worried she had been for you and that you had been very unhappy."

"My mother liked Mirella at first, but over time she started to notice things about her that made her worry. She didn't want to interfere directly, but she would tell me to be more supportive, to travel less and spend more time with my wife. I did exactly the opposite, which made things worse. I just thought Mirella was being possessive and unreasonable. It never occurred to me that she needed help."

"What did Mirella say to you?"

"I don't really—"

"It was about me, wasn't it?"

Luca clenched his jaw but didn't answer.

"Okay. I can guess what she said."

"I'm embarrassed. In all the time we were married, I'd never heard her talk like that."

"Luca, *you're* not a bigot; that's all that matters to me."

"I am sorry. She ruined a nice evening."

They didn't talk much for the rest of the evening. He seemed deep in thought, and Jada took great pains not to intrude. At first, she thought they would not make love; Luca lay still in bed, not touching her and making her feel she shouldn't touch him. They didn't have to make love, but she felt so emotionally distant from him, she wanted to cry. But later he turned to her and kissed her slowly, passionately. He then began making love with a tenderness so profound, goose bumps appeared all over her body. He never said a word, but his eyes spoke the depth of his feelings for her.

Her time in Torino was flying by. Jada finally broke down and called the office to check in. What she heard was pretty much the same old stuff: people contemplating the future of her accounts, people wondering where she'd gone on vacation, and people speculating about her apparently neglecting to submit work for the Beanies. Annie admitted she had not bothered to correct any misconceptions about that.

"Well, no one asked me *directly* about what you had done before you left, so I didn't see any reason to volunteer information."

"Annie, don't go stirring the pot!"

"I can't wait until next month when they all get to the Beanies and see the finalists in each category and discover that your stuff is up there! It will be great." Annie chuckled.

"Well, I'm glad everything is okay. I'll be back in a couple of days."

"Have a safe trip back home and I'll see you Friday, bright and early. And Jada? Don't take this the wrong way, but don't call back. If anything needs your attention, I'll call you."

"If I didn't know better, I'd think you've been talking to Luca. I get the message. You won't hear from me again. Thanks, Annie."

Jada was determined to enjoy every moment of her remaining four days in Torino. She left bright and early Monday morning with Luca and enjoyed wandering in and out of boutiques and sitting in cafés, listening to the musical charm of the Italian language. At times, she felt as if she understood what people were saying; other times, she just smiled politely or said, "*Non parlo italiano*" –the standard response of tourists who didn't speak Italian.

Jada was walking happily along via Garibaldi when she saw her. Hoping she would just walk by, she tried to duck into a boutique, but it was too late. Mirella walked up to her, smiling, but it was clear the smile was not meant to be friendly. Jada did not know if she spoke English; she hoped she didn't because that would guarantee that their encounter would be brief. Luca was supposed to meet her in a little while for lunch. She was hoping there would not be a repeat of the restaurant scene a couple of nights ago because she seemed intent on causing a confrontation.

"Well, it's Luca's new girlfriend," Mirella said in perfect English.

Jada considered what Luca had told her about Mirella, and decided that it wasn't even worth it to engage her in conversation.

Stepping aside to pass her, Jada said, "Excuse me."

Mirella was aghast that Jada would walk away from her without really speaking. She pulled Jada's shoulder and, when she turned, Mirella slapped her across the face. Jada was stunned.

Luca had just caught a glimpse of Jada walking toward him after she had passed by Mirella, so he hadn't noticed his ex-wife mere footsteps behind his girlfriend. But when Mirella grabbed her suddenly and slapped her, he sprinted toward them.

"Mirella, what in the hell do you think you're doing?" he demanded, speaking in English so that Jada could understand exactly what they were saying.

"What am I doing? Your *girlfriend* is insolent. Why did you bring her here? I told you the other night to make sure that I didn't see her anywhere I go in Torino, and I find her walking down the street window-shopping!"

Well, it's official. Now I know exactly what she said the other night.

"Apparently you didn't hear what *I* told you the other night, either. I told you that what I did was not your concern. Let me remind you again: we are divorced. We have been divorced for ten years, Mirella! *Ten years.* My life was hell when we were together! If you ever talk to me again or come near Jada again, I will kill you."

The ice-cold look in Luca's eyes and his fierce tone frightened Jada. "Luca! Please don't sink to her level.

Come on, let's go," she said, taking his hand and gently pulling him away. She was absolutely mortified.

"I'm glad she pulled you away, Luca. I could press charges against you for threatening my life. Here!" she said, gesturing at the curious onlookers drawn to the scene. "There are witnesses!" The crowd quickly dispersed, as those who understood English wanted no part of the quarrel between the two women and the man.

Jada at his side, Luca walked closer to Mirella to avoid having to yell. "It looks like you lost your witnesses. In case you forgot, you hit Jada. *She* can press charges against you, too. Look, just go away, Mirella. What I do is of no concern to you. I have a reputation that I care about as much as you care about yours, so you don't need to worry about what anyone says about Jada or anything else I do. You will still be one of the most admired women in Torino."

It was amazing. With Luca's assurance that she still mattered in Torino, Mirella's temperament appeared to have changed. She even smiled slightly before turning and walking away without another word.

Jada watched, perplexed. *All this because she was afraid she wouldn't matter anymore in this town?*

"Jada—"

She was feeling embarrassed and angry and at that moment, with people still walking by and staring at them, she wasn't prepared to discuss things.

"Luca, please take me somewhere we can talk."

"She hit you. Are you all right?"

"I'll be okay. Right now I just want to get out of here, and then I want you to explain, if you can, what just happened."

He took her hand and they walked silently to a quiet restaurant off the busy pedestrian zone. A friendly waiter came over to take their order, but his smile disappeared when he saw their grim faces. He quickly took Luca's order for aperitifs and left. Jada then looked at Luca and lit into him.

"Luca, I've got to tell you, I don't do drama very well. You said Mirella had some emotional problems, but she seems a little . . . nuts. I want to know what the hell is going on. I was walking along minding my own business, and suddenly Mirella was standing in front of me, ready to pick a fight."

Luca hung his head and took her hand. "I'm really sorry . . ."

Jada pulled her hand away. "Her behavior isn't normal. Is something wrong with her?"

"I don't know. She has not really let go. She had a bit of a breakdown after our divorce. As you can tell, her reputation means a lot to her."

"Well, as you know, my reputation means a lot to me, too, and I don't appreciate being hit by some woman in the street. Has she had any other relationships since your divorce?"

"Sure she has. I am not sure she didn't have other relationships while we were married. None of her liaisons have developed into anything serious. As for me, I can only apologize for how I reacted. I went a bit too far."

"I have to admit, you really scared me. It was even worse than the other night when Mirella came up to us at the restaurant."

"Jada, I know I keep saying the same thing over and over, but I *am* sorry."

"I guess I know what she said now."

"I want to make this up to you somehow."

"Luca, what can you do? I would never have expected that an ex-wife of ten years would be so wound up about what her ex is doing. But it comes down to this: I don't want to walk around here being afraid that Mirella is going to jump out from behind some bush and go after me again. I was having such a nice time, but maybe I should go back home a few days early."

"No. No, Jada, please don't leave. I don't think she would dare bother you again."

"I need to think about it, Luca. Let's just have lunch."

Luca didn't want to press her, so he dropped the matter and they ate without saying much else. But Jada was still fuming. *Do I really need this at my age?* She looked at Luca and knew that the answer wasn't nearly as clear-cut as she might have liked. She was in love with this man. He had been married, and every married person carries with him or her some kind of baggage from past relationships, some heavier than others. Mirella was an irritant, but if she was really a deal-breaker, then Jada had been kidding herself about being in love with Luca in the first place. That realization had a calming effect on her, and she resolved not only to stay but to never let Luca feel that he couldn't talk to her about his ex-wife. Jada emerged from her reverie to find Luca looking anxiously at his watch.

"What's wrong? Do you have a meeting this afternoon?"

"Yes, I have an important meeting that I cannot postpone. I don't want to leave you alone, though, and I do want us to talk more about this situation. My mother is in town. I'm going to call her and ask if she'll meet you. Is that okay? As for continuing our conversation, I'm hoping we can do that this evening."

Jada managed a weak smile. "Thanks for looking out for me. I know none of this is your fault. Of course we can talk some more when you get home."

"I will always do what I can to protect you, Jada. That is a promise."

Olivia wasn't far away and she arrived at the restaurant quickly. Luca greeted his mother and then said goodbye to Jada.

"*Ciao, amore mio.* I'll see you tonight."

"*Ciao*, Luca."

Olivia ordered espressos for both of them. "Jada, I'm afraid you're not getting the best impression of Italians, thanks to my ex-daughter-in-law. This incident must have been frightening for you."

"It was."

"Luca told me you're thinking of going home early. I do understand why you're upset, but I hope you will stay. Luca would be heartbroken if you were to leave even an hour before you're supposed to. Lorenzo or I will personally take you around town when Luca isn't able. That should help."

"That's really nice, Mrs. Alessandri. I've thought about it, and I've decided that I'm staying. But Mirella really frightened me, as did Luca. He was so angry he told her he would kill her if she came near me again. I was going to leave because I figured if I stayed, I might run into Mirella again. I really don't want to be the cause of Luca having any more problems with his ex. But I now realize that I can't let her chase me away from here or, more importantly, from Luca."

"Oh, Mirella! She does know how to push all of my son's buttons, as you say in English. Probably what upset him more than anything was that he had let her get to him. Luca prides himself on his control and discipline, and she has always been able to rattle him. But my dear Jada, Luca doesn't see you as the cause of anything but incredible joy in his life. You mustn't even think that you're the cause of anything upsetting to him, because you are not."

"Thanks for saying that, Mrs. Alessandri. Luca has talked to me a little about her, but I sense there's more to the story than he's been willing to share. One of these days, perhaps he will be more forthcoming."

"I'm sure it will help him to talk more. Of course, he has said very little to Lorenzo and me about his marital situation over the years. His usual response whenever we tried to talk to him was that they were 'working on their relationship.' I will speak with Mirella's family, too. They are wonderful people, and I'm sure they would be horrified when they hear what she did today."

"Mrs. Alessandri, Luca mentioned that Mirella had some kind of breakdown after they divorced. How bad was it?"

"Sadly, bad enough for her parents to send her to a retreat in Switzerland—what we used to call a very nice sanatorium. But I honestly believe the girl was unstable long before she and Luca ever met. Anyway, she seemed to be much calmer when she came back a few months later. For Mirella, maintaining her status in society means more to her than anything. When she and Luca divorced, she feared she would no longer get invited to the 'in' parties and dinners. For a long while, that was not the case, and she was better, more stable. But now that she is an older woman nearing fifty, she sees younger women, beautiful and single, being invited in her stead. Perhaps that is why she has such a strong reaction to you and Luca."

Jada thought about how difficult her own life would be if her entire self-worth depended on getting invited to social events. She imagined she would be despondent, perhaps more so than Mirella. Being older and single can do weird things to your mind—if you let it.

"Mrs. Alessandri, Mirella scared me, and I really hope I don't see her again—ever. But I do feel a little sorry for her."

Olivia patted her hand. "That's because you are a wonderful person with a kind heart."

Jada and Olivia strolled through the busy pedestrian zone for a while, and then Olivia returned Jada to Luca's apartment, and it was not long before he called to check on her. They chatted briefly, but he didn't ask if she had made a decision about leaving. She watched television for a while, but when seven o'clock came and she hadn't heard from Luca, she became a little concerned and called his cell phone; the call went to voice mail. He returned home late in the night.

"I'm sorry I am so late getting back to you. I was on a never-ending conference call with Hugh."

"I know you have to work, Luca. It's not a problem."

"So . . . have you made any decision? I really hope you will stay."

"I decided to stay."

Luca smiled, visibly relieved that Mirella's behavior—or his own—had not chased her away. "Jada, you have made my day. I was so worried that you would leave. I promise she won't bother you again."

"You can't promise that, Luca."

"You're right; I can't promise that."

"Luca, so much has happened so fast. We're building this wonderful relationship, but the reality is that we're still getting to know each other. Every day, I learn something new about you. I've gained a lot of insight into your marriage over the past week, and you've probably learned more about me, too. I realized that if I'm really serious about us, my place is here, with you, because our time together is precious. I love you and you're worth fighting for. Even if I have to duke it out on the streets of Torino to keep you," she added, laughing at the absurdity of the thought.

"You shouldn't have to do that, but I'm glad you're willing to do it for me," Luca said, also laughing.

"Now, since I've decided to stay, I want to enjoy my last few days as much as I can. So let's work out what the plan will be."

They agreed that when she wanted to go into town, she would always go with either Luca or one of his parents. Jada was touched by his parents' willingness to look out for her, realizing also that it would enable her to get to know them in a way that otherwise might not have been possible.

CHAPTER 27

The rest of her days went by quickly. Luca's parents were gracious about taking her wherever she wanted to go—to the Museo Egizio to explore the priceless antiquities, to the cathedral to actually see the Shroud of Turin. She couldn't go home and tell people she'd spent almost two weeks here and not seen it. She also did some last-minute shopping, picking up gifts for her team at the office and some Italian chocolate for her friends. All in all, it had been an unforgettable vacation.

On Wednesday, the night before her departure, Jada awoke in the middle of the night to find herself alone in bed; Luca's side of the bed was almost cold.

"Luca?" she called. When there was no response, she wrapped herself in Luca's fluffy terry robe and went looking for him. She found him sitting in the living room, staring at the cold fireplace.

"Luca, honey, it's freezing in here. What are you doing?"

"I couldn't sleep and I didn't want to wake you. I'm okay. Go back to bed."

"I won't be able to fall back asleep without you there." She sat on the sofa and snuggled close to him.

"But you'll have to get used to it."

"Believe me, I won't get used to it, but it won't be for that long. I know we'll make the most of this time apart.

You'll do what you can to wrap up your projects, and we'll be talking and figuring out what makes sense for us. We're blessed to have found each other and to have come this far. I refuse to see the coming months as a bad thing; it's just the next phase."

"I'm coming for one week every month, without fail."

"I'll be counting the days until you come next month. The Beanie Awards ceremony is the last big event before things slow down a bit during the summer months, and it happens to fall during the week you're there. We'll get to walk the advertising red carpet."

Luca actually laughed. "Even if the awards were at a different time, I would fly over. I wouldn't miss that event for anything; I've never walked a red carpet."

"We're going to have lots of fun. You're going to get to meet lots of the quirky people in the ad biz. Some are incredibly bright and creative; others are sharks."

"Sharks?"

"Yes, advertising has more than its fair share of them—those people who will sell their soul for a client or a bonus. Some of them are really harmless; they're just petty. Others are a little more predatory."

"They don't sound like the greatest people."

"Some of them aren't. But I shouldn't be talking about them that way. It's a fun industry to be a part of."

"Hmmm. I'm not so sure."

CHAPTER 28

Jada couldn't believe she was already back at the office. She hadn't fully appreciated until now how nice it had been to be away. She had arrived at the office earlier than usual. She'd found all her day-to-day correspondence on her desk, and she quickly thumbed through the stack. She had kept her promise to Luca to stay away from work while on vacation, but she had taken almost daily glances at her e-mail and had actually responded to critical ones with copies to Annie. So she set about filing or tossing the ones she had ignored. When Annie arrived, she would get to the important mail, which was kept locked up after they'd discovered that someone had been routinely rifling through her mail.

The sun was just coming up over the city, and, as much as she hated the idea of being in the office so early, she actually enjoyed the tranquility of this time of day. She thought of calling Luca—it was lunchtime in Italy—but she decided not to, as they had spoken not long after she'd arrived home the evening before, and she didn't want to seem clingy or desperate. Just then, the phone rang; it was Luca.

"Luca! I was just thinking about you."

"Don't think I'm following your every move, but I called you at home and you weren't there. Why are you at work so early, *amore mio*?"

"I'd planned to be at the office early to get a head start on things, but I had a little jet lag and woke up even earlier, so I just came in. I wanted to be so on top of things, Gene would have no reason to complain about my having been away."

Luca laughed. "You are as driven as I am."

"Yeah, I guess I am."

"Jada, I'm sorry, but I have to go. I just needed to hear your voice."

"It's good to hear yours, too."

"*Ciao, amore mio.*"

"*Ciao.*"

Annie arrived moments later. Placing her bag on her desk, she quickly went into Jada's office. "Jada, you're here already!"

"Hey, Annie! It's good to see you!"

Jada pulled two packages wrapped with bright, paisley paper out of her tote bag. "Here, I brought you a little something from Torino."

"Thanks so much, Jada."

"I know you love chocolate and my God, Annie, this is some of the best chocolate ever! And what's a trip to Italy without something leather, so you've got a wallet and a pair of gloves. I hope they fit."

"Jada, this is so thoughtful. It's too much."

"No, it's not. Annie, if you weren't here watching my back and keeping an eye on things, I couldn't have gone to Italy for almost two weeks."

"No thanks necessary, really," Annie said, going to her desk and retrieving her keys. She unlocked her secret file and got Jada's private correspondence.

"So what's on today?" Jada asked. And with that, they fell naturally into their usual routine.

"No meetings today; you've got a free Friday to catch up in peace. Gene the Mean may have made you come back early, but anyone who wants to see you can wait until Monday."

"Thanks, Annie."

"Let's see . . . You'll meet with the copywriters and art directors on Monday after the directors' meeting. Oh, there's a letter in your personal correspondence from Dan Egleston, the head of Rize agency. He's very interested in talking to you. He's called a couple of times, too. If you ask me, you're a very hot commodity, Ms. Green!"

"Do you think so? Rize is a very hot agency."

"Your winning the Burrows account is the talk of the office, and from what I hear, around town, too. The fact that you're not out there blowing your own horn at every professional event just adds to the buzz. You've got this mystery about you that keeps people talking. *And*, all your accounts are thriving. It's a good time to be you!"

Jada laughed. "Let's hope that it stays that way."

CHAPTER 29

"Hugh, this is wrong. It's completely off strategy!" Fiorella was so exasperated she wanted to scream. After all her work in putting the proposal together, he had gone and screwed it all up.

"Fee, if I'm going to take the US office of Allegro and make it my own, I've got to establish my own way of doing things: follow my own vision."

"Hugh, if you do that, you're not working at a company called Allegro. That's something completely different."

Hugh had heard enough. "Look! Just draw up the fucking designs for our meeting. We're going to do this my way. I don't care what you think about it."

"And I'm telling you Luca is not going to like it, and neither will the client."

Hugh snorted disdainfully. "We'll see."

Now thoroughly furious, Fiorella stormed out of Hugh's office, slamming the door behind her. The power that came with being president of the US operation seemed to have gone to his head. When he was president-in-waiting, they would have intense disagreements about a project's direction, but he had always been willing to listen to a dissenting view, to consider an idea different from his own, or even to change his mind completely.

What he was asking her to do was not going to go over well with the people at Case & Battle, and it was going to infuriate Luca.

Fiorella had been the principal at a small interior design company when Luca approached her about joining Allegro. Since she specialized in home interiors, not commercial design, Fiorella had been surprised by the offer; but the timing was perfect, because she had been planning to close her company. She was a designer, not a salesperson, but as a company owner, all she did was sell. Her first assignment, when she joined over four years ago, was to create a distinctive Allegro image. Working with Luca, she had painstakingly pinpointed the elements that defined the Allegro style, and it had helped propel the company to its present success. A commercial interior with a distinctive look was the best marketing tool Allegro had for attracting future business. All her hard work—and Luca's—was at risk of being cancelled out by a silly power play. She picked up the phone.

"Luca, it's Fiorella. Look, I am in a difficult position, but I wanted you to know what's going on here." She described the situation, as well as the problems she thought would inevitably ensue. Despite his best efforts, Luca began a slow burn.

"Fiorella, please put Hugh on the phone."

"Luca, please. If I connect you, he'll know that we have talked about this. I have to work with him every day . . ."

"And sleep with him every night?"

"How did you know?"

"It doesn't matter; I shouldn't have even mentioned it. Okay. I will not speak to him now, and it's probably better if I don't, but I'm ordering you *not* to show the client anything that is off strategy. You'll have to manage how you do that with Hugh. I'll be there in about a week. I can't believe that a month has gone by already."

"You have my word, Luca. The client will not see anything that's off strategy. I'll get Hugh to understand somehow. Luca, I hope you don't mind my asking . . . how are things going with you and Jada? Daniele and Elena told me they had met her; they liked her very much."

"It was a nice evening until Mirella—"

"I know; they told me. Look, Luca, I wish you and Jada every happiness. We have always kept our social and professional lives separate, but I wanted to say that to you."

"*Grazie,* Fiorella. I appreciate it. Jada means everything to me. Meeting her has changed my life."

"I'm happy for you. Anyway, as I said, I will deal with Hugh. But I felt you needed to know what was going on."

"I appreciate it, Fiorella. I'll see you next week."

"*Ciao.*"

Luca was livid. It was as if all his worst nightmares were coming true. He was beginning to feel more and more that he was the only man who could successfully establish a US presence for Allegro. His life was beginning to feel like an emotional yo-yo. Just yesterday, he had been envisioning a life with Jada in Torino one day. It had all gone so well when she was there with him.

Jada had two concerns about moving to Torino. Time would take care of both of them. First, they had met and fallen in love quickly. Although he had no doubts, it made sense to give their relationship more time to grow before anyone moved anywhere permanently. The second was Jada's concern about being able to speak Italian. He was sure she would be speaking functional Italian in no time. But right now, it seemed that he might well be the one making the move. If Hugh continued on his egocentric path, he would destroy Allegro's credibility. Luca could not let that happen.

In the meantime, Luca had plans to put into motion before his return trip. He had gone back to the pedestrian zone on via Garibaldi to purchase the Byzantine necklace Jada had admired the first day that he'd taken her sightseeing. Through friends, he had found an amazingly talented artisan designer named Marco Tuccini to translate the intricate pattern on the necklace into a setting for a ring. Marco had done some preliminary renderings of the ring, and they'd agreed on the stones required to achieve the desired look.

Sketches in hand, Luca traveled to Amsterdam, the gemstone capital of Europe, to select a diamond and two smaller rubies. Marco needed one month to perfect the design and complete the ring. That timing worked for Luca. He could take care of the other things he had to do on his upcoming trip to Boston. And the next time he traveled there, he would be able to take the ring with him.

The Tuesday before leaving, he called Jada's parents and asked to meet with them when he got into town.

They were surprised to hear from him, but didn't ask any questions, agreeing to talk when they were face to face.

Now, the day before his departure, he was on the way to his parents' house for dinner and to reveal his plan for the future.

After chatting briefly with his mother, he went to his father's office.

"Papà, how are you?"

"I'm doing well, son. It's good to see you. How are you?"

"A little frustrated, but I'm okay."

"Things aren't going well in Boston?"

"Actually, they're not. Hugh is proving to be a little bit of a problem. I told you he'd brought in a new account on his own—Case & Battle?"

"Yes."

"Well, he was planning to present some designs for their offices that were completely off strategy."

Lorenzo frowned. "I told you . . . I never liked that man! What does he think he's doing?"

"I'm going to deal with him when I go to Boston next week."

"Good. I tell you, Luca, if you need to fire him, do it. We'll get by without him if we have to. And if he keeps doing things like this, he's no help to us, anyway."

"I agree."

Olivia stuck her head into the office. "It's time for dinner, you two, so finish your discussion. I don't want to hear about work at the table."

"We'll be right there, *amore*," Lorenzo said. After so many years of marriage, he knew better than to fool with

Olivia when it came to dinner conversation. She loathed business talk at meals and was especially strict about it when it was just the three of them.

She would always say, "Ask me to delay the meal if you need to, but I do not want to hear about Allegro throughout my meal. Meals together are meant for pleasant conversation about things that are interesting to everyone at the table. If you must talk about work over lunch and dinner, then don't come home. Dine out somewhere."

"Do what you need to with Hugh," Lorenzo said as they left his office. "I know that whatever you do will be the right thing."

"Thank you, Papà. I will let you know what happens."

For a time, they chatted pleasantly about whatever subject came up and then Olivia asked, "How is Jada, Luca?"

"She's fine, but very busy at the moment. I'll be attending a big advertising awards event in Boston with her called the Beanies."

"Beanies?"

"Yes. Boston is known for a dish called Boston baked beans, so the city's nickname is Beantown, and that is why the award was dubbed a Beanie."

"Oh?" Olivia thought it all sounded a little strange. *Who ever heard of naming an award after a dish? Advertising people have a very odd sense of irony.*

"Anyway, Jada's accounts are nominated for awards in five categories."

"That's wonderful!"

"Jada is very good at what she does, Mamma. I'm sure Papà told you about how he persuaded Ambrose Burrows to take his business to Jada at Honoraria."

"Yes, he did."

"Well, they won't regret having her in charge."

Lorenzo thought before he spoke this time, careful not to divulge the extent of his knowledge about Jada.

"After all the things you told me about how smart Jada is, I knew I wasn't really going out on a limb by pushing to have her in charge of the Burrows business. Really, it was nothing."

Luca was suddenly very nervous. He was sure his parents would be happy for him and supportive. Still, it had been a long time since he'd had this kind of conversation with them. In fact, he'd expected to never again have news like this for them.

"I want to tell you both about some decisions I've made."

Somewhat surprised, Olivia and Lorenzo looked at each other, pushed their plates aside and gave Luca their full attention.

"When I return to Boston, I will be meeting with Mr. and Mrs. Green to get their blessing before I propose to Jada."

"Luca!" Olivia exclaimed, standing up to embrace her son. "Jada is such a lovely girl. I like her more than any other woman you've ever dated. Or married. I so enjoyed getting to know her when she was here in Torino. I wasn't going to mention it, but I spoke with Mirella's parents about her behavior when Jada was visiting."

"Mamma, you didn't have to do that. It is my responsibility to find a way to deal with Mirella and her antics."

Sitting down next to Luca again, Olivia said, "I know it is your responsibility, *figlio mio*, but as a parent who was concerned for my child, I felt that I had to say something to them. They are lovely people, and they were truly horrified to hear about what she had done. Mirella has taken over her parents' business and she's under a lot of pressure. She has been in a more fragile state than usual lately. They are going to send her away again."

"I hope Mirella can get the help she needs. I wasn't the most supportive husband when things took a turn for the worst; it would be fair to say I ignored all the signs that she needed help. Our marriage wasn't the right thing for either one of us, but I want her to be healthy and happy. She is a beautiful and talented woman."

"Have you talked to Jada about this?"

"A little. I don't want to keep secrets from her, but there is a delicate balance between sharing what's happened in the past and complicating the present by talking too much about all the bad things that happened before. I've been honest with Jada; I've told her that my divorce was my greatest personal failure. I'm sure as time goes on, I'll have reason to tell her more details about my marriage. My marriage and divorce have made me the man I am today; I think it's helped me learn more about what it takes to make a relationship work."

"If you and Jada can continue to communicate this way and work things through when problems arise, you will be just fine. It's what your father and I have always done," Olivia said. Suddenly, it occurred to Olivia that, thanks to the dossier they'd received right after Luca met Jada, neither she nor Lorenzo had asked what Jada's parents did.

"Her father is a retired postal worker; her mother is a nurse. They were pleasant enough when we met. I had a bigger problem with her brother, who is not very happy at all about our relationship. At least he's willing to give me a chance."

Lorenzo patted his son's shoulder, saying, "Well, I've told you that I have my concerns about all the differences you will have to sort through, too. But I know you are both determined to be together. Mirella is the past. She is probably lonely and resents that you've found someone else. I am sorry that she is somewhat fragile, but I am glad you've moved on now. I like Jada, too, and I'm happy for you, Luca. I hope she will make you very happy."

"She already has, Papà. I bought a beautiful Byzantine necklace she had admired, and commissioned Marco Tuccino, who is a great designer, to create a ring inspired by the necklace," Luca said, pulling out a copy of Marco's initial sketches. "I bought the stones he'll use in the setting a couple of weeks ago."

"So that's why you went to Amsterdam?"

"Yes, Papà. I just wasn't ready to talk about it."

Olivia admired the sketches. "Luca! This is lovely. I've heard wonderful things about Marco Tuccino. He is one of the most talented young designers in Torino, and he's booked solid with commissions, so your request must have been very persuasive. Jada will love it."

"I hope so. The ring will be ready next month, so I will propose when I get it. I'm excited, but nervous. I didn't think that I would marry again."

"We certainly hoped you would, Luca."

"We had hoped you'd give us some grandchildren, though—"

"Lorenzo!" Olivia scolded.

Luca was quiet for a moment and then, in a somber tone, said, "I know you have always wanted grandchildren. With Mirella, when I wanted to try, she wasn't ready, and when she wanted to try, I was unhappy and pretty sure that our marriage would not last. I don't know . . . if I'd met Jada even five years ago, maybe we would have had children right away. But we're both older, so I'm not sure if children are in our future. And maybe I'm selfish, but I just want us to enjoy our lives together. I'm sorry if the possibility of not giving you grandchildren has left you disappointed."

"Luca, it is true we desperately wanted grandchildren, but what we want even more desperately is for you to be happy. When you were married to Mirella, it broke my heart to see you so unhappy. Thank God that you and she had no children, because you might not have left her, and God only knows what your life would have been like. We have seen how you are when you're with Jada; she brings you great joy. Disappointed? It would be impossible for you to disappoint us. You are our greatest blessing," Olivia declared, her eyes brimming with tears.

"Thank you, Mamma."

CHAPTER 30

When the plane touched down at Logan Airport, Luca could hardly contain his excitement. So apparent was his nervousness, he wouldn't have been surprised if the customs officer had pegged him as someone fitting the profile of a drug dealer or a terrorist—or at least someone with something to hide. The wait for his bag seemed interminable, and he wished he hadn't checked it. As soon as the double doors opened into the arrivals lounge, he began scanning the crowd for Jada. Then he saw her, and like a scene from one of the sappy movies he enjoyed so much, they rushed into each other's arms.

"Jada, *amore mio* . . ." When words failed him, he just savored holding her again and tasting her lips, touching her face. They stood at the exit ramp for so long someone walking by muttered, "Get a room." So they finally set out for the parking lot.

"You look great," Jada said. And that was the absolute truth. She thought she had committed every detail about Luca to memory, but she was nonetheless struck once again by how incredibly good-looking he was. *Wow, this man is with me.* "Did you get any sleep on the plane?"

"I tried to, but I was too excited about seeing you."

When they reached Jada's car, Luca reluctantly let go of her waist and kissed her lightly on the lips. "I am so happy to be able to see you, touch you and kiss you. I missed you so much."

Playing catch-up on the drive to Jada's house, they realized how much they hadn't discussed while apart.

"It's amazing how many things we haven't told each other, even though we talk on the phone at least once a day," Luca remarked.

"I know. But there never seems to be enough time. Sometimes I want to call you, but I don't want to be a pest."

"Jada, you could never be a pest. You can call me any-time."

"I guess I know that, but I'm still sensitive about not wanting to smother you. I could do it pretty easily, you know."

"Smother away. I'll tell you if it bothers me, but remember I come from a country where men are smoth-ered first by their mothers and then by their wives. It's like a way of life." He laughed.

"Hmmm. I'll keep that in mind. You know, I'm always learning something new about you! Anyway, are you hungry? I made us a light dinner just in case."

"I ate on the plane, but I suppose I could eat a little something. What I really want is to make love with you—all night, all day tomorrow, all week."

"Whoa! We have to come up for air sometime."

"Do we?" Luca smiled. "Why?"

"Well, we do tomorrow. I promised Renie that we'd meet her and the others for brunch. And then tomorrow night we've got the Beanie Awards to attend."

"Ah, our coming-out party with your colleagues."

"Yes. It should be most interesting. You know, no one at work has ever seen me at one of these professional events with a date. Some people at work may well think I'm a lesbian."

"You're kidding! They *really* don't know you, do they?"

"No, they don't, so seeing me there with you is probably going to set some tongues wagging."

"Well, I have often wondered what it's like to be a 'celebrity.'"

Jada had daydreamed about what it would be like to be with Luca again, fretted about whether she'd unwittingly exaggerated how things had been in Torino. While she loved making love with him, she especially enjoyed the times when they were just talking, making dinner or watching TV together. They had an undeniable connection, something she had never experienced with anyone, and she was very protective of that bond. But she couldn't help wondering if it was real or romantic wishful thinking. Toward the end of the drive home, Jada finally decided to just trust her instincts and to let go of her worries and concerns.

Jada turned on her MP3 player, which was hooked up to wireless speakers throughout the house. Then she busied herself, putting the finishing touches on the light dinner she had prepared for Luca. The kitchen table was already set, complete with candles and a small vase of roses.

Luca watched her adoringly as she moved around the kitchen. "The music is really nice. What is it?"

"It's a compilation of chill-out music. There's a little bit of everything in the collection, and it's all nice and relaxing. This song is by a group called Silk 23."

"It's perfect. What can I do to help?"

"Nothing. Just sit here and talk to me. We're having salmon, so it will only take a few minutes."

Taking the time to enjoy a simple meal and reconnecting was the best thing they could have done. Despite his excitement about seeing Jada, Luca, too, had wondered if the past two months had all been a pleasant dream. But as they fell into their familiar rhythm, they knew with certainty that what they had could only get better.

"You look really tired, honey; something beyond jetlag," Jada said, caressing his face, which was beginning to show traces of a five o'clock shadow.

"Things have been busy. There was a lot to get done this week since I lost a day by leaving on Friday, but I'm fine, just relaxed and happy to be here with you." Talvin Singh's "The Traveler" played softly in the background, setting a romantic stage. Luca sighed, "I think this was the longest month of my life."

"Mine, too." Jada held his hand and Luca kissed it tenderly.

"Jada?"

"Yes."

"Dinner was wonderful."

"Thank you."

"I'm ready for dessert."

Surprised since Luca often passed on dessert, Jada rose and picked up the plates to clear the table. "Okay."

Luca stood up as well, took the plates from her and put them back on the table. "That's not the dessert I was talking about," he said amorously. Slowly, he led her down the hallway and upstairs to her bedroom.

They made love with an abandon that left them both exhausted. Their climax had come in wave after wave, and they had shouted, groaned, laughed and even shed tears.

Few words were exchanged between them, and none were needed; they were content in the certain knowledge that nothing had changed. The silence that fell between them was not that of awkwardness, but of a oneness so profound that words seemed redundant.

Nine o'clock the next morning, the phone rang. Jada cursed herself for forgetting to turn it off, as she usually did at night. She considered letting the machine pick it up, but that would have meant having to endure another infernal ring.

"Hello?" Jada half whispered. Mumbling something incoherent, Luca, tried to pull her deeper into his embrace but did not awake.

"Hey, girl! How are you doing?"

"Renie?"

"In the flesh! Good morning! Sorry to call you so early, but I didn't want to call last night since I know Luca just arrived."

"It's okay. What's up?"

"I wanted to confirm our plans for brunch today."

Jada pulled away from Luca, who was then instantly awake.

"I'd mentioned it to Luca yesterday, but I think we're going to bail on you."

"Jada—"

"Renie, Luca *just* got here, and we've got the Beanies tonight, too. I shouldn't have booked so much for his first day in town."

While Luca whispered to her, "It's okay. Let's do whatever you planned. I am fine," Renie was talking in her other ear, saying, "Come on. Just come for a little while. It will be fun for all of us to get to get to know Luca a little better."

"All right, Renie, Luca says it's fine."

"Since you're being such a good sport, you can pick. Where do you want to go for brunch?"

"How about Gloria's?"

"Gloria's diner? Are you sure Luca is ready for that?"

"Well, there's a first time for everything. A diner is a very American experience. I certainly didn't see any place like it while I was in Torino."

"All right, then, you can't get more all-American than Gloria's. India and Liz are going to join us; Carmen has respectfully declined. See you at around eleven?"

"Sounds good."

CHAPTER 31

"Okay, tell me, Jada, what *exactly* is a diner?" Luca asked.

"Well, once upon a time, most diners were open twenty-four hours; you could get any kind of food any time of day. Nowadays, most aren't open around the clock, but it's still a place where people go for generous helpings of whatever kind of breakfast, sandwich or dinnertime meal that you want any time of day. Diners are great for brunch because you can have a little bit of everything. The menu consists mostly of comfort food—dishes that are often rich and fattening but really, really good. Everyone should go to a diner at least once. You'll like it."

"Well, we'll see," he said skeptically.

Jada chuckled. "It's not a surprise that you've never been to a diner in all your visits to the States. Diners aren't exactly places that people want to entertain potential clients." Jada parked the car. "Here we are. This is Gloria's, one of the neighborhood's gems."

"*This* is it?" Luca asked. He hadn't known what to expect, but it certainly looked like nothing special from the outside. In fact, it looked like a place he would have driven past without giving it a second look had he been on the road looking for a place to eat.

Jada put her arm on his shoulder and smiled. "Just be open-minded, okay? I think you'll really like it."

"I'm going with the flow, *amore mio*. Don't worry."

Watching unbroken lines of people coming and going through the doors of the restaurant, which looked like a super-sized trailer home, Luca felt overwhelmed. The food had a distinctive aroma that was unidentifiable to him. He also didn't know what to make of the overflowing plates of food waitresses were carrying to the tables.

"See what I mean? Comfort food, hearty and palate-pleasing."

Both India and Liz had jumped at the invitation when Renie called, so the five of them were seated in a large corner booth that looked like something straight out of the 1950s.

"So what's the best thing to have at a diner?" Luca asked, flipping through the oversized menu, not knowing where to begin.

"Pancakes."

"French toast."

"Hash browns."

"Thanks, ladies. That was very helpful." They all burst out laughing.

The waitress came to the table to take their order. "Luca, why don't we share a breakfast platter? Then if there's something you really like, we can order more," Jada suggested.

"Good idea."

"Got it," the waitress said, looking to the others at the table.

"Well, I order the same thing whenever I go to a diner, French toast with a side of ham, so I've got to keep the tradition going!" Liz said.

"Blueberry pancakes and bacon for me," chimed in Renie.

"And I'll have the breakfast omelette with peppers, spinach and cheddar cheese and a side of ham."

"Just so you know, all your orders come with hash browns on the side. I'll get you all some coffee. Your food will be out shortly."

One by one, the waitress brought their orders, each heaped high with generous servings of hash browns, syrup and other side orders, all now seldom a part of their diets.

"My trainer would *kill* me if she knew I was here eating this stuff," India said. "But it tastes *so* good!"

Renie asked, "So, Luca, what do you think of diner food?"

"Well, there's more than enough of it, that's for sure. It's quite tasty. I really like the French toast. In Italy we usually have something sweet for breakfast, so I guess it reminds me of home."

Between bites of food, Luca and Jada shared jokes and stories. Jada mentioned the memorable dinner that she and Luca had when she'd visited him in Torino and her nervousness about the Beanies that night.

"So you're up for awards in *five* categories? That's pretty amazing," India said.

"It's exciting. Everyone can submit work to be nominated in as many categories as they like, but then the award panel selects the finalists who compete against one another for the awards. It's unusual to get selected in so many categories."

"What are you nominated for?" Liz asked.

"Best business-to-business direct-mail campaign, best online ad for a consumer product, most memorable radio spot, best corporate print campaign, and . . . I don't remember what the last one is."

"It's best short-length television spot," Luca said.

"Yes, that's it. Thanks, honey. It's nice to have my very own cheerleader."

"I think I'm more excited about these awards than Jada is. I'm sure tonight is going to be a big night."

"I've got my fingers crossed. My three-year anniversary as a vice president is coming up soon. I'd like to make senior VP before my fourth anniversary, if I can. Winning big tonight will help me to reach that goal."

"Well, aren't you the ambitious one?" Liz teased.

"Yes, I am, and I make no bones about it. I want to get to the next level before I turn fifty. Ageism is a real phenomenon, and it's particularly acute for women in the advertising world."

"Especially for black women," Renie said.

"I disagree with you, Renie. I think being over fifty burns *all* women pretty equally. If it hasn't happened for you by then, it's just not happening, no matter what color you are."

"Maybe you're right."

"Let's put it this way, I'm not waiting around to find out."

"That's one of the nice things about having your own company. You can give yourself the title you want and work yourself to exhaustion as much as you like," Luca said. They all laughed.

Jada said, "Can I change the subject? What's going on with Carmen? She missed our get-together the other night, and you said she couldn't come today. Is she okay?" India, Liz and Renie all shifted uncomfortably. "What?" Jada asked.

Renie started off, "Well, she didn't come the other night because she knew you would be talking about your trip to Italy. And she didn't come today because she didn't want to spend time with you and Luca."

"I see. She's been pretty clear since the beginning that she didn't think Luca and I were a good idea, but for heaven's sake . . ."

"You should talk to her, Jada. You two have been close ever since you met."

"I'll call her."

Sensing her upset, Luca put his arm around Jada's shoulder. "Everyone is entitled to their opinion, *amore mio*. That's just the way it is."

"I know. I just feel that she's making a judgment about you without ever even trying to get to know you. She can think what she wants, but a friend should at least do that."

"Well, girlfriend, that's why we're here!" Renie said, trying to cheer her up. "It's getting late. You two need to get out of here so you have time to relax before you have to get ready for your big night. Good luck, girl! We'll all be sending up our prayers to the universe that you win and win *big*!"

CHAPTER 32

Jada smoothed her red knee-length silk crepe dress down and spun in front of the mirror. The dress, one of her favorites, was an homage to 1950s vintage fashion, with a draped V-neckline and a well-defined waist. It flared slightly and stopped right at the knee. Jada had spent weeks looking for the perfect dress for this event; she thought this was it, but now she needed reassurance. "Luca, I know it's hard for you to be objective, but I need you to try. Does this look good?"

"No."

"No?" she asked, turning again to check her reflection. "What's wrong with it? Does it make me look fat?"

"What's wrong with it is that you're wearing it, and I wish you weren't because you look even better with nothing on. But since that isn't an option, let me just say you look fantastic—as you always do. Don't worry."

Jada punched his shoulder. "Luca! You nearly gave me a nervous breakdown! I'm anxious enough as it is."

"Sorry, *amore mio*. I couldn't resist teasing you, but you don't need to be anxious. I have a feeling you're going to do fantastically well tonight. Just relax. I'm going to enjoy spending an evening out on the town with you."

"Aren't you worried about meeting my colleagues?"

"No, not at all. You know, in a way, it's very easy for me. I don't know any of them personally, so I can meet them, say hello and move on. I look forward to seeing your boss again, though. I will be able to continue my campaign for promoting Jada that I began when we first met."

"Luca—"

"I promise you, Jada, I will be charm personified, just as I was before."

The awards ceremony was being held at the Marriott—right next to the Top of the Hub, where they'd gone on their first secret date. They decided to go there for a quiet drink before heading to the Beanies.

"I reserved our special table again so that we can enjoy the view."

"Luca, when did you do that? This place is quite popular on the weekends. I'm surprised they even agreed to hold a table."

"Well, I can be persuasive," he said mysteriously.

She looked at him curiously. "Hmmm. Yes, you certainly can be."

"I said it before, but you're going to win a lot of awards tonight. I just know it."

"Luca, I think you're a little bit biased."

"I am, but I also know that you are really good at what you do. Tonight you are going to get some well-earned recognition for all your hard work."

"You say that with so much confidence."

"Well, my father is very intuitive, so perhaps I inherited some of his special talent. I know I'm right. You can marvel at my abilities when we're home later."

Jada laughed. "Luca Alessandri, you are a dirty old man."

When they arrived, the expansive reception area in front of the grand ballroom was already abuzz. People who needed to be seen were making themselves conspicuous, while others mingled casually amongst advertising's who's who. There were a few well-stocked bars set up in the area, and most everyone had a libation in hand. Waiters circulated through the crowd offering a delectable array of appetizers to whet everyone's appetite. A jazz quartet jammed softly near the ballroom entrance. The main room had not yet been opened, a tactic used by the organizers to ensure that people took full advantage of the opportunity to socialize before being seated for ceremony.

Jada encountered several of her colleagues and introduced them to Luca. Some people recognized his name, having been associated with the Allegro pitch; others were just surprised to see that Jada had turned up at a professional event with a date.

They had just gotten their drinks when she saw Gene and David Heath walking toward them.

Actually, Gene had cleaned up pretty well. His slate-grey double-breasted suit fit nicely; it didn't pucker as such suits sometimes do. He wore a white shirt with mid-sized blue stripes and a striking blue tie. David was his usual unkempt self, only tonight he wore a suit. A brown suit. Brown! A fair-skinned man carrying twenty-five more pounds than he should was wearing a brown suit with a yellow shirt. Good God! Didn't the man have friends? Someone needed to help him with his wardrobe—not to mention taking him to a barber. His hair needed at least a wash and a trim, and his beard, well, it just needed help.

"Oh, God," Jada said. "You wanted to see Gene; well, here he comes, along with one of my colleagues, David, who is irritating but harmless. Are you ready, Luca?"

"*Amore mio*, I'm ready when you are. Let's go." They then began walking toward Gene and David rather than waiting for the two to reach them.

"Gene, David, it's good to see you both."

"Jada! You look great," Gene said.

"Yes, great," David echoed.

"Thank you. Gene, you probably remember Luca Alessandri; David Heath, Luca Alessandri."

"Of course I remember you, Luca. Good to see you again."

"And it's good to see you, Gene. Nice to meet you, David," Luca said.

"Same here."

"Luca, I understand you've given your business to Cornerstone?"

"Yes, that's right."

"They're a nice shop. I'm sure you'll be happy with their work."

"After Honoraria was no longer in the running, Jada thought they would be our best alternative. So far, so good."

Gene turned to David to explain. "You probably remember that we had to pull out of the Allegro pitch at the last minute when we got the offer from Burrows." Turning back to Luca, he said, "I'm sorry about what happened; we would have loved to have your business."

Luca raised his hand to stop him. "There is really no need to apologize. It's business; it worked out as it was supposed to. I believe in destiny." He looked at Jada and winked. "I think we're all happy," he said, running his hand up Jada's back.

David listened to the conversation with seeming interest, but his mind was on something else. *Jada's such a smug bitch. She thinks her rich boyfriend will stop Gene from being furious with her. I'll show her!*

"Jada, I was just about to tell Gene that it's a shame none of your team's work is in the competition."

"David, what makes you say that?" Jada asked, feigning surprise.

Sensing that something might be wrong, David turned red and shifted uncomfortably. Gene looked at him, puzzled by his remark.

"What are you talking about, David? All of Jada's team's pieces made it to the finals and are noted right here in the program," Gene said, pointing to the page where Jada was mentioned.

Obviously rattled, David tried to explain, "Well, I thought you had missed the deadline for the nominations because you were away on vacation. In Italy!"

"Oh. I submitted all of my team's work for consideration days before I left. I wouldn't miss the opportunity for them to get some well-earned recognition."

"That's good to hear," Gene said.

"Actually, David, all five of the pieces we submitted are up for awards. It should be a fun night!" She knew it was really a little mean to rub David's face in his error, but she couldn't help herself; he played subtle games of one-up with her often, and just once, she was giving it back.

The look on David's face was just priceless. Jada wished there was a roving photographer around to capture his stunned expression. Still, she didn't want to stand there and gloat. That wasn't what the evening was about.

"Well, they've opened the doors now. We're going to make our way to our seats. Enjoy the evening," Jada said in the sweetest voice she could muster.

"Yes, you do the same. Nice to see you again, Luca," Gene said.

"I hope we meet again soon," Luca said, trying to match Jada's breezy tone.

Jada laughed heartily. "Is it awful for me to say that I enjoyed that encounter immensely?" She glanced back to see David Heath still frozen in the same spot, gawking.

Luca chuckled. "I enjoyed myself, too, mostly because I could tell you were having so much fun. Tell me more about David."

"He's been around for a long time and he's actually brought in a lot of business for the agency. He's very old school and hierarchical; he doesn't think VPs should do much of anything except entertain and present to clients, and he's *very* protective of his relationship with the partners. While he's yet to be promoted to senior vice president, he's definitely one of the boys. When he's not in his office, he can usually be found in the office of Sam

Blackstone, one of the partners. He's *very* competitive, but never overtly mean. Still, I wouldn't want to be stuck in an elevator with him. He gives me the creeps."

They had almost reached the entrance to the grand ballroom when Jada heard her name. She turned and saw Dan Egleston smiling broadly at her.

"You are a hard lady to pin down."

"Dan, I was out of town when you called, and things have just been crazy since I've been back. Dan, this is Luca Alessandri."

"The president of Allegro Europe, right?"

"Yes, that's right," Luca replied, somewhat surprised that Dan knew who he was.

"I've been following your company's progress for a few years. I met your US president, Hugh, a couple of weeks ago. If you ask me, I think your company will have a lot of success in this market. I think the time is right for a company like Allegro to have a big impact here."

"I certainly hope so." *So Hugh really has been getting out and meeting all kinds of people since he's been in Boston. That's good to know.*

"Jada, since you're so hard to pin down, I'm just going to blurt it out: I'm very interested in talking with you about coming across town to join Rize." Looking directly at Luca, Dan said, "This woman is phenomenal."

"Yes, she is."

"Look, all I want to do is have a conversation with you. I'd like to at least get the chance to tell you about Rize and why I think it's where you need to be. Can we at least do that?"

"I think we can make that happen. Maybe I've been hard to reach, but please don't think I'm not interested in talking. I really do want to talk with you."

"Good. I'll give you a call early next week to set something up."

"Thanks, Dan. I'll look forward to it."

"He seems like a nice guy," Luca said.

"Yes, he does. Rize is building a great reputation in town. Dan has been very persistent, too. He sent a letter and called a few times while I was away."

"Hmm. It looks like you had an audience for your conversation," Luca said, gesturing casually to where Gene and David were standing. Obviously, they had watched Jada's brief encounter with Dan Egleston.

"Oh, well, there's no crime in chatting with competitors."

Finally making their way into the ballroom, Luca said, "If you think there's interest now, just wait until you win some awards later on tonight."

"Luca! Don't jinx me."

"Jada . . . you are *good*. You're better than good; you're phenomenal. Dan Egleston just said so. You're going to win. There's no jinx on the planet that's going to stop you from doing well tonight. Trust me."

They settled into their seats, introducing themselves to the other people at their table. In another effort to promote networking, agency teams were not seated together. They chatted casually with the others and waited for the ceremony to begin in earnest. The room was awash in hues of blue, and twinkling lights gave a festive accent to the ceiling. Each table was dressed with sparkling napkin rings decorated with the word "Beanies" and an elaborate orchid floral arrangement. Stills of the nominated works and candid shots of recognizable people in the Boston advertising world flashed on giant screens around the room.

"This is a very elaborate setup for an awards ceremony," Luca whispered.

"The industry puts everything they've got into these awards. It's the pinnacle event in town."

Like most awards ceremonies, this one was long and only sporadically interesting. Jada's categories were all clustered together, and there was no need to stay the entire evening. She was already plotting their early escape.

The first time Jada heard "Agency: Honoraria; Account team lead by Jada Green, vice president," she was overjoyed. She kissed Luca and strode to the stage to accept her Golden Beanpot. The second time, she was surprised. The competition had been stiff in the business-to-business direct mail category; she was up against David Heath's team, too, and she'd decided to submit something only because her team members wanted to see how their work would fare in competition with similar work from other agencies.

"I told you this was your night. I'll get my reward for being right later," Luca whispered.

She was stunned when she heard her name called a fifth time—maybe even a little embarrassed. Luca led a standing ovation, and the emcee noted that Beanie records confirmed that no team up for consideration in five categories had ever won in every one. Jada and her team at Honoraria had made Beanie history.

Luca hugged her when she returned to the table with her fifth golden Beanpot. "*Amore mio*, I am so proud of you. I knew that nothing was going to stop you from doing well tonight. You earned every one of these awards. Never doubt that."

"Thank you, Luca."

A stream of well-wishers came up to offer congratulations. Team members had their pictures taken with their respective Beanpots out in the reception area and everyone seemed to enjoy reveling in their individual and agency success. Gene stood close by Jada, trying to soak up some reflected glory. A few competitors came over, too, including Dan Egleston.

"Now, Jada, remember that I was interested in having you come to Rize even before this amazing showing tonight! Congratulations."

Laughing, Jada said, "Thank you so much, Dan. We'll talk soon, I promise." Gene couldn't have heard what Dan had whispered to her; nonetheless, Jada sensed his nervous curiosity, based no doubt on her response to the Rize executive. *Well, good. He needs to be a little bit nervous.*

After staying at the event for a decent stretch, Luca and Jada made their escape. Later, they lay in bed rehashing the evening's highs and lows.

"*Amore mio*, you were just wonderful. I'm so happy I was there to see you win all those awards. *And* to see you in that beautiful red dress. You were by far the most beautiful and well-dressed woman there. I must say I was surprised there was not a greater sense of style on display at such an event."

"Luca, this is Boston, not Los Angeles, New York, Paris or Milan. Our fashion sensibility is what it is—uniquely ours."

"Almost all the women wore black. There was no creativity. Don't women like dressing up?"

"Some do, but some don't."

Luca chuckled, "And David looked as if he'd closed his eyes and grabbed whatever his hand touched in his closet. But Dan Egleston's suit looked as if it might have come from Italy. It was very nice."

"You would think that, wouldn't you?" Jada teased.

"Well, yes, I guess I would. So, what will you do about Dan Egleston? He seems determined to get you to move to his agency."

"It seems that way. I'm not sure exactly what I'll do. All I know for sure is that I don't want to go somewhere new and have to go through the same old thing all over again."

"The same old thing?"

"Yes, having to prove myself all over again. Did I get the job because of some quota or fluke or because I slept with someone?"

"Do you really think it's possible that anyone could feel that way about you anymore? Some people may have thought that five years ago when you started at Honoraria, but surely no one could be so stupid now, especially not after what happened tonight."

"I suppose."

"That concern aside, what do you think? Are you interested in working at Rize?"

"I don't know. I need to really think about it. Before, it seemed like a bit of a game—you know, he wrote and called and we kept missing one another. Now that I've had a face-to-face conversation with him, I know he's serious; he's not just making small talk. I need to really think about what I want my next move to be and where it makes the most sense to be to achieve my goal of becoming a senior VP."

"Well, remember you are in control. Whether you stay or go to Rize or somewhere else, make sure you get everything you want."

"Speaking of getting everything I want . . ."

CHAPTER 33

They were not off to a good start.

"Hugh, these designs are not in keeping with the Allegro brand! Since we're just establishing ourselves in the US market, it's more important than ever that our work consistently reflects our strategy."

"Luca, I got this Case & Battle account all on my own. I've got three other accounts poised to sign with us as well."

"You do?"

"Yes. I figured I'd tell you when the deals were closed, but since we're talking . . ."

Impressed that Hugh had been able to get so much potential new business in such a relatively short time, Luca exclaimed, "Hugh, that is fantastic. It's really great news. Congratulations. I applaud the initiative, but neither Case & Battle nor any of those other new accounts will remain our clients if we don't meet their expectations."

"Look, Luca, this is the States, not some place in Europe. I doubt they even know what authentic European style really is, so we don't need to be so narrow in how we define Allegro."

"I disagree. And if you really believe that Americans as a whole are that unenlightened and gullible, we have a real problem. Anyway, our target is really those who *do* understand what the term 'European style' actually means. Allegro will never be a mass-market commercial-design enterprise."

"Luca, I have to ask you, am I the president of the US office or not?"

"Well, Hugh, you are the president of the US office now, but if you're really asking if you will be the president in the months ahead, I'm not sure of the answer to that question. If you're willing to stay on strategy and run this office the way it was meant to run—an offshoot of the European entity—the answer is yes. If you want to do what you like, ignoring the consistent design philosophy that we worked so hard to establish, then the answer is no."

Hugh had not expected such a blunt answer from Luca, although he realized he should have seen it coming. Luca had always made a point of calling things as he saw them. He believed the truth was always the best path, no matter how upsetting it might be initially. But in spite of knowing that, Hugh did not react well.

"Right. Well, Luca, if you want to move here to be with your girlfriend, why don't you just say so?"

Luca was stunned. He had never once mentioned Jada to Hugh. His relationship with her was not a secret; it was simply not his colleague's business. Luca surmised that Hugh and Fiorella had probably talked about it, but even she, an old friend, had made measured comments about his relationship when she had finally mentioned it. He realized, however, that he had to temper his anger before things got completely out of control.

"Hugh, I'm going to ignore what you just said because I know you're upset. My personal life is of no concern to you, nor yours of any concern to me, unless it prevents you from doing your job effectively." Luca decided that was as far as he wanted to go with Hugh on the subject of his interoffice relationship for now. Maybe Fiorella had told him that he knew about them; maybe not. He really *didn't* care if they were sleeping together as long as things at Allegro weren't affected.

"Quite frankly, I would like nothing more than to remain in Torino. But it's all up to you. I'm afraid this is your last warning, Hugh. Either run this office in a way that is consistent with our existing strategy, or you will no longer be president of Allegro USA."

With that, Luca got up and walked out. Furious, Hugh stood and looked out the window, where he saw Luca hailing a taxi.

"Fuck you, Luca, and as for your bloody girlfriend, I wish she would just disappear."

"Hugh? Who are you talking to?" Fiorella had overheard what he'd said and was surprised to find him alone and not on the phone.

Without turning around, he said, "I was talking to myself. Luca is playing games with the wrong man. He's threatening to kick me out of the job! This is all his girlfriend's fault. Jada fucking Green. She needs to just *go away*, then he'll probably back off and let me do what I do best."

"Hugh, you shouldn't say that. Jada doesn't have anything to do with this; you've done it to yourself."

He turned and glared at her. "Fuck you, too, Fee." Stunned, she ran from his office in tears.

CHAPTER 34

Trying to ward off a headache, Luca pressed his long fingers against his temples and took a deep breath. He was beginning to think it hadn't been the smartest idea to schedule this important meeting with Jada's parents right after a crucial meeting with Hugh—one of the most exasperating people he'd ever met, always, it seemed to him, on some ridiculous ego trip.

Luca took another deep breath, and before he knew it, the taxi was pulling over and coming to a stop in front of a modest house with a well-maintained lawn; he knew he was not that far from Jada's house.

"Hey, are you sure this is where you're supposed to be, buddy?" the taxi driver asked, looking back and forth from the house to Luca. The driver was white and clearly thought that the elegantly dressed businessman with the foreign accent would have had no reason to be in this part of town. Luca understood the implication of his question. He had never been to the Greens' house, so he checked the address once again just to be sure.

"Yes, this is it. Thank you." The driver shrugged. Luca paid him and got out. He took yet another deep breath before ringing the bell. *Oh, God. Please let this meeting with Jada's parents go off without a problem.*

Ida Green opened the door.

"Luca, hello! I hope you found us okay!" she exclaimed, drawing him into a warm embrace.

"Hello, Mrs. Green. It's good to see you. No, I didn't have any problem. The taxi driver seemed to know his way."

"Well, consider yourself lucky! Most taxis don't have any idea where anything is in this city. The first thing they ask you is: 'How do you get there?' Not much help for people who aren't from around here. Come in! Come in! Mr. Green is just down the hallway in the living room." Ida Green led Luca into the room, where Horace Green was in an easy chair watching TV. The room was about the size of Jada's living room, but it seemed smaller because of the knick-knacks that seemed to fill every shelf and table in the room, as well as the oversized chair, no doubt one of Horace Green's favorite spots in the house.

"Horace, Luca is here," Ida said merrily.

As Horace Green eased slightly out of his comfortable throne, Luca stepped forward to shake his hand. He could feel the dampness on his hand when Mr. Green grasped it. He was so nervous! Everything had gone well with their parents so far, but the few negative things that had happened—the encounters with Darren and Mirella, as well as Carmen's apparent disappointment in her friend's choice of a partner—seemed to have become magnified tenfold in his mind, and he found himself plagued with fear that things would unravel for some unexpected reason.

"Good to see you, son. Sit down, sit down. Let me turn off this TV." Horace got the remote control from the end table next to his chair and turned off the television. He then gave Luca his complete attention.

"Thank you, Mr. Green." Then Luca froze; he didn't know how to start, what to say. Why hadn't he thought about how he would start the conversation?

Sensing his discomfort, Mrs. Green thought she would help him out . . . by stalling.

"Luca, can I get you a bite to eat? I can make you a sandwich or a salad if you'd like. Or maybe something to drink?"

"No, thank you, Mrs. Green. That's very kind of you. I wanted to speak to you about Jada."

"Is something wrong with Jada?" Ida asked, a trace of worry in her voice. She hadn't spoken to her daughter in a couple of days; maybe something had happened. But then, Luca had called them days ago from Italy to arrange a time when he could speak with them. *Stop worrying so much, Ida. The boy has come here to give you good news.*

"No, she's fine. I—Mr. and Mrs. Green, I hope you know that I have been very serious about my relationship with Jada right from the start. I am here to ask for your blessing before I propose to Jada. It's old-fashioned, but—"

"You want to *marry* Jada?" Horace Green asked, immediately realizing he shouldn't have been surprised. After all, he'd seen them together at the party and knew that the guy didn't seem to be playing games. Still, so many men today seemed to enjoy playing around and dragging the whole thing out, sometimes for years. The skeptic in him hadn't thought he would ever actually get around to asking Jada to marry him.

"Yes, sir, I do. We—we've not known each other for long, but I really love your daughter. I am ready to commit myself to her, and I look forward to building a wonderful life with her. We aren't children and life is so short . . . I don't see any reason to procrastinate about this. I am having a ring made for her, and I would like to ask her next month when I come back to town."

Ida Green clasped and unclasped her hands. She had suspected this was what he'd wanted to talk about, and was happy that this man cared so much about her daughter he wanted to make it official and marry her. She was no doubt a little biased, but Ida thought Jada was an extraordinary woman, at times watching her from a distance and marveling at her style and grace. And she had always been an exceptionally thoughtful and kind girl. When she was growing up, Ida often imagined the man Jada would marry. He didn't look like Luca. He looked more like a young Sidney Poitier or Denzel Washington. She didn't have anything against Luca; he seemed like a wonderful fellow. But she did worry about his being a foreigner. Where were they going to live? The thought of her baby living far away in a strange country where Ida had never been scared her.

Horace realized that Luca's news had propelled Ida into her own world of worry. Meanwhile, the guy was waiting for one of them to say something. *Ida always does this when things like this happen. She did the same thing when Craig came home and told us he was getting married. I guess it's up to me to keep this conversation going.*

"Luca, it's nice of you to do this the right way—asking our permission. But in the end, our opinion doesn't matter; Jada is a forty-five-year-old woman."

"Mr. Green, your opinion *does* matter—to Jada and to me. She is as close to you as I am to my parents, and it would sadden both of us if we didn't have your blessing. I'm hopeful that you'll be happy for us."

Nodding thoughtfully, Horace said, "Well, I think that I can speak for both Mrs. Green and myself when I say that you have our blessing. When you called and said you wanted to see us without Jada, we kind of thought you wanted to talk to us about your future together, but we weren't sure. We're happy for you. But, son, we've got some concerns, too."

"Concerns about us?"

"No, concerns about other people's reactions to you as a couple. You got a sampling of it from our own son at the anniversary party. Luca, you're not from around here, so let me tell you: black/white couples still raise eyebrows in this country—a lot. You two both have high-powered careers, so maybe it'll be a little bit different, maybe even a kind of buffer. But rest assured, race still matters here. Your relationship will be bound to rub at least some people you'll encounter the wrong way."

"I know, sir," Luca said and nodded. "I've spent enough time in the States over the years to see that first-hand. To a degree, the same is true in Italy. But as I said before, we are not young kids and we're not naïve, either. I feel we have the experience in life to deal with those kinds of situations."

"Well, I certainly hope so, because if you're not prepared to deal with it, it can trip you up and cause you some real problems."

"Luca, where are you going to live when you get married?" Ida asked, finally finding her voice again. She'd listened to Horace go on and on about racism. Of course, he was right, but Luca was right, too. Neither he nor Jada was naïve, and she was satisfied they would be able to handle anyone who might have issues with them being a couple. But where they were going to live? *That* was a problem.

"We don't know, Mrs. Green. Jada doesn't know that I am planning to propose. We have never really had a serious talk about marriage, even though it's something that I have been thinking about almost from the first day we met. But we have talked a lot about how much we want to be able to live in the same place. We are both open to either Boston or Torino. There are good reasons to choose either city, but at this point I'm honestly not sure."

"I'd really hate to see her living so far away in Italy," Ida said, more to herself than to Luca.

"Mrs. Green, I promise you, if we live in Italy you will see us almost as much as you see your son Craig— maybe even more. I'm building a business in the States, and Boston is my headquarters. I fully expect it is going to be successful. There will *always* be a reason to be here. You can count on that." Luca's words gave Ida some much-needed reassurance and brought a bright smile to her formerly frowning face.

Luca still had another appointment before he could call it a day. Glancing at his watch, he said, "Well, I should go. Is it best to call a cab or can I hail one in the street?"

"Well, you can hail one, but I think it's easier to call one of the cab companies. I'll take care of that for you," Ida Green said, hurrying off to find the phone number.

"Thank you, Mrs. Green."

"One more thing, Luca," Horace Green said, his raised hand signaling him to stay seated.

"Yes, sir?"

"I wasn't too crazy about this relationship when I first heard about it. It's probably fair to say that I felt a little bit like Darren did—that you were some rich foreign guy who'd come to town looking for a good time at the expense of my daughter. But you've proved your commitment to Jada. I—we—believe you really do love her. You've treated her and us with respect, and we hope that will continue in the future."

"I always will, Mr. Green. I love Jada with all my heart, and I will do anything I can to make her happy. I told Jada when I first met her that I am an honorable man, and I am; I will always treat you with respect."

"I am glad my daughter met a man like you, son. I hope the two of you will have a wonderful life together," Horace said, ending the conversation with a firm handshake.

"Thank you, Mr. Green."

Jada picked up Luca at his office. As soon as she looked at him, she could tell he'd had a long day. "What's wrong?"

"Nothing is wrong." But as soon as he uttered the words, he realized that while some frustrating things had happened during the day, he had a lot to celebrate. Jada's parents had given him their blessing, and nothing could ever come close to overshadowing the importance of that news. His mood lightened almost instantly.

Jada looked at him cynically. "Haven't we been down this road before? Is it the same problem as the last time?"

"Really, nothing is wrong. Seeing you has made me realize that I need to relax a little. Everything is going to work out."

Jada smiled. "Well, I'm glad I can have such a magical effect on your mood, Mr. Alessandri. You really do look happier than you did when I first walked in the door."

"Believe me, I have never been happier than I am today," he said, kissing her on the forehead.

"Allegro USA looks totally different from the last time I was here. Luca, it looks fantastic. And I love your office."

His modern-style desk was up on a small platform set far back into the space. A sleek slate-grey leather sofa, comfortable chairs and an oval-shaped table that could be used for meetings were on the other side of the room. A striking abstract-art wool rug spotted with bright orange, red, gold, black and blue separated the two spaces. If Luca had described it to her, she might have told him that the rug was too much for an office space, but it worked, and the style fit his personality perfectly.

"I'm glad you like it. Since the space is so open, it seemed to make sense to divide it up this way. I like having a casual meeting area like this, and then there's a table over in the corner that folds out from the wall if I need to put up a model or lay out a large drawing."

"This is fantastic. Show me the rest of the office."

"Okay." He took her hand and walked her through the rest of the space, introducing her to people as they went along. He knocked on Hugh's door, which was closed and, oddly, locked. He had to wait an awkwardly long time for him to open it. Hugh stood in the doorway.

"Luca, hello," Hugh said with a brightness that somehow betrayed his nervousness. Normally impeccably dressed, Hugh looked less crisp.

"Hugh, I'm sure you remember Jada."

Hugh couldn't believe he had brought her to his office—not after they had quarreled about her only hours earlier. "Yes, of course. Good to see you again," he said, extending his hand. Jada found his handshake clammy and cold.

"I was looking for Fiorella."

"Oh, she's here." Fiorella appeared behind Hugh. She saw the look on Luca's face and was embarrassed. So she didn't let a moment pass before introducing herself and starting to babble about the weather, the city and anything else that popped into her head. The two men stood by, looking everywhere but at each other until the conversation ended.

"Well, I was just showing Jada around the office. I'm leaving now."

"See you tomorrow, Luca," Fiorella and Hugh said almost in unison.

"Looks like a little love in the afternoon to me," Jada whispered to Luca.

"Yes, I know. I don't like it, but I'm not going to hold it against them unless it starts to interfere with work. That little display came pretty close."

"Luca, if you're going to be okay with it, then you can't say anything about what just happened. They did not put on a 'display,' as you said. They were in his office with the door locked. You knocked and he answered. I mean, you have every right to say that your company will not tolerate office relationships—many companies do— but otherwise, you've got to lighten up. They were actually being discreet."

"Yes, I suppose you're right." If Hugh only knew that Jada, the woman he had complained about earlier in the day, stuck up for him almost every time they had a conversation about Allegro. What irony, Luca thought.

"Let's go. I've had enough of work for today."

The rest of the week seemed to pass in a flash. Jada and Luca were both drowning in work, so they were overjoyed when evening came and they could spend quiet time alone, eating dinner and talking about whatever came to mind.

They retreated to the living room to listen to music after enjoying takeout from a Thai restaurant they had recently discovered. "I finally set up a meeting with Dan Egleston from Rize. We're having lunch in three weeks."

"Three weeks? I thought he was so anxious to see you."

"He is. He'd hoped we could meet this week, but I was booked and now he's got vacation and some out-of-town meetings, so he can't do it until then. It works for me. I was trying to put it off as long as I could anyway."

"I don't know why you would want to put it off at all. It will be good to meet with him and hear what he has to offer."

"I suppose."

"Jada, you're doing that doubt thing again. I can hear it in your voice. This is a good opportunity! Three weeks? What's the date of your meeting?"

"June twenty-fourth."

"Oh, that's too bad. That's right before I am due to come back. I wish I were going to be here. You will have to call me as soon as you leave the meeting."

Jada hugged him tightly. "I can't believe you're leaving already. I can only hope the month goes by as quickly as this week did."

"Me, too."

CHAPTER 35

Led by the hostess to an obscure corner of a nice but unremarkable restaurant, Jada saw Dan Egleston's lean frame come into view as they approached. The place was definitely not an ad-industry haunt. *He is not taking any chances that we'll be seen—unless someone is looking for us.*

Smiling affably as he rose to greet her, Dan said, "Jada, I'm glad I was finally able to pull you away from the office for this conversation."

"Dan, I know this meeting has been a long time coming, but I'm glad we've finally been able to sit down to talk. It's been absolutely *insane* at the office since the Beanies! At times like this, I really have to wonder where the time goes. Three weeks just zoomed by."

Truth be told, Jada had stalled just a little bit in making this business lunch happen. She had wanted to see how things would unfold at Honoraria after her triumph at the Beanies. In the past, when her peers had won Beanies, promotions and new responsibilities followed within days for them and their team. She had made herself accessible in the days following the ceremony and had even sent Gene a note saying that she was interested in talking with him about future opportunities. But the result of her efforts was a huge helping of status quo. After all of Gene's fawning over her and Luca the night of the Beanies, he hadn't had much to say to her about anything since then. Everyone had gone silent. Even David Heath had stopped his games of one-up; he had been unusually cordial at the weekly directors' meetings. It seemed as if all her hard work and success would get her nothing without a little leverage, and that is what an offer from Dan Egleston would provide. Because in spite of all that *hadn't* happened, Jada's preference was still to stay at Honoraria. She had carved out her own little niche there; she worked well with her team, had fantastic clients and appreciated the partnerships she'd forged over the years. But it was beginning to dawn on her that if Honoraria had nothing to offer in the way of continued growth, she might have to move on. She was loyal, but she wasn't foolish.

Trying to gauge Jada's bullshit meter—whether she was truthful about how busy she'd been or just putting on an act—Dan Egleston studied her closely, but he really couldn't tell.

"It doesn't matter, Jada. What matters is that we're talking now. Once again, I wanted to congratulate you on your team's phenomenal success at the Beanies."

"Thanks, Dan. It's funny that the account person gets all the praise; I've got an amazing team working on my accounts."

"But we all know the account leader drives the strategy and keeps the team motivated and focused. You're too humble."

Jada didn't comment, but she did mentally note that Luca had told her the same thing more than once.

"Anyway, Jada, I've been pretty transparent about my interest in having you join the team at Rize."

"Yes, you have."

"I think we've got a lot to offer, too—excellent accounts, a growing business, one of the most creative shops on the East Coast. And one of the most diverse. Rize runs circles around Honoraria and any other agency that comes to mind in terms of in-house diversity and commitment to multicultural advertising."

"I know Rize definitely helps drive the diversity in advertising numbers in the New England area, that's for sure."

"Not just in New England, Jada; in the *Northeast*. In an industry that has only a shameful 2 percent of non-white hires, Rize has almost 20 percent. No general-market agency in the area—and few in the nation—even come close. We've got more women in the upper tier of our agency than any other in town."

"That's very impressive, Dan," Jada said.

Sensing that he may have gone on too much about diversity and not enough about career opportunities, he quickly moved on. "Rize can offer you great opportunities for advancement, too. I'm proposing to bring you on at a senior VP level. I believe that's a level higher than where you are at now, right?"

"That's correct."

"Of course, at that level, you would immediately become a member of our management team—what your shop calls the steering committee. The most senior people at the agency have the opportunity to have equity in the company. That would also be available to you after an agreed-upon tenure with us. I don't know the specifics of your salary demands, and I don't want to even get into money right now. Tell me that you're coming, and we'll work it out."

Jada sat silently, taking in everything Dan had said. Not sure how to read her silence, he continued: "Jada, to paraphrase a line from Sally Field, 'We like you; we really like you!' You won't regret making the jump. I can guarantee it, and everyone in the ad biz knows that business people do not guarantee anything unless they believe their product is foolproof. We are."

"Dan, you've given me a lot to think about; I really appreciate the offer. I hope you'll give me some time to consider my options and talk to some of my key advisors."

Dan was reasonably sure that Luca Alessandri was one of her key advisors. He had spent time in Italy as a student in business school and had studied the growth of Allegro under his father, Lorenzo, for a project. He'd followed the company since then, and he knew that when Luca joined the company, Allegro had stepped up its game and had become a European powerhouse in the field of commercial design. It was one of the best-run businesses of its kind. He wasn't surprised when he heard that, under Luca's leadership, Allegro had decided to make a move into the US market.

Dan had wanted to pitch for the Allegro business, but his agency had not made the short list. He understood that if Jada and Luca really were a couple, the chances of the Allegro business coming to Rize were further diminished by the realities of mixing business and professional relationships. But that didn't matter; Jada was a superstar and he wanted her on his team. In any case, Dan was fairly certain that if Jada asked Luca, he would advise her to make the move to Rize. If anything, the relationship between Jada and Luca made him want her on his team even more. Both were exceptional at what they did.

"Take the time you need, Jada. But I'm hoping you can give me an answer within a couple of weeks."

"You'll have my answer by then, Dan. I appreciate it. Thanks for lunch, too."

"It was my pleasure, Jada. We'll talk soon."

Jada returned to the office in a state of panicked euphoria. Dan's offer had exceeded her expectations. Senior vice president! Management committee! Equity! It was way more than she could have hoped for. He had given her a lot to think about. Still, it bugged her that she felt so concerned about making a move; something was giving her pause. She pulled out her cell phone and pushed the familiar numbers.

"Jada, I was just thinking about you! How are you, *amore mio*? How did your lunch with Dan go?"

"It went well. Really well. Luca, he offered to promote me to senior vice president and to give me an equity option after a period of time that we would have to work out."

"Jada, that's fantastic!"

"Yeah, it is."

"What's wrong? You don't sound that happy about it."

"I don't know, Luca. It's such a good offer, but I guess I'm a little scared."

"Scared of what, *amore*?"

"I'm afraid of starting over, of failing. I mean, I *know* what I'm up against where I am—"

"But Jada, you can't just stand still because you are afraid, and you *know* you're not going to fail."

Jada bit her lip and considered what Luca had said.

"Come on, you are fantastic. You just won five awards, more than anyone has ever won at one time."

"Yeah, I know—"

"Jada, where is this lack of confidence coming from? Why this fear? It's a side of you I haven't seen."

She felt her eyes welling up with tears. It was impossible to answer his question. Even though thousands of miles separated them, Luca could sense her anxiety.

"Jada, you have something else to do that should help you make your decision."

"What's that?"

"You need to tell Gene about your offer."

"I don't know—"

"Jada, you have to do this. Remember what I told you before I left? You have the power in this negotiation. It's up to you to use it. Tell Gene what Rize has offered you and see what Honoraria will offer to get you to stay. You have nothing to lose, and you will learn a lot about how much Honoraria really values your work."

"I wish you were here, Luca. I don't know if I can do this. You make it sound so easy."

"You can do it, Jada. I know you can. It will be all right. Besides, I'll be there Saturday, so put everyone off until next week, and we can talk through all the pros and cons when I get there."

"Okay. Thank you, Luca. As usual, you've made me feel better and talked me off the cliff. I love you."

"I love you, too. More than you will ever know."

CHAPTER 36

Luca looked out the window of his office in Torino. Time was flying. Three weeks had disappeared in the blink of an eye. He was scheduled to return to Boston in a couple of days. It felt as if he and Jada had barely spoken to one another, the demands of work having stretched them both to the limit. It made him feel good that she had called him for advice and support. He hoped she would use her power to the fullest in any negotiation with Honoraria.

The situation with Hugh was nagging at Luca, so much so that he'd barely taken time to celebrate the things in his life that *were* going right: In spite of the issues he had with Hugh, they had successfully launched Allegro USA, a longtime dream. His future in-laws had given him their blessing; he was free to ask Jada to be his wife. At his age, just as he'd felt like giving up, he had found a woman whom he loved completely and who loved him in return. This was an exciting time in his life.

Luca's thoughts turned to Jada's friends, remembering brunch at the diner and how much he'd appreciated getting to spend some time with some of the people who were an important part of her life. They were witty, honest and supportive and he looked forward to the next time that they'd all be able to get together. He hoped that

Jada would also get to know his friends better, and indeed, to spend more time in Torino, whether they ultimately lived there or not.

As usual nowadays, Luca's thoughts circled back to Hugh. He was genuinely impressed that his US president had been able to sign one account and bring three others to the table in less than two months. According to Dan Egleston and others, he had been everywhere in Boston, making himself known and drumming up business in his smooth and charming way. Clearly, he wasn't completely useless. But what he proposed to do with the accounts once they came in the door was potentially disastrous. It had to stop. He needed to choose the moment, but he was going to have to do it when he returned to Boston.

"Luca, you look troubled, my son. What's on your mind?" Lorenzo asked, walking into the office and embracing his son. Luca had appeared distracted since his return from Boston and hadn't been talking much. This disturbed Lorenzo, but he had decided to give him some time to work through whatever was bothering him. But now, he was determined to get him to open up before he once again left for Boston.

Lorenzo had always been proud of the close relationship he and his son had, always able to talk about everything. A wall of silence appeared only when a woman was complicating his life. So he naturally wondered if Luca's withdrawn mood had something to do with his relationship with Jada. But he wanted Luca to feel comfortable enough to tell him willingly.

"Papà, I know I've kept you in the dark about what's been happening."

"Yes, you have, and it's not like you."

"I know. I just needed to think; there are a lot of implications."

"So this is about work?" Lorenzo didn't know whether he was relieved or worried that his son's pensive mood didn't concern his personal life.

Luca smiled knowingly. "You thought this was about Jada? No, it's not. She's wonderful; we are doing fine, and it's magic when we are together. I hate being apart from her, but we talk at least once every day. I haven't told you, but I met with her parents when I was there."

"Did that go well?"

"Yes, they were very happy and supportive—just a little worried about difficulties we might face because we are different races, as well as some concern about where we might end up living and how often they would see Jada if she lived here in Torino. But it looks like they were worrying for nothing."

"What do you mean?"

"Papà, it's Hugh. I think I have to fire him. I know you never liked him in the first place; hiring him was my decision—"

"Wait a minute, Luca. Tell me why you want to fire him now. When I suggested it, you thought it was a bad idea."

"He is incapable of being a president who appreciates Allegro's strategy and design aesthetics. You should see what he'd proposed for Case & Battle, the new client that he brought in. If Fiorella hadn't intervened, it would have been a disaster. Now he's got three new accounts poised to sign with us—"

"Three?"

"Yes. He really is thriving when it comes to making the rounds in Boston and bringing in new business. Maybe it's his English accent, who knows? I even met someone at one of Jada's business events who had met him. But what's the point in bringing in new clients, showing them what we do and then proposing whatever suits his taste on that particular day? That's no way to build a business!"

Lorenzo was quiet for a while, and then he started to pace as he pondered Allegro's options.

"I am just thinking, Luca."

Despite being in the midst of a serious conversation about Hugh, Luca couldn't help smiling, as he was actually having the pleasure of seeing his father "just thinking."

"Luca, I think you need to consider another alternative. If Hugh has brought in *that* much potential business in a little less than two months, he's not as useless as I had thought. That is good work—*impressive* work. But it's clear that he is an idiot when it comes to design strategy and building an image for Allegro."

"Yes, but that is probably an understatement."

"The title of president means a lot to Hugh, doesn't it?"

"Yes, but he is not—"

"Luca, I think you are imagining the role of what a president is as how *you* would handle it, not how it would work best in this situation."

"What do you mean?"

"Hugh is good at bringing in business; he's basically a salesman."

"Yes."

"But he is very good at it. Why not let him remain president?"

"Because, Papà, that is not all a president is supposed to do."

"For *you*, Luca. What I'm saying is let him keep the title of president. Why not make the role of president of Allegro USA primarily a sales job? On the other hand, Fiorella created the strategy along with you, and she's capable of seeing it through, but she's not a salesperson."

"She's our creative director; I cannot imagine her going out and doing sales for Allegro. At a minimum, it's not what she does best," Luca said.

"Yes, I would agree. But why don't we promote her? We can give her the title of vice president and creative director. She can take over for Hugh the minute the client signs on. At that point, the selling is done and staying on strategy takes on the greatest importance. Hugh can then go on to find the next prospect, and he can still check in with the clients he's signed on. Take them to lunch, make sure they're happy and all the things he likes to do. Meanwhile, Fiorella will be responsible for the designs, and she can come to you for final approval on all the designs that come out of the US office. So what if you would do things differently if you were president of Allegro US? It doesn't work for the team in place now. As long as Hugh continues to bring in new business and is keeping the clients already in our portfolio coming back, he can call himself 'God of Allegro,' for all I care. Don't get so hung up on the responsibilities and the titles. If it works, it doesn't matter."

Luca thought this made a lot of sense. In fact, it was a painfully obvious way to work things out.

"It's a perfect solution, Papà. Why hadn't I been able to see it?" Luca was almost embarrassed that he had not come up with the answer on his own.

"Luca, that's why it's always good to talk to people, to share ideas with another person. Sometimes we're so committed to the way we believe things should be that we're not able to see the way things *could* be."

He gave his son a hearty embrace. "Luca, sometimes I think you worry too much about what *I* think. You were afraid that I was going to criticize you for hiring Hugh because you know I don't like him. Well, I still don't like him, but your instincts were right. He was a good choice to play a part in developing our US business." Lorenzo laughed. "He can't help it if he's a pompous Englishman."

"Well, I'll talk to him about the new organization structure when I'm in Boston. Thank you for your help, Papà."

"That's what I'm here for. Oh, I hear he and Fiorella are having a difficult time in their relationship. She's looking for her own place. Just information to keep in your pocket!"

"*Where* do you hear these things, Papà?"

Lorenzo shrugged, smiled knowingly and walked out the door.

CHAPTER 37

After a full day of strategizing for the four partners—Gene Bradley, Erwin Stone, Alison Samson and Sam Blackstone—and the three SVPs—Michael Bradley, Casey Rayburn, and Greg Walters—the Honoraria steering committee meeting was finally coming to a close. Everyone was anxious to leave the small but well-appointed conference room. Gene just wanted to get to the last item on the agenda: Jada Green. After Honoraria's triumph at the Beanies, thanks to Jada, he was more concerned than ever about keeping her in the fold. She was a hot commodity. Her popularity with the competition had not been lost on him the night of the awards ceremony. He'd seen many, especially that snake Dan Egleston, trying to charm her. The truth was, Gene had known for some time that she was a hot commodity, but he had done his best to make her feel that she was only marginally better than average. There was no point in her moving up the ladder too quickly if he could keep her unsure, motivated and challenged. But the reality was that after only a few years she was so good at what she did that the agency would be significantly diminished were she to leave. He needed to get the steering committee to approve her promotion to SVP sooner, rather than later.

The last year had been something of a turning point for Jada. When she had first come to Honoraria, she had been reticent to hold her ground when conflicts arose. Now she pushed back more aggressively, taking less crap from the guys and letting them know that she would not be bullied. It took some of them by surprise when she started giving as good as she got, but they respected her for it. Jada had always worked hard, but she'd upped the ante when she made VP. She sharpened her ability to pin-point the most effective strategy; her team was highly motivated, their work was creative, memorable and delivered results. That was the essence of what an ad agency did. Jada did it well. Very well, indeed.

Sam Blackstone, the managing partner, said, "Next item on the agenda: Jada Green." Hearing her name brought Gene's focus back to the meeting.

"What's this about, Gene?" Sam asked.

"Well, the time has come, gentlemen . . . and Alison. We've got to promote her."

"Why?"

"Because she has earned it."

"Because her team won some Beanie Awards? Come on, Gene. You're putting too much weight in those things," Erwin said dismissively.

"No, she has *earned* it. Beanies be damned, Jada is one of the top producers at the agency."

"Yeah, well, that is why she's a VP."

"Now hold on a minute. The reality is that because of those Beanies that you're scoffing at, Jada has become one of the hottest commodities in town. She won five of them—*five*. Every piece she put up for nomination won. No one, here or at any other agency, has been able to do that. The competition is knocking at her door. If we don't up the ante, she's going to walk."

After listening to Gene's argument with interest, Michael Bryant asked, "Gene, people—good people—walk all the time. Why should we jump through hoops for her?"

"Well, she is just about our only diversity hire."

"Hey, we're living in a post-racial society now, didn't you hear? Those things don't matter anymore." Erwin and Michael chuckled. Gene was flustered. He looked to Alison, who had remained silent throughout the discussion, for help.

Alison said, "Hold on, you guys. It seems you just really don't want to promote her, yet I know many others in this agency have been promoted with less cause and less debate than we've had already. What's the problem?" She looked around the table for a reaction.

Grateful for the support, Gene added, "On top of that, if Jada walks, we have the potential of losing about sixty percent of her satisfied clients within a year, and at least three key people on her team would likely follow her wherever she goes."

"How do you know?"

"Well, clients have told me her management of the business is one of the reasons they're staying with us without putting the business up for review. As for the staff, it's the word around the office. Her team is pretty loyal to her. Guys, I'm telling you, we need to do this."

"I agree," Alison said. "Demonstrated ability deserves to be recognized."

"Okay, what should we offer?"

"SVP. Just give her the title; role stays the same." Gene winced as he threw the offer out on the table because he knew she deserved more. But at that point, he just wanted to get the deal done. Besides, he didn't want his peers to think he was carrying the banner of diversity. They had already scoffed at the mere mention of the word, except Alison, of course.

"Gene, I can't believe after that impassioned argument to promote her, that's the offer you've put on the table." Alison shook her head in dismay. Gene didn't respond.

"No equity offer?" Erwin asked.

"Well, I think we should mention it as a future intent—you know, a carrot. We don't have to offer it as part of the promotion."

"Gene—" Alison was in disbelief.

"Steering committee?"

"We can say that it will come within a year or something—proof of performance."

"Money?"

"A fifteen percent increase."

"Only fifteen? For an SVP?" Casey Rayburn, one of the SVPs, asked.

"Okay, Gene, so what you're saying is that we can keep Jada on board and get her to buy into this promotion with just a title change, no increased responsibilities, a pittance more money and nothing else, is that right?" Sam Blackstone asked.

"Yes, I think it will be enough."

"Well, you know her better than I do, but I've never had the impression that Jada was solely motivated by money and her title. I thought she would be looking for more responsibility."

"I agree," Alison chimed in. "I would be *very* surprised if Jada went for this offer."

"She will want more responsibility at some point, but I think we'll be able to keep her on board with the promise of more in the future," Gene retorted.

Sam looked at Gene skeptically. "Okay, we'll save the other stuff as incentive down the road . . . if you think that will work."

"I have a high degree of confidence that it will work." Gene plowed ahead, in spite of Alison's concerns. "If we're all agreed, I'll make her the offer later on today."

"Since you think that we have to do this in order to keep her on board, I'm all right with it," Sam said. "Is everyone agreed?"

Several people muttered, "Yeah," "Sure" or "Fine with me."

Shaking her head in disgust at her colleagues, Alison said, "I want to go on record that I think this is a travesty. But I'd rather Jada get something rather than nothing, so I won't block this since everyone else agrees."

And with that, the meeting was adjourned.

CHAPTER 38

Jada sat in her office kicking herself. Having known that Dan was going to make her an offer, she should have done this homework *before* she had her meeting. Had it been something related to any one of her accounts, she would have been all over it weeks in advance. But this was something for herself and, in typical fashion, she'd put aside her own interests for the sake of everything else. If she had to be honest, her procrastination had been helped along by her fear of having to make this decision. In the end nothing had stopped this moment of truth from coming, and now she was sitting in front of her computer doing invaluable research. Better late than never.

She found a host of websites that provided information on average salaries by city for various professions. She focused on two sites that had a fair amount of detail on the advertising industry. What she found surprised her. Jada was *significantly* underpaid for what she did, versus the average salary in Boston for advertising VPs.

While she had gone to the mat for more money twice in the five years since she had joined Honoraria, those increases barely put her in the low average range of pay. *No wonder they were so happy to give me those salary bumps.* The revelation made Jada pretty angry with herself. As hard as she'd worked and fought for the benefit of her team members, she had shamefully and inexplicably neglected herself, and unlike her team, she had no one advocating on her behalf.

Further research produced an article that suggested a monetary value should be added to every professional award received—no matter how trivial. She had just won *five* that were considered a big deal in her profession. No, she was going to fix this and fix it now. Where she had once felt fearful and somewhat timid about pushing for more money and responsibility, she was now angry and ready to fight for what she was due. Jada remembered a scene from one of her favorite movies, *The Joy Luck Club*, in which someone tries to buy a character's favor with a string of pearls. In recounting the story to her daughter, the character tells her, 'Always know what you're worth.' *Indeed.* She had always remembered the line, and now she understood exactly what it meant. Just then, there was a knock at her office door.

"Come in."

Jada knew it was Gene before she saw his face; she could smell his pungent cologne as soon as the door opened.

"Jada, do you have some time to talk?"

"Of course, Gene. Actually, I was just coming to see you."

"Really? Well, this won't take long and it's good news, so I'll go first."

This was the moment Jada had been waiting for: he was about to put an offer on the table. She was curious to hear what it was, so she nodded her consent. "By all means, bring on the good news!"

"Well, I've just come out of the steering committee meeting, and I wanted you to know that everyone was really pleased with the great result the agency had at the Beanies."

The agency, indeed! "Gene, I am so thrilled that *my* team won five of the most coveted awards in advertising. *Five.*" Maybe she was being overly sensitive, but Jada had the feeling that Gene was trying to downplay her direct contribution to Honoraria's success at the Beanies, and that is why she had subtly corrected him.

"Yes, it was pretty impressive. So in recognition of your hard work, the steering committee agreed unanimously to promote you to SVP. That's pretty amazing, since you've been a VP for only a few years."

Jada waited, expecting to hear more about what the new role entailed—salary, anything. Instead, Gene sat there waiting for her reaction.

"Wow! That's great. I'm really amazed." At first, she hoped that he hadn't heard the sarcasm in her voice. But then, she simply didn't care. "Tell me, Gene, what new responsibilities come with my new role?"

Gene shifted uncomfortably. *Damn. Sam and Alison were right. A bigger title and money alone would not be enough to satisfy Jada. Why did I try so hard to convince them otherwise? I should have at least gotten the go-ahead to offer more if need be.*

"Well, it's an in-place promotion, Jada. Your roles and responsibilities will stay essentially the same."

"Essentially the same?"

"Well, they'll stay the same for the near term. We would like to give you the opportunity to join the steering committee in a year or so—" Gene realized right away that his offer couldn't have sounded more meager, even if she had yet to receive an offer from a competitor. In his zeal to get the steering committee to agree to promote her, he had disregarded whom he was dealing with. While an in-place promotion would be fine for some people, for Jada, it was insulting—basically a slap in the face, especially after her recent triumphs.

"I see. And what about salary?"

"Er . . . of course the promotion comes with a generous salary increase. As you know, our average promotion increases are between eight and ten percent; you'll get a fifteen percent increase."

Jada did the math in her head. That still didn't get her even comfortably into the average range for an advertising vice president in the city.

"So what do you say, Jada? All of your hard work has really paid off. I'm happy for you." He had no choice; he had to at least try to make the offer sound a little more exciting and upbeat than it actually was.

The conversation was way more awkward than it should have been, crystallizing for Gene the fact that he and Jada had spent very little time together just shooting the breeze and getting to understand each other as people. He knew nothing about her except what he'd heard through the rumor mill. Thus, they had no rapport and nothing to fall back on to lessen the awkwardness of the situation.

Jada took a deep breath and summoned up a visual image of Luca watching the whole thing and cheering her on. It was now or never . . .

"Well, Gene, it's an interesting offer, and it dovetails nicely with what I wanted to talk to you about."

"Oh, really?" Gene had a feeling this was not going the way he'd hoped.

"Since the Beanies I've had calls from a couple of agencies, and just a little while ago, I had a firm offer from Rize."

"Oh?"

"Yes. Quite frankly, I had been putting them all off, because I was curious to see if Honoraria would come forward with any kind of recognition of my achievements; hence, my calls about getting together. I have to tell you, Gene, Dan Egleston at Rize presented an offer that was very interesting: an SVP position with membership on their steering committee—effective immediately, equity to be negotiated and salary to be negotiated, but at a level commensurate with salary averages in Boston. As you are surely aware, my current salary is *well* below average for the area."

Gene felt sick. He was going to pay for not having asked for latitude from the steering committee to negotiate with Jada. He had been foolishly confident that he wouldn't need to. But he had been way off-base. Rize's offer was fantastic, and, if Gene were honest, it was in line with what she deserved.

"That's an impressive package, Jada. We certainly don't want to lose you without making a counteroffer, so let me go back to the steering committee and talk to them before you make a decision. Can you just give me the weekend?"

"Sure, Gene. For what it's worth, I want you to know that I would like to stay at Honoraria. I'm proud of what I've achieved here. I think I've got one of the best teams in town; their recent success validates that. But I also have to tell you that this experience has been an eye-opener for me. I was really a little shocked to discover how significantly underpaid I am compared to my peers in town. Given my track record, I think I deserve the same chances for career growth, development and compensation that they have."

Gene swallowed hard. "Understood. Let me get on it. Thanks for being so honest and for hanging in there with us, Jada."

"No problem, Gene," she said, watching him all but run from the office.

Actually, it *was* a problem. Despite what she had just said to Gene about wanting to stay at Honoraria, the exchange with him had convinced her that she had to leave; she didn't have a future there. If Gene could come to her with an offer as anemic (and insulting) as he had when he had seen with his own eyes that she was being courted by other agencies, Honoraria would never take her seriously. While she had fretted about having to go somewhere else and prove herself all over again, she saw that she would *always* be fighting an uphill battle for respect at Honoraria. Even though she had basically made up her mind about leaving, she was perversely curious about what kind of offer Gene would have when he came back to her on Monday.

Gene left Jada's office in a complete panic. He had really screwed up. He walked straight to Sam Blackstone's office to discuss his options. Sam chaired the steering committee, and this situation required that he call an emergency meeting to deal with it. He hoped he could do it before the close of business for the weekend. Sam's door was open and he walked right in, determined to get this mess taken care of immediately. He didn't look to see if anyone was in the office before he started talking.

"Sam, I'm afraid you're going to have to pull the steering committee together for another meeting. We've got to have another conversation about Jada's promotion—" When Gene glanced around, he saw David Heath sitting on the sofa. "Oh, sorry. I didn't realize you had someone with you."

David felt as if he was going to blow. He turned beet red. "You're *promoting* her?"

"Way to go, Gene," Sam said. Turning to look at David, he said, "Hey, David, please keep this under your hat; this is confidential information."

"You're *promoting* her?" David repeated and then stormed out of the office.

CHAPTER 39

Awaiting a call from Luca, Hugh was on edge. They hadn't spoken much since Luca's meeting with him in Boston. Hugh was angry, feeling Luca wasn't appreciative of the work he'd done to bring in so much new business so quickly. The phone rang and he snatched it up.

"Luca. Hello."

"Hello, Hugh. How are things?"

"Going well, Luca. I'm working on even more new client opportunities. Keeping the ones we've got happy . . ."

"Good. Good. Hugh, I'll make this brief. I'm coming into town this weekend. I'd like to talk with you on Monday morning if you're free."

"Yeah, sure, I've got time. Anything in particular you want to discuss?"

Luca didn't want to get into it with Hugh on the phone, so he chose to be cryptic.

"No, just some ideas about the organization that I want to discuss with you."

"Okay," Hugh said, his voice hesitant.

"I'll be in Boston tomorrow at midday if anything comes up."

"All right. Short of that, I'll see you Monday morning then."

"*Ciao.*"

"Yeah, *ciao*," Hugh responded. "What the fuck is that about—*ideas about the organization?*"

Fiorella knocked and walked in.

"Hugh, I'm beginning to worry about you. Almost every time I walk past your office, you're talking to yourself."

"That was Luca. He wants to talk Monday about ideas about the organization."

"What does that mean?"

"I'm fucked if I know, Fee. I was hoping you might have some idea. I think he might be firing me."

"Firing you? No."

"Why not? He told me last month if he didn't see changes, I'd be gone."

"That's not Luca's style. If he were firing you, he would have told you over the phone and asked you to be gone by the time he got here. He wouldn't be asking you to meet him Monday morning. We Italians don't like to start a week with bad news; it's bad karma."

Fiorella continued, "No, Luca wouldn't be so considerate of someone he didn't plan to keep around."

"Hmmm. I like your assessment better than mine. He's coming to Boston tomorrow, undoubtedly for another weekend of hot sex with Jada Green."

"Hugh, what have you got against that woman?"

"I don't like her. I don't know why. From the moment she came on the scene, things have gone pear-shaped. If she weren't a part of Luca's life, he wouldn't be running back here every time I turn around."

"That seems a little simplistic, don't you think?"

"Maybe it is, but it works for me," he said, laughing heartily. "Fuck it. If I could possibly be fired, I'm going to start my weekend early. Fancy a drink?"

"Hugh, it's only three o'clock in the afternoon!"

"And it's Friday. Have you got any appointments later?"

"No."

"Then come on. We're calling it a day and starting our weekend early . . . by order of the president."

CHAPTER 40

On his way to Marco Tuccino's studio to pick up Jada's engagement ring, Luca was running late. He couldn't wait to see it; he couldn't wait to be back in Boston with Jada. As the time got closer to his departure, he was spending large portions of the day imagining how he would propose to her. Much of the rest of his days were spent thinking about making love with her. That left very little time for getting work done. His reputation as a man who thought about "business and only business" was going up in flames, and he couldn't have been happier about it.

"Marco, sorry I'm late. The traffic was horrible."

"It's not a problem, Luca, not a problem. But I'm afraid I don't have good news about the ring. I'm a little behind schedule—"

Luca's heart sank. "Marco, I'm leaving tomorrow morning to go to Boston. I need the ring tonight."

"I know, Luca, and I am really sorry about this. Let me show you what the problem is." Marco took him into his atelier and showed him the challenge he'd had getting the band to match the intricacies of the necklace on the outside while keeping the inside smooth. "I could let you take it like this, but I know you want it to be perfect. I'm afraid that unless I work the gold down more smoothly, this little ridge could irritate your fiancée's finger. It just takes time to sculpt it properly."

Luca smiled to hear someone call Jada his fiancée. But this news complicated his plans. "Marco, it has to be perfect. If it will take you another day, I'll move my flight back by a day."

"I'm terribly sorry about this, Luca," Marco repeated. "I had planned out my time assuming that everything would go to plan, which was a mistake on my part. But I knew you would want it to be done properly, and so do I. My reputation is at stake! I promise you I will have it the way it should be by tomorrow afternoon."

"Fine, Marco. See you then." He could barely contain his disappointment.

Luca got back in his car and dialed Jada's cell phone number. "Pick up, Jada . . . please." Her voicemail picked up.

"*Amore mio*, I'm sorry I missed you. Something has come up that will keep me here for another day, so I will have to fly in on Sunday instead of tomorrow. I am so sorry. But I'm going to extend my trip on the other end so we're not cheated out of any time together, okay? I'm going to call your office number now. I want to talk to you. I love you. *Ciao*."

He hung up and dialed her office number, which also went to voice mail.

"Jada, I left you a long message on your mobile phone. Call me after you hear it, okay? I love you. *Ciao*."

He glanced at the clock in his car. It was going on four o'clock in Boston. He was anxious to hear how her talk with Gene had gone. She hadn't called or left him a message, so she must have been very busy. He hoped she'd be able to get out of the office a little early so she could talk to him from home.

CHAPTER 41

Jada got back to her office from her meeting just in time to hear her cell phone switch over to voice mail.

"Damn! I'm sure that was Luca." She checked the number and saw that indeed it had been. "I'll call him from the car; I'm so out of here," she said out loud. After the day she'd had, she was *owed* an early quit. Clearing the messages from her office phone, she heard Luca's.

"I really love that man," she said, continuing her conversation out loud. Though it was relatively early, the agency was almost empty; many people tried to slip out early on Fridays. Annie was already gone for the weekend, which was a refreshing change. She was usually there burning the midnight oil right alongside her. Jada reminded herself to make bringing Annie over to Rize with her a part of her negotiation with Dan. The thought of leaving Annie at Honoraria made her cringe.

As crazy as the day had been, she was in a good mood. It was the weekend. Luca would be there with her in a matter of hours. Could she ask for anything more? She walked through the cavernous garage to her car, cell phone in hand, and hopped in, oblivious to the world around her. She nearly jumped out of her skin when David Heath suddenly appeared at her passenger window, peering in with his beady, bespectacled eyes. *Oh, my goodness. What on earth does he want now?* She rolled the window halfway down.

"David? What are you doing?"

He looked at her with his eyes narrowed. Jada thought he looked stranger than usual, at the same moment noticing his gloved hand held a gun.

"Oh, my God!"

"Get out of the car, Jada."

"David, what?"

"I said get out of the car!"

His shrill voice scared her almost as much as the gun. In her entire life, Jada had only seen guns in the holsters of police officers. She'd never seen one close up, much less had one pointed at her. She was terrified and felt as if she could faint. She opened her car door and got out, but had the presence of mind to put her purse on the floor of the car and to tuck her keys and phone into the seat. They were hidden enough from view to discourage the random thief, but anyone searching her car would find them fairly easily.

David led her at gunpoint through the garage to a service tunnel leading to the warehouse building tucked away in the recesses of the building complex. Few people knew this building within a building even existed. Honoraria stored old files and creative work there. She looked back at him briefly. He didn't seem to be looking at her or at anything else. It was as if he were on autopilot. Still, she couldn't trust that he was so out of it, she could risk trying to run away from him.

"David, why are you doing this?"

"Shut up. Just keep walking until I tell you to stop."
She walked on and reached a small damp room with a
dim light and a chair in the corner. She stopped and
looked back at him questioningly.

"Sit there." She did as instructed. He held the gun
pointed directly at her chest.

"I figured it out."

"Figured what out?"

"I heard."

"David, you heard what? I don't understand . . ."

"Lorenzo."

"Lorenzo?"

"Don't pretend you don't know who Lorenzo
Alessandri is!"

"Luca's father?"

"Yes, your boyfriend's father. He got you the Burrows
account."

It all came flooding back to her. After her first
meeting with the Burrows team, when Ambrose Burrows
had said, "I'm going to call Lorenzo and thank him for
telling us about you." She had suspected that David had
heard the conversation, but she had convinced herself
that he hadn't since he had said nothing about it. Now
she knew better.

"I don't know—"

"Liar! You do know."

"No! Ambrose Burrows and Mr. Alessandri know
each other. *I* know that because Ambrose Burrows told
me so. But beyond that I really don't know anything
about their relationship. And why would Mr. Alessandri

go to bat for me? I've only met him once, and that was *after* the Burrows account came to Honoraria."

The argument seemed to give David a little pause, and he seemed to be considering what Jada had said. But then he continued.

"Still, you got promoted."

"Gene talked to me about a promotion."

"You got *promoted!*"

"But I—"

David yelled, *"Shut up!"* At the same time, he raised his hand and swiftly struck Jada with the butt of his pistol. Her world faded to black.

CHAPTER 42

"Jada, *amore mio*, I know you're not happy that I've been delayed. I can't tell you how sorry I am about it, but your silence is torturing me. Please call me any time tonight. I need to hear your voice. *Ciao*."

It was eight o'clock in the evening in Boston and there was still no word from Jada. Was she really that angry with him for postponing his trip? Maybe she'd gone out with her friends to celebrate her job offer and she didn't hear the phone? But why hadn't she even called to let him know what had happened when she talked with Gene? He called one more time; the phone once again went to voice mail. It was 2 a.m. in Italy. He forced himself to go to bed, though he was certain he would not sleep.

He woke in the morning around 10 a.m. and called her cell phone. Again, the call went to voicemail. He called her landline, but knew that she usually turned that phone down when she went to bed. *Jada, where are you?* By now, all kinds of thoughts were running through his mind. More than anything, he was getting seriously worried.

By noon—six o'clock in the morning in Boston— Luca was beyond frantic. She was often awake by six, even on weekends, and the first thing she did was turn on the ringer and check her landline for messages. He'd left several. This just wasn't like Jada. He looked through his papers. He had written down Katrina's phone number somewhere. But where? It had to be in his files somewhere.

"*Grazie a Dio!*" Luca shouted when he found the number. He dialed anxiously, hoping that Katrina would have news that would calm his now frazzled nerves.

"Hello?" Renie was only half awake and sounded more than a little pissed off when she answered the phone.

"Katrina, it's Luca. I'm sorry to call you so early—"

"Luca? Where are you?" Her question made Luca even more anxious because it meant that Jada had not told Katrina his arrival had been delayed, and he knew the two friends spoke every evening, almost without fail.

"I'm in Torino."

"What's up?"

"I was wondering, have you spoken to Jada recently?"

"No, I haven't. You know, we usually talk in the evening, but yesterday I didn't hear from her. I tried to call her but the calls all went to voice mail. I'd figured that she was off doing something, since you're—Hey, aren't you supposed to be on a plane or something?"

"I had to delay my trip by a day. Katrina, I'm really worried. I haven't heard from Jada since early yesterday—before I had to change my flight. I've left messages for her everywhere, and she hasn't called back. And now you say she hasn't called you, either. That's not like her. I hate to ask you, but—"

"Luca, you don't even need to ask. You're right. This is all slightly strange, and I'm worried, too. Let me get in touch with Annie and see if she can help so we can check out her office. It wouldn't be the first time she's burned the midnight oil at work, but she usually lets someone know that she's doing it."

Luca felt ill. He seriously doubted that she was working at the office. If she had been, she would have checked the messages on her cell phone and called him a long time ago. What would he do if something happened to her?

"Please, Katrina, call me back as soon as you know something."

"I will. Bye."

Renie got dressed while dialing Annie's cell phone number. It was a good thing she'd stored her number in her cell phone; otherwise, she might end up at the police station for breaking and entering at Honoraria. This was not like Jada at all; something was wrong.

Annie knew it, too, when Katrina explained the situation. She told her husband that he'd have to forget about his day of golf with his buddies and deal with their boys. She then raced off to meet Katrina at Honoraria.

Everything looked fine in the office. The lights were off, her desk locked up as usual; nothing was out of order. Jada's purse was gone. There were no clues to her whereabouts there.

"Let's check the garage," Annie suggested. They rode down to the garage level in nervous silence.

"She usually parks over here—There's her car!" They raced over to the car. Katrina looked in and tried the door, which was unlocked.

"Oh, my God," she said when she saw Jada's purse, keys and cell phone.

"Annie, call the police! I've got to call Luca."

CHAPTER 43

"Hello, Katrina?"

"Luca—" Suddenly, Renie couldn't speak and burst into tears.

"Katrina, what's happened? Please, calm down and tell me!"

"We found Jada's car at the office. Her purse, keys and phone were in it. We've called the police. Luca, I'm so scared!" Katrina knew that her hysteria could only serve to make Luca more upset, and he was thousands of miles away. She tried hard to control herself for his sake, but she didn't have much success.

"Oh, my God. I'll be there as quickly as possible. Please call me again—every hour. I've got to go."

"I promise I'll call you. Get here soon."

Luca didn't know where to begin. He called the airlines and learned he had already missed the last nonstop flight to Boston. He might still be able to make a flight to Milan that connected to a flight to Boston from London. He booked it and then called his father.

"Papà, I don't have much time. Something has happened to Jada."

"What? What's happened?"

"I don't know for sure. She is missing. I changed my flight because the ring wasn't ready. I should have been there already."

"Luca, you cannot blame yourself."

"What could have happened to her, Papà? Her friends have called the police; I'm on a flight to Boston via London. I have to leave soon."

"No! Don't do that."

"I *have* to go, Papà. I have to be there."

"I know you do, Luca, just—I will get you a plane to take you there. Your uncle, Pietro, has access to planes."

"Papà, you and Uncle Pietro don't even speak."

"This is one of those times when family is more important than the disagreements that families may have. He loves you like his own son. He will do it. His planes are at the airport near here, so meet me here. I need to see you before you leave."

"Papà, I don't have time—"

"Please, Luca, let me do this. I will set everything up. It's important that I see you before you leave. I wouldn't ask you otherwise."

"Okay. I'll be there shortly."

"Good. I will have everything arranged with your uncle by the time you arrive. And Luca?"

"Yes, Papà?"

"Please drive carefully."

"I will."

Lorenzo had to look up his younger brother's phone number; it had been that long since he'd last called him.

"Pietro, *ciao. Come stai?*"

"Lorenzo?"

"Yes. It has been a long time."

"What do you want? You have made it clear that you want nothing to do with me."

"Your nephew has an urgent situation. He needs to get to Boston immediately."

"What's happened?"

Lorenzo quickly told him about Jada, Luca's plans to propose and her mysterious disappearance. Pietro didn't even let him finish.

"One of my planes was due to be flown to New York tomorrow, anyway. I will have them get the plane ready to leave for Boston within the hour."

"*Grazie,* Pietro."

"Thank you for letting me know and for letting me help Luca. I would do anything for my nephew. He is very dear to me. Please tell him I'm praying for the safe return of his fiancée."

"I will tell him. *Ciao.*"

Lorenzo then found Olivia and told her what had happened.

"Oh, no, Lorenzo," she said, tears forming in her eyes. "If anything happens to Jada, I don't know what it will do to Luca."

"I know, Olivia. But this does not sound good."

"I pray that they find her and that she's okay." Lorenzo took his wife into his arms to comfort her.

"Me, too. I will make some phone calls." Olivia pulled away from her husband and looked at him.

"Lorenzo! You must give Luca the file from the detective agency. It may have information that could be helpful somehow. Lorenzo?"

"Yes, yes, I know. I was just thinking—"

"Well, what you need to think about is how you're going to explain why you were having detectives follow her around and investigate all of her colleagues in the first place. You cannot let him go without the file! Lorenzo?"

"I *know*. I know. I really do hate it when you're right."

Luca arrived moments later. He broke down when he saw his parents, sobbing uncontrollably.

Olivia embraced him gently. "Luca, I am so sorry to hear this news. They will find her, *figlio mio*. Don't despair."

"I delayed my trip so I could bring the ring with me. Marco was trying to make it perfect and I wanted perfection. Now I'd give anything to be there now. When she was here, I had promised her that I would always do everything I could to protect her. I failed when she was here, and I've failed once again. One of her friends has called me twice with updates, but there's no news. All they can tell me is that there was no sign of blood in the car. The police have nothing."

It devastated Olivia and Lorenzo to see their son in such emotional distress.

"Luca, you have to have faith that they'll find her and that she's all right. My darling son, have faith in your love."

His mother's words helped to calm him down. He knew he had to hold himself together, and if nothing else, he did have deep faith in his love for Jada.

"I've got to go. Thank you, Papà, for talking to Uncle Pietro. I will call him and thank him later."

"Certainly, Luca. He sends his best wishes to you and to Jada."

Olivia was giving her husband dirty looks because he had yet to give Luca the file.

I might as well get this over with. "Luca, one more thing before you go; please take this file with you. Don't ask me now how I've come to have it; we'll talk about it later, but there may be things in here that can be of help to the police."

Luca looked at the thick file questioningly, but he took it without opening it, shoving it into his briefcase.

"Thank you, Papà."

"Go now. Your uncle said the plane would be ready to take off within the hour. Good luck. And let us know what's happening. We really do adore Jada, and we know that she has made you very, very happy since she has been in your life. We pray that she is found safe."

"Thank you." Luca hugged them and left for the airport.

CHAPTER 44

It had been almost two hours. David looked at the still passed-out Jada. He really hadn't thought this out. All he had wanted to do was to get her to agree to quit the agency. What was he going to do with her now? As usual, she was nothing but trouble to him. He laughed. "As tough as you *think* you are, one hit and you passed out cold. I wish I'd known that sooner . . . I would have cracked you one the minute you came on my turf. Mine!"

Everything had been fine until the agency started worrying about not being diverse enough. " 'Not enough women . . . not enough people of color,' " he mocked. "No one had a more solid portfolio of accounts than me. No one! That is, until you came along. Manager to director in two years? Two years! But I'm a VP; I'm feeling things are still going pretty well, and then what do they do? They promote *you* to VP! To make it worse, everybody *loves* you. All I hear is 'Jada Green is great. Jada Green is the best boss ever!' Well, what about *me*? And now, because of your rich boyfriend's father, Lorenzo, you're getting promoted *again*! That is not going to happen! I tell you, I wouldn't mind if *all* the other uppity women got lost, but *you* are the worst of the bunch. You've got to go. You've got to go. But you need to wake up first. There are a few things I've got to say to you. So wake up!" Jada was slowly regaining consciousness, but she remained silent and immobile.

My God. David is really insane. How am I ever going to get out of here? Please, please . . . someone help me!

CHAPTER 45

It was Luca's first trip on a private jet. His father and uncle had a falling out when Luca was in his early twenties. That was around the time when his uncle's high-tech business had begun to flourish, eventually becoming one of the largest in Italy. Luca's family was rich, but his uncle's family had become obscenely so. Despite the bad feelings between the brothers, his uncle had always doted on him and treated him like one of his own children. Luca had never taken advantage of the situation; it was awkward, since his father had made it clear that he wanted nothing to do with his brother. He had no idea what had caused the rift, but it had seemed irreparable. Yet in spite of that, the first thought Luca's father had was to ask his brother for help. It touched Luca a lot that his father was willing to swallow his pride to help him. Maybe it was also a sign that so much time had passed that the two of them didn't really know why they weren't speaking to one another.

After takeoff Luca paced the aisle of the plane, willing himself to stay calm. His stomach was in knots. Then it started. He rushed to the bathroom and vomited. He spent most of the flight there. The crew offered him tea, ginger ale, every kind of remedy they could think of, but he couldn't hold anything down. No one was more grateful than he when the plane finally touched down outside of Boston just before two o'clock in the afternoon.

He called Katrina and joined her and Jada's parents at the police station.

"Sergeant, this is Luca Alessandri, Jada's boyfriend," Katrina said. Looking Luca up and down, the sergeant said, "Have a seat, Mr. All-is-sand-ree," pronouncing the name in his distinctive Boston accent.

"I arrived from Italy a few moments ago. Is there any more information about what happened to Jada?"

"Nothing new, I'm afraid. We brushed her car for prints, but only found hers and Ms. Culver's. We believe that whoever took her was probably armed and wearing gloves."

"Armed? Oh, my God. Sergeant, are there cameras in the garage?"

"Yes, the cameras are trained on the entrance and the exit of the garage. We found Miss Green on the tape entering in the morning, but we haven't found anything on tape that shows her leaving in another car. Her car is running fine; it didn't break down. I'm afraid at the moment we're at a bit of an impasse. We're matching up the entrances and exits of everyone at the agency and we're trying to track down and interview all of her associates. It's a little more involved since it's a nice summer weekend and a lot of people head out of town. We're also going through a list of other potential suspects and leads. Tell me, Mr. All-is-sand-ree, do you know of anyone who had a grudge against Miss Green? Anyone who had a problem with her?"

"Aside from my ex-wife, no one comes to mind."

"Your ex-wife?"

"Yes, but I'm pretty certain that she is still in Italy."

"That may be, Mr. All-is-sand-ree, but I'm a thorough guy. I've already checked you out, so give me her name, anyway."

Luca's bright blue eyes looked at Sgt. Casey, not sure whether to be insulted or not. But he saw a man who simply took his work very seriously. "Mirella. Her maiden name is Montavani, but she still goes by my last name."

"We'll check that out." The sergeant nodded to one of the detectives listening in, who hurried off to check out the information, "Tell me, did Ms. Green happen to mention any of these people to you: Erwin Stone, Alicia Delgado, Steven Thomas, David Heath or Casey Rayburn?"

"Yes, I remember Jada telling me about Erwin Stone and Casey Rayburn; they're on the steering committee at Honoraria. David Heath is a colleague of hers; I don't recall her mentioning either Steven Thomas or Alicia Delgado. Why do you ask?"

"They're a few of the people we're having difficulty locating. Did Ms. Green ever mention having a problem with any of them?"

"No, not exactly."

"What does that mean?" Sgt. Casey asked, raising a bushy brow.

"Well, David Heath. He has a strong business rivalry with Jada. Sometimes he made her feel uneasy."

"That's interesting. Mr. Heath has a summer house on Nantucket, but he's neither there nor at his home in town. You're also the third or fourth person who has characterized his relationship with Ms. Green that way. He's at the top of the short list. Anything else?"

Luca's mind went back to his last meeting with Hugh, recalling his comment about Jada.

"Mr. All-is-sand-ree?"

"It's probably nothing—"

"Let us determine that. Right now, we've got nothing."

"Well, the president of my company here in the US, Hugh Laws, has been upset about my relationship with Jada. He felt it was a threat to him keeping his job."

Sgt. Casey perked up. "Do you know where Mr. Laws lives?"

"It's in the Back Bay. I don't have the address, but I've got his home phone number."

"Excellent. You'll have to give it to me. Then we'll go have a talk with Mr. Laws."

CHAPTER 46

Two unmarked cars pulled up in front of Hugh's apartment and four officers scurried out, hands on their holsters. The lead officer pounded on the door.

"Mr. Laws, Boston Police. Open up!"

Hugh and Fiorella were asleep in bed.

"What the fuck?" he said, pulling on his robe and going to the door.

"Hugh Laws?"

"Yes. What do you want?"

"Boston Police. You're going to have to come with us, sir."

"What the fuck for?"

"Hugh!" Fiorella had thrown on her clothes and walked up next to him. "It's really not wise to swear at policemen here. They have guns. This isn't England."

"You should listen to the advice of your lady friend, sir. You're going to have to come with us. We'll allow you to get dressed."

"Well, thanks for that," he mumbled.

They shoved Hugh into one car and put Fiorella into another. As they got closer to the police station, Hugh became more and more agitated. He asked the officers a few times if they could tell him why he was being brought in for questioning, but his queries were met with a stony silence. *What the fuck is happening?*

They took Hugh and Fiorella into separate interrogation rooms and the grilling began.

"Mr. Laws, what can you tell me about Jada Green?"

"Jada, Luca Alessandri's bird?"

"Bird?"

"Yeah. Girlfriend. I can tell you that they've been seeing each other for a few months now and that my life has been fucking hell since he met her. You dragged me down here to ask me about that?" he asked, brushing his hair off his face with two quick sweeps. "By the way, aren't I supposed to be able to call a solicitor?"

"A who?"

"A solicitor, you know, a lawyer."

"We haven't arrested you yet. We just want to talk to you. Can I ask you, though, what do you mean by what you said about Jada, Hugh? May I call you Hugh?"

Hugh noted that the officer had said that he hadn't been arrested *yet*. That subtle warning was enough to make him change his tone. "You can call me whatever you like. I mean that from the time Luca met Jada, Luca's been angling to take back his offer to make me president of Allegro USA."

"So you really don't like Jada Green, do you?"

"Like her? I don't really know her at all. I've only met her twice, actually. I saw her the last time a few weeks ago when Luca was in town. But the *idea* of her is a pain in my arse."

"Where were you yesterday from about 3 p.m. on?"

"That's easy. I was in the office, then I went to a couple of hotel bars with Fiorella Fontana. Afterwards, I was in bed with said mademoiselle trying to make up for being such a complete asshole to her over the past few weeks."

The officers in the room almost started laughing. This English guy had a way with words.

"Officers, please, can you tell me what's going on?"

"Jada Green is missing, Hugh, and we're trying to determine what has happened to her."

"And you think *I* had something to do with it?"

"We have witnesses who heard you say that you wished she weren't around anymore."

"I say all kinds of things. I talk. I swear. I blow off steam. Any problems I have on my job are with Luca, not her. Bloody hell. You think I'd harm a woman over a fucking job?"

"You just said being president of Allegro is important to you."

"Yeah, and it is, but not *that* important. I'm telling you, you're barking up the wrong tree here, mates."

Fiorella was getting a similar grilling in the other room.

"Miss Fontana, have you heard Mr. Laws say that he wished Miss Green weren't around?"

"Yes, but . . ."

"But, Miss Fontana?"

"Hugh talks a lot of nonsense all the time. He's a somewhat insecure man. Being president of Allegro means a lot to him, and when he started having difficulties with Luca—Mr. Alessandri—he blamed everyone he could think of for it, including Jada. When Luca started seeing Jada, it meant that he had more reasons to come to Boston, and that made Hugh feel uncomfortable."

"Where were you yesterday from 3 p.m. on, Miss Fontana?"

"I left the office early with Hugh and we went to two hotel bars and had drinks. Then I went back to Hugh's apartment, where we were until your officers knocked on the door. We used to live together; I only recently moved out. Please, tell me what's happened?"

"Jada Green is missing."

"Hugh didn't do it."

"How do you know that, Miss Fontana?"

Fiorella laughed. "Honestly, I've never met a man who talks more nonsense than Hugh. He says mean things and swears a lot, but he's really a nice guy. He doesn't even really know Jada, and, even if he did, he could never hurt her. I'm sure of it."

"Their stories check out, sir. There's no record of either of them entering or exiting Jada's office building or the garage. He's got the receipts in his wallet, and the hotels have verified that they were there. Unless the time-line is wrong, they're clean. Also, sir, Mr. Alessandri's ex-wife is still in Italy."

"Let the lovebirds go then," the sergeant said.

Luca and Hugh passed each other in the hallway of the police station but said nothing. Fiorella followed just behind.

"Luca, I'm so sorry to hear about Jada. I hope they find her soon."

"Thank you, Fiorella. Thank you."

"You look terrible, though. I think you need to get some sleep."

"I will a little later."

The sergeant overheard the conversation and came over to them. "Mr. All-is-sand-ree, Miss Fontana is right. You've been here since your plane landed. We'll continue to track down Ms. Green's colleagues and follow up some other leads. Why don't you go home and we'll call you if we find out anything new?"

"Go, Luca, you look like a zombie."

Luca was reluctant to leave, but he was beginning to feel the effects of hours without sleep. He thought about going to Jada's house; he had the key. But the thought of being there without her made him change his mind. He decided to stay at the Ritz. He had wonderful memories of their time together there, and he wouldn't have to see her clothes hanging in the closet or smell her familiar perfume in every room, which would be more than he could handle without breaking down completely.

Though he was exhausted, he found that he couldn't sleep, so he tried doing things insomniacs often do. He read magazines, he tried to watch TV. Then he remembered the file his father had given him. What was in it anyway? He'd been in such a daze when his father had handed it to him that he hadn't paid it much attention. He rifled through his briefcase until he found it. To his surprise, when he looked closely, he saw that the folder had a name: Jada Green.

"What is this?" Luca wondered. The inside of the file bore a stamp reading "Kingsley Detective Agency, New

York, New York." Flipping through the pages, he saw pictures of Jada's driver's licenses from the time she was a teenager; her college transcript; a copy of her university degree; job reviews from what looked like every company she had ever worked for. Then he came to a section called Honoraria. There was a company organization chart with pictures; a floor plan and write-ups on her boss, Gene Bradley, and on each of her colleagues and team members.

Luca paused for a moment to try to figure out why his father had this information, but he quickly put the question out of his mind. When his father had given him the file, he'd said that there might be information in it that could help him to find Jada. *That's all I'm going to focus on right now.* He rubbed his temples and started reading.

He took out all the write-ups and sorted them into three piles: people he had met, colleagues Jada had mentioned, and others.

He read about Gene, Annie and several others he had met at the Beanie Awards. Then he came to David Heath. He'd always heard Jada's point of view: an old-school adman who loved the power and prestige of being a vice president and confidante of the partners. From his fact-based biography, Luca got a different view. David had been with Honoraria for twenty years. At first his career progressed rapidly, from associate to director in a little more than five years. But then he spent almost another five before getting promoted to VP. Almost everyone on the steering committee had started at

Honoraria in a more junior role than him. "No wonder he resents Jada," Luca said aloud. "After working there for so long, I'd be furious, too, if so many people were getting promoted before me." Luca stopped reading, threw on his clothes and hailed a taxi back to police headquarters.

CHAPTER 47

After tracking down leads and extensive interviews with Jada's colleagues, all evidence pointed to one man: David Heath. Several hours into the investigation, he was still missing in action, and he was one of two people whose departure from the building had not been matched with his arrival; the other was Jada Green. The building, constructed in the 1950s at the height of the Cold War, had been swept twice, but no sign of either of them had turned up. Sergeant Casey knew there must have been fallout shelters or secret hideaways that they were missing.

After 9/11 a concerted effort had been made to put digital floor plans of all office buildings in the city into a database. Somehow, Honoraria's building had been overlooked. Sgt. Casey was almost apoplectic. "Dammit! Where's that building plan?" he bellowed. "I want it now!"

Luca walked into the station in the midst of the pandemonium. "Mr. All-is-sand-ree, I thought we sent you home?" Sergeant Casey asked.

As Luca started to answer, he realized that he couldn't mention the file his father had given him, because he didn't know how he would explain having it if someone asked. "Yes, you did. I've just come back because . . . I think David Heath concerns me more than I had first thought."

"He concerns us, too, Mr. All-is-sand-ree," he said as an officer ran in with the floor plan.

"At last!" Sgt. Casey scrutinized it carefully.

"What's that?" he asked.

"The garage, sir."

"No, *that.*" He pointed to the box within the box. "Get someone in here or on the phone who can explain it to me. I need an explanation. Now!"

"Yes, sir!" About five officers scampered off to find the answer.

Luca was running on fumes. He stayed out of the way and let the officers do their work. He prayed that they were really on the brink of finding out what had happened to Jada.

Moments later, an officer returned with news. "Sarge, we just spoke with one of the engineers for the building where Miss Green works. It seems that the space on the plan is a bunker. It's used now as a warehouse for some of the companies in the building, including Honoraria, but hardly anyone even knows it exists. The entrance to the bunker was intentionally disguised, and it's accessed only through the garage."

"Bingo! Let's move!"

CHAPTER 48

David Heath paced the floor, considering his options. He was weary, hungry and totally confused. "I need a plan. Think, think, think." He and Jada had been there for hours. She had finally come to and asked to use the restroom. He obliged, showing her to the toilet in the adjoining room and standing guard at gunpoint. Since then, he knew he had dozed off, and perhaps Jada had, too, but she'd been too fearful of what he might do if she tried to escape. *Well, that's good. She should be afraid.* Still, David knew he wasn't a killer, but he was damn angry.

Jada was, indeed, paralyzed with fear. While she sensed David resented her, nothing in his demeanor had prepared her for this. She sat quietly in the corner of the damp room, watching him as he strode back and forth, muttering. Her only hope was that someone would figure out where they were. Meanwhile, she decided that getting David talking might be her best chance to stay alive. But it was not without risk; if she said the wrong thing, he could snap.

"David?" The unexpected sound of Jada's voice caused him to jump.

Pointing the gun at her, he asked, "What do you want now?"

"I just—I'm sitting here wondering why you dislike me so much," she said, her voice trembling.

David laughed bitterly. "Well, Jada, you're just the unlucky one. You're the last straw."

"What do you mean?"

"I've been at Honoraria for more than twenty years. I've played the game. I've been damn successful at it, too. Do you know how many years I was the VP with the largest portfolio? Do you?"

"No."

"Ten. Ten years. Do you know what's happened in ten years? Ten years ago, Alison Samson was a director; ten years ago, that good-looking jock Casey Rayburn was in college. Ten years ago, you weren't at Honoraria and no one there gave a damn that we didn't have any women or people of color in the higher levels of the agency. How is it that people like Alison, Casey and now you all end up passing me by? You were just the unlucky one. Winning that account did it for me. But you could have just as easily been one of them."

Talking seemed to be calming David down, so she listened, hoping he would continue.

"I learned to play golf, I became friends with all the partners—I bet *you've* never been to Sam Blackstone's house, have you?"

"No, I haven't."

"See? And yet, despite all of that, Alison gets promoted, that punk Casey gets promoted and you get promoted. If we're supposed to be making things more fair, where's the fairness in that?"

In spite of her circumstances, Jada could understand how he felt. Advertising was evolving, and people had come along with skills better suited to today's demands. David had been left behind. In his fragile state of mind, each colleague's promotion had to hurt, not to mention her winning a plum account and a boatload of professional awards at his expense. Scared as she was, Jada actually felt sorry for him.

"David, this isn't going to end well if you don't let me go."

Glaring and aiming the gun at her, David said, "Do you *really* think I care?"

"Police! Drop the gun, Heath!"

David swung around and pointed his gun at the officer, who fired twice. David Heath was dead before he hit the ground. Jada screamed at the top of her lungs, saw David's bullet-ridden body fall right in front of her, and faded to black once more.

CHAPTER 49

Luca had been ordered to stay at the station; he was a bundle of nerves as he waited for news. An officer walked over with Sgt. Casey.

"It's all over, Mr. Alessandri. Jada Green was found alive," the officer said.

"She's alive? Thank God." Luca buried his head in his hands as tears of joy fell uncontrollably. He didn't care what anyone thought. The emotional relief was overwhelming.

Sgt. Casey patted him on his shoulder. "She's at the hospital, Mr. All-is-sand-ree. Gunshots were fired. She wasn't injured, but I understand that she had been assaulted and then fainted. She's been admitted to Mass General Hospital."

"Assaulted? Oh, no. I have to go. Sergeant, thank you. Thank you very much." He shook Sgt. Casey's and the officer's hands and ran off to catch a cab to the hospital.

Luca called Katrina and his father with the news as he made his way to the hospital.

"Papà, Jada has been found alive."

"*Grazie a Dio!* Thank God."

"Papà, that file; it had so much information. Jada's school grades, employee reviews? Why did you have such a file and how did you get it?"

"Luca, I know you must have questions about it. We can talk when you come back. But I hope it was helpful."

"No, it was not. Papà, I want to know now. Why were you investigating the woman I'm going to marry?"

"I investigate everyone who is close to me and my family. How did you think I knew so much information about Hugh and Fiorella? I hired an investigator when you first met her. I just wanted to find out about her—to be sure that she wasn't out to get your money."

"Papà, Jada is my concern. I'm a grown man! I don't need you to hire investigators on my behalf!"

"I know you are a grown man, son. I'm sorry you feel I was interfering, but I'm not sorry that I did it."

Suddenly, Luca was too tired to argue. Besides, he knew there was nothing he could say to convince his father that what he'd done was wrong.

"Papà, you're right; we'll talk about it later. I'm on my way to the hospital now. Please tell Mamma the news. I'll speak with her later."

"I will. Luca?"

"Yes?"

"I'm very happy that Jada is all right."

"*Ciao,* Papà."

He raced into the hospital and tried to go into Jada's room but was stopped by the nurse.

"I'm sorry sir, only family members are allowed in unless you have her parents' consent."

"Where are they?"

The Greens were just walking up the hallway with Katrina when they saw Luca talking to the nurse outside of Jada's room.

"Luca?"

"Please, Mr. and Mrs. Green, I've been so worried. I must see her."

Horace and Ida were taken aback by how tired and haggard Luca looked. It seemed like he'd aged twenty years since they'd last seen him at the police station. He had dark circles under his eyes, which looked glazed and bloodshot, and he was in desperate need of a shave.

"Son, are you all right?" Horace asked.

"I will be fine. I just haven't slept since before I arrived here in Boston. Please, Mr. and Mrs. Green . . ."

Horace and Ida looked at one another in silent agreement. "Go ahead. Go spend some time with your fiancée. They had to sedate her, so she may already be sleeping deeply."

Luca nodded. It didn't matter; she was alive. He walked into the room slowly, quietly.

"Jada, *amore mio.*" His hand was shaking so much, he was afraid to touch her. She had a gash on her hairline where David had apparently hit her; otherwise, she looked just like she always did—so beautiful. He held her hand, which felt warm, even a little clammy. "I was so worried about you. Oh, Jada, I am so grateful that he didn't hurt you too badly. Just get better soon and know that I love you." He kissed her hand gently.

"Luca?" Her voice was hoarse and croaky. As soon as he heard it, his tears started falling uncontrollably once again. "Shhh. Don't try to talk, Jada. Just rest."

"I—I was scared."

"I'm sure you were, *amore mio,* but it's okay now. You're safe. He cannot hurt you. Your parents are here,

Renie is here and I am here. Just sleep now. I'll be here when you wake up. I promise." Jada nodded her head, closed her eyes and went back to sleep.

Ida Green walked in to check on her daughter.

Luca was sitting in the chair next to her bed. "She woke up for a moment and we spoke, then she went back to sleep."

"I think she needed to speak to you as much as you needed to speak to her. Luca, Jada is going to be okay. The doctor said she'll sleep for at least four hours, and, right now, I'm worried about you. I have to tell you, honey, you look worse than she does! Please go get some rest. Do you have a place to stay?"

"Yes."

"Well, please go there and sleep for a little while . . . for me? You won't be any good to Jada when she wakes up if you collapse from exhaustion, and you're on your way there right now."

"I am really tired," he admitted.

"Go on then. If anything changes, Katrina has your number. I can call you."

"Thank you, Mrs. Green. I don't know what I would have done if I'd lost her. I get frightened when I think about it."

"I know, Luca, I know. We'll see you a little later on, okay?"

"All right. I'll be back soon."

He made his way out of the hospital and glanced at the newspaper in the honor box at the entrance: "Ad Exec

Missing," the front-page headline read. He imagined that the kidnapping of a beautiful female ad exec—and a black one at that—by her mentally disturbed, misogynist, white colleague was indeed a juicy news story. He was grateful that in their haste to get the story out quickly, the reporters hadn't discovered his relationship with Jada and that he had been able to stay under the radar throughout this ordeal. He knew his name would come up now and he'd just have to deal with it. But he would never have been able to deal with news reporters asking him for comments about what had happened before she'd been found alive. Right now, all he wanted to do was see Jada get better and for them to get on with their lives. When he got back to the Ritz, Luca asked them to give him a wakeup call in four hours. He was asleep before his head hit the pillow.

He returned to the hospital after showering, shaving and changing quickly. Horace Green was standing outside the hospital room with a worried look on his face.

"Is everything all right, Mr. Green? How's Jada?"

"They thought she would be stirring by now, but she still hasn't woken up, Luca. Go in there, son. Maybe she's waiting to hear your voice again." He nodded and went into the room. Luca approached her bed silently, kissed her forehead and gently held her hand. He was sure he hadn't imagined it; she had squeezed his hand back, but she didn't move. So he whispered, "Jada, *amore mio*, I have a question for you. Are you awake yet?"

Her eyes opened slowly and she spoke softly.

"I told you before, you're a dirty old man, Luca Alessandri." She smiled weakly. Luca actually laughed. He was so overcome with relief that he didn't know what to do.

"I'm so glad you've come back to us. You're going to be okay."

CHAPTER 50

They spent hours just sitting together. Sometimes they talked; sometimes they just sat quietly. The mere presence of the other was enough. The police were the first to be let in. Gratefully, they were efficient and brief. Renie, India, Liz and even Carmen stopped by. Jada and Carmen had the chance to chat and clear the air. Luca left them alone, happy that they were speaking again. Later in the day, Gene and Sam Blackstone came by to visit. Mrs. Green hadn't wanted to let them in, but Jada overruled her mother. Gene started the conversation.

"We just wanted to say how sorry we are about this. I, we, had no idea that David was so disturbed."

"I'm sure you didn't."

Sam then took over the conversation.

"Look, Jada . . . I know you were in the midst of talking with us about your promotion when this happened." Then, he faltered. Seeing Jada lying in bed in the hospital with a gash on her head from David's gun filled him with overwhelming guilt. While he truly had not realized how unstable David was, he knew that David had been extremely frustrated by how stagnant his career had become at Honoraria. David no longer fit the mold of an advertising executive in terms of either style or substance. But because he had such close relationships with some of the partners, no one had the heart to tell him it was time to move on. Sam had not been a true friend to David, and his silence only served to fuel David's anger and delusional jealousy.

"Ummm. Jada, we want you to stay with us. We really do. But that's not the most important thing right now. Even more than that, we want you to take as long as you need to get well and recover from this. Everyone at the agency wishes you well."

"Thank you, Sam. I appreciate it."

He and Gene left the room quickly after that. Jada turned to Luca. "I had already decided that I wasn't going to stay at Honoraria. I had the phone in my hand to listen to your message and to call you and tell you about my decision. They were underpaying me and they didn't want to give me more responsibility. I thought about what you'd said to me when we'd talked . . . about being scared. I realized I was . . . That's why it was kind of ironic."

"What was ironic?"

"David. He'd heard that I was getting promoted; that's what set him off. I was trying to tell him that I was leaving Honoraria when he hit me and I blacked out. When I came to, I was too scared to bring it up again."

"It probably wouldn't have mattered to him, anyway. He was insane. Being passed out in the beginning may have saved your life."

Jada was quiet for a while. "I hadn't thought about it that way." Suddenly, she started to cry.

"It's okay . . . let yourself cry . . . you need to let it out. It's okay, Jada." Luca stretched out on the side of the hospital bed and held her in his arms. "You are safe, *amore mio*. It's okay."

"I was afraid he was going to kill me." She was starting to hyperventilate.

"I know, Jada, but you're all right now. Take a deep breath." Luca was worried about her emotional recovery, but grateful that was his only worry. He knew that Jada was the kind of woman who would try to fight through any problem quickly and on her own. He hoped that she would really take the time to heal and that she would let him help her. After a while her breathing regulated, the tears subsided and she fell asleep. And so did Luca.

Jada was released from the hospital the next day. Luca took her home. In some ways, it seemed very routine; they hung out in her house, listening to music and eating takeout food. Luca longed to make love with her, but he was afraid to touch her since he didn't want to rush her after her ordeal. So he busied himself cleaning her house, making her tea, chatting about mundane things. Jada thought he was walking on eggshells around her and she didn't know why.

Finally she had to ask him. "Luca, what is *wrong* with you?" Jada almost laughed, because it was the first time she'd ever used her "girlfriend" tone with him.

"Nothing. I'm just . . . I don't want to overexcite you."

"Luca, I'm not a geriatric patient! Lighten up. Weren't you the one asking me if I was awake just yesterday?"

"Yes, but—"

"Oh, so you're all about seduction and nothing else?"

Luca smiled. "*Amore mio*, I haven't even begun to seduce you. Be assured of that." He slipped his arms around her waist and pulled her in for a slow, deep kiss.

"I just didn't want to rush you; you just got out of the hospital."

"I am going to be fine. I'm *determined* that I'm going to get my life back. Luca, one of the things that kept me alive was you. I could hear your voice telling me to stay calm." She kissed him softly. "I could taste your kiss . . . I dreamed of making love with you again, so don't keep me waiting."

That was all he needed to hear. Luca took her into the bedroom, undressing her as they walked up the stairs. He kissed her hair, her nose, her neck and finally, at length, her lips. He took a deep, steadying breath. "*Amore mio*, I missed you so much when I was away and when you were gone . . . I was so scared . . . Jada, I love you. I love you." He lifted her onto the bed and quickly put on a condom. Luca looked down on her lying there, silently taking in her beauty. Then he slowly pulled her into his embrace. His eyes filled with tears as his heart filled with a whirlwind of emotions—relief, joy, worry, passion, uncertainty and desire. They were all there for Jada to see and feel. His hand wandered everywhere on her body. He couldn't get enough of her. He touched her scar which was beginning to heal and kissed it tenderly.

"Jada, I'm so sorry this happened."

"It wasn't your fault, Luca."

"I should have—" She covered his lips with her fingertips.

"It wasn't your fault. Just be with me . . . please."

Slowly, gently, he entered her, his eyes riveted to hers, watching for any sign that making love was taking too much of a toll on her. Seeing none, he relaxed and kissed her deeply, savoring the taste of her lips as he steadily increased his tempo.

Her nails dug into Luca's back as she felt the restlessness brewing within her body. Luca's pace grew faster and faster. Their climax was like a hushed gasp; so much emotion had been expended by both of them. After they parted, they kissed and caressed, choosing not to break the magical silence they shared.

Later on Luca lay watching Jada sleep, once again captivated by her steady breathing. He felt there was no limit to the depth of gratitude he felt having her there with him. She stirred a few times throughout the night, jumping up in a panic. Luca calmed her and held her tightly until she fell back asleep.

Jada woke up slowly to find Luca smiling at her.

"What's wrong?"

"*Amore mio*, nothing is wrong. I'm infinitely happy."

"Good. Luca?"

"Hmmm?"

"I was thinking about what the doctors and other people have said about taking time to recover."

"Yes?"

"I think I need to get out of town for a while. I don't feel like I can get perspective here."

"I can understand that." He pulled her close. "Where would you like to go?"

"Can I come to Torino and stay there with you? I know you have to work—"

"Don't worry about my work, Jada. Of course you can come to Torino! My house is your home in Italy. I have to ask, are you concerned about Mirella? I don't want anything to upset you."

Jada laughed. "After all of this, Mirella is the minor league. I'll be able to deal with her if we have another encounter."

"Okay. When do you want to leave?"

"Soon."

CHAPTER 51

They decided to leave in two days. Both Jada and
Luca had to scramble to get things in order before they
left. The doctors had wanted Jada to have a follow-up
examination, and they insisted that she come in right
away since she was planning to take an overseas trip. She
went to visit her parents to tell them about her plans.

"Jada, this is your home! Why do you feel that you
have to go away to get better?"

"Mom, I just feel like too much has happened here. I
can't think straight. I'll be able to clear my head and get
away from it all if I spend a little time in Torino. It's not
like I'm moving there!"

Ida Green nodded, but she knew there was a possibility that one day she would indeed be moving there.
She just didn't like the idea of her daughter being so far
away.

Horace decided he had to step in before his wife
spilled the beans about Luca's plan to propose and
blurted out all her fears about Jada moving to Italy
permanently.

"Look, Jada, you know how your mom worries about
you. I think we both understand why a change of scenery
might do you good. Hopefully, you understand that day

when you were missing was the scariest in our lives, too. We just wish you weren't going to be so far away right now, because after what happened, we just don't want you out of our sight."

"I understand, Dad. I really do. I don't know exactly when I'm going to come back, but I doubt I'll be gone more than a few weeks."

"Have a good time and be careful."

"I will, I promise."

"We both love you very much," Ida managed to whisper as Jada was leaving.

"I love you both very much, too."

Jada hadn't been driving since she got out of the hospital, so she hopped in a taxi. She'd thought she was brave enough to go to Honoraria to talk to Gene about her plans, but halfway there she found herself filled with fear. Jada had the taxi stop at a coffee shop where she went to call him on her cell phone.

"It's good to hear your voice, Jada. How are you doing?"

"I'm okay." Jada had always found it hard to make small talk with Gene, and it was even harder now. She'd had a lot of time to think about things—his lack of real support for her, his apparent endorsement of her feeble pay scale and his anemic job offer. No, she could not pretend that they were best buddies now. She just wanted to get what he and Sam had promised when they had visited her in the hospital.

"Gene, I want to take you up on Sam's offer for me to take as much time as I need to recover from this nightmare. I would like to take an indefinite leave of absence from Honoraria."

"Okay," Gene said slowly. Once again, he had not correctly anticipated what Jada was going to do. He'd expected that she would take a few weeks off and come back tougher than nails, defying anyone to try to rattle her again. That had always been her modus operandi. Apparently, that wasn't going to happen.

He knew that Sam had been sincere in his offer to have her take as much time as she felt she needed to recover and he'd been happy to endorse his plan because he never thought he'd have to face a long period of time without her. The steering committee had unanimously agreed to match Rize's offer and to throw even more money in to get her to stay at Honoraria. He hadn't even had the chance to tell her that. Now he didn't know when he'd get the chance to talk with her about it . . . and he was down not one, but two executives for the foreseeable future. No, this was not going to plan. This had to be that Italian boyfriend's influence. Those Europeans could never get enough vacation or sick leave.

Even though she knew she shouldn't have to explain, Jada felt obliged to do so.

"Gene, I was on my way over to talk to you personally, but as soon as I got close to the office, I was petrified. I was kidnapped and almost killed by the man who worked two doors down from me. I'm going to take the time I need to deal with what's happened to me; otherwise my life will continue to be ruled by it. If Sam's offer wasn't sincere, tell me now. I'll resign and take further action if I have to."

Jesus. Please don't do that! Honoraria's gotten enough bad press as it is! "No, Jada. Sam meant it. Take whatever time you need. Whenever you're ready to come back, we'll be happy to see you."

"Great. Thanks." Jada was still almost one hundred percent certain that she was going to leave Honoraria, no matter what they offered her to stay. They had already shown their hand where she was concerned, and she didn't like what she'd seen. But she could deal with that when she got back from Torino.

"I'm not sure how long I'll be out, but I'll keep you posted over the coming weeks."

"That's all we can ask for, Jada. Thanks for calling."

She hung up her cell phone, hailed a taxi and made her way over to Rize to meet with Dan Egleston.

"Jada, it's been all over the news and in the papers. I'm glad to know you're doing okay."

"I'm fine physically, but it probably won't shock you if I say that I'm pretty emotionally traumatized."

"With good reason. You were kidnapped and held at gunpoint by someone you worked with every day, and then you saw him shot right in front of you. That's more than most of us have to deal with in a lifetime."

"That is so true. Dan, I don't want to take up too much of your time. I just wanted you to know what was happening with me . . . I was all set to make the move. I liked the job offer you put on the table and I was ready to sit down with you to iron out the details . . . Now I'm not sure what I'm going to do. Since I don't think it would be fair to come over to Rize with so much up in the air in my life, I've asked for an indefinite leave of absence from Honoraria. I don't think 'indefinite' will end up being that long, but I'm afraid that under the circumstances, I don't want to make any decisions about what's next for me right now."

"I totally understand, Jada. We still want you at Rize. Whenever you're ready, the offer will stand."

"Thanks, Dan. I appreciate it."

"For the record, I think you're right to take some time to work things out. It will probably take you longer than you think, too. One of the worst things we can do to ourselves is not take the time that we need to heal."

Jada nodded. "Thanks for understanding, Dan."

Luca checked in with his father and his uncle, who insisted that Luca and Jada take his private jet back to Torino.

"Luca, the story even made the international news! What a nightmare for your girlfriend. Thank God none of her injuries were that serious. Still, you both need to have as little stress as possible right now. You must take the jet back here. I'm happy to be able to offer it to you."

"Thank you so much, Uncle Pietro."

"I hope you and Jada will visit when you're back in Torino." He laughed. "I have to meet the woman who has finally captured my nephew's heart. She must be pretty special."

"She is very special, Uncle Pietro, and I promise we will come by to visit."

"Excellent. I will look forward to seeing you soon."

He then finally had his meeting with Hugh. Luca wasn't sure what it would be like; he was certain that Hugh didn't appreciate being identified as a potential suspect in Jada's kidnapping. Also, according to Fiorella, Hugh believed he was going to be fired when they met.

He knocked on Hugh's office door.

"Hugh?"

"Luca, come in." He walked over to shake his hand, and Luca was somewhat taken aback. Hugh was actually happy and upbeat.

"I wasn't sure when we'd see you, given all that's gone on over the past several days. What a nightmare. I do hope Jada is doing better?"

"She's going to be okay. She's still very traumatized by everything, but she's handling it well."

"That's good then . . ."

"Yes. Hugh, I won't take much of your time. I wanted to finally talk with you about my ideas for the organization."

"All right." Luca had the impression that Hugh was bracing himself for the final blow. He didn't want to string out what he had to say, so he laid it out as simply as he knew how.

"Well, you've done a fantastic job bringing in new business, and we've clashed over design direction. I'm proposing that you remain president but focus exclusively on bringing in business and keeping clients happy; Fiorella would take over responsibility not only for design but alignment to strategy, and I would bless the final proposal. That way, you're able to focus on what you do best and I can ensure that the brand develops here the way I want it to."

"*That's* your organizational change?"

"Yes. How does that seem to you?"

"It's fucking fantastic—sorry. I'm trying to cut back on my swearing. Bad habit . . ."

Luca laughed. "It's okay."

"Look, Luca, the past few days have been a real eye-opener for me. I know that I was hauled in by the police because I had been going around saying to you and anyone else who would listen that I wished Jada would disappear. I understand why I was a suspect. I shouldn't have said those things. I owe you an apology about that. Fee—Fiorella has been telling me for a while that I need to think before I talk and I fobbed her off—I ignored her. This experience has made me realize that she's right. I really apologize."

"Apology accepted. I've come to realize that not everyone sees things my way and I need to be a little more flexible. The US business is yours to run with this new division of responsibility. I'm still not sure what will happen with Jada and me—where we'll live—but we'll work that out when the time comes, okay?"

"That sounds reasonable."

"Jada and I are leaving tomorrow for Torino. She needs to get away."

"I know you'll enjoy having her there with you."

"I'm happy that she wants to be there to recover and, yes, it will be great to have her there with me so I can look after her while she gets better."

The final thing that Luca did was call Marco Tuccino to arrange for the ring to be delivered to his parents' house.

"I need to get that ring, Marco. It feels like I'm going to continue to have problems until she's got it on her finger!"

CHAPTER 52

"Luca, this is such an amazing treat! I've never been on a private jet."

"Well, it's only the second time for me, and honestly I don't remember much of my trip here."

Jada entwined her fingers with Luca's. "This trip will be better."

"I know it will be." He smiled.

They slept most of the way; the toll of the past several days finally caught up with both of them. Just before landing, they woke up and had a coffee.

"If you don't mind, we'll stop briefly at my parents' house on the way home. The airport where we'll land is close to their house, so we don't even have to go out of our way."

"That's fine. I'll be happy to see them."

Just as before, Olivia met them at the door with a big hug for each of them.

"Jada, I was so happy to hear that you were safe." She said as she cupped Jada's face with her hands. "God bless you."

"Thank you, Mrs. Alessandri."

"How are you, Luca?"

"I'm much better now than when you saw me last, Mamma."

"I'm glad. Come, let's find Lorenzo."

"Jada!" Lorenzo came walking quickly down the hallway. Even he was too excited to wait patiently for them to find him. He hugged her warmly.

"Mr. Alessandri, it's good to see you!"

"Welcome back to Torino. Luca, I'm glad you're back, son."

"Good to see you, Papà."

Lorenzo whispered in his ear as he embraced him, "Your package is on my desk in the office."

Olivia had already taken Jada by the arm into the parlor. Luca slipped quickly into the office to pick up the box. He looked at the ring closely. It was perfect. The necklace was there, too. He slid them into his briefcase and joined Jada on the comfortable Venetian-style sofa. Jada was recounting her ordeal to his parents.

"It must have been a nightmare, Jada."

"Thank God they found you."

"It's an experience that I wouldn't wish on my worst enemy. I don't know how I'll get over it, but I'm determined not to let what happened change how I live my life. That's why I asked Luca if I could pay him a visit here in Torino."

"I'm sure my son would be happy for you to stay as long as you like," Lorenzo said, smiling knowingly at them both.

Luca got nervous. "Okay. We're going. I'm not going to repeat my mistake of the last time when Jada was about to fall asleep at the table. We'll see you later."

"It was nice to see you again, Mr. and Mrs. Alessandri."

"We'll see you soon, Jada. I hope your jet lag isn't too bad."

"I'm sure it won't be. The flight was wonderful!"

They drove to Luca's house in silence. In fact, Jada was a little tired and Luca was becoming more nervous by the minute. After giving it some thought, he had decided to propose immediately. He didn't think that he had the composure or the patience to plan some elaborate event. He'd learned that every moment mattered, and he wasn't going to let any more time pass before he asked her to be his wife. He'd almost proposed in front of his parents, but decided that he could at least wait until they were alone.

Jada smiled when they pulled up to his building. It felt familiar; it felt like home.

"Thank you for letting me hide out here." Jada kissed him softly.

"*Amore mio*, I cannot imagine a better place for you to be." He gathered their bags and they went upstairs. So much had happened since she had been there the last time. She went to the balcony to look at his spectacular view of the city and the mountains. While she was in silent reflection, Luca put their bags in the bedroom and went to join her with his package in hand.

"Luca, it's just so beautiful here. I thought my memory had served me well, but it's even more beautiful than I had remembered it to be."

He put his arm around her waist. "I'm so happy you're here. Jada, I'm too nervous to be romantic, so I just have to do this."

"What?" Luca handed her the box with the necklace.

"Here, open it."

"Luca—" Jada carefully unwrapped the paper and opened the box. "Oh, my God, it's the necklace I'd seen that day when we went sightseeing! It's so beautiful." She bit her lip and was fighting hard not to cry. "Luca, thank you. I love it. I love you." She kissed him softly.

"Let me help you put it on. I'm glad you like it."

"I love it. You know I do."

"Actually, there's more."

"More?"

He handed her the other box, which was not a typical ring box but rather one the size of a bracelet box. Jada went through the same ritual of carefully unwrapping the paper and opening the box. When she saw the ring, she looked at him questioningly.

"It's a ring, Luca—"

"Jada, from the moment I met you, you have changed my life. People ask me why—why you? And I cannot answer. I can only say that it *is* you. I love you. After my first marriage, I never dared to dream that I would meet someone like you. I never thought that I would want to share my life with anyone ever again." He caressed her face and wiped her silent tears. "But I did meet you. Then I almost lost you before I could ask you if you would marry me."

"Luca—"

"*Amore mio*, I know that a lot has happened and you need time to make sense of it all. But I want us to have a life together. I want to marry you. I cannot imagine my life without you."

Tears continued to roll down Jada's cheeks. She struggled to find the right words.

"Luca, I don't know what's going on in my life, and I don't feel like I'm capable of making many decisions."

Luca's heart sank and he physically slumped. He shouldn't have been so selfish. He should have waited for a better time.

". . . except this one. I love you and I want to be married to you." He couldn't hide the relief he felt when he heard those words. He smiled and caressed her face.

"Jada, we'll work through all the things that happened to you together. I know it's been an ordeal, and maybe I was very selfish to have asked you now. But I couldn't wait. Where we live doesn't matter, either. I will live anywhere that you'll be happy. We will work it out. All you have to do is say yes."

"Yes!" Jada exclaimed. Luca then slid the ring on Jada's finger. It was a perfect fit, and the diamonds glistened in the moonlight.

ABOUT THE AUTHOR

Adora Bennett is the pen name for an international business executive whose career encompasses experience as a copywriter at a world-renowned New York advertising agency, fashion writing for a major department store, global marketing for a Fortune 500 company and a masthead position at a major metropolitan newspaper.

She has traveled around the world extensively, lived in several cities across Europe, and divides her time between homes in Boston, Mass., and the south of France.

2011 Mass Market Titles

January

From This Moment
Sean Young
ISBN-13: 978-1-58571-383-7
ISBN-10: 1-58571-383-X
$6.99

Nihon Nights
Trisha/Monica Haddad
ISBN-13: 978-1-58571-382-0
ISBN-10: 1-58571-382-1
$6.99

February

The Davis Years
Nicole Green
ISBN-13: 978-1-58571-390-5
ISBN-10: 1-58571-390-2
$6.99

Allegro
Adora Bennett
ISBN-13: 978-158571-391-2
ISBN-10: 1-58571-391-0
$6.99

March

Lies in Disguise
Bernice Layton
ISBN-13: 978-1-58571-392-9
ISBN-10: 1-58571-392-9
$6.99

Steady
Ruthie Robinson
ISBN-13: 978-1-58571-393-6
ISBN-10: 1-58571-393-7
$6.99

April

The Right Maneuver
LaShell Stratton-Childers
ISBN-13: 978-1-58571-394-3
ISBN-10: 1-58571-394-5
$6.99

Riding the Corporate Ladder
Keith Walker
ISBN-13: 978-1-58571-395-0
ISBN-10: 1-58571-395-3
$6.99

May

Separate Dreams
Joan Early
ISBN-13: 978-1-58571-434-6
ISBN-10: 1-58571-434-8
$6.99

I Take This Woman
Chamein Canton
ISBN-13: 978-1-58571-435-3
ISBN-10: 1-58571-435-6
$6.99

June

Doesn't Really Matter
Keisha Mennefee
ISBN-13: 978-1-58571-434-0
ISBN-10: 1-58571-436-4
$6.99

Inside Out
Grayson Cole
ISBN-13: 978-1-58571-437-7
ISBN-10: 1-58571-437-2
$6.99

2011 Mass Market Titles (continued)

July

Rehoboth Road
Anita Ballard-Jones
ISBN-13: 978-1-58571-438-4
ISBN-10: 1-58571-438-0
$12.95

Holding Her Breath
Nicole Green
ISBN-13: 978-1-58571-439-1
ISBN-10: 1-58571-439-9
$6.99

August

The Sea of Aaron
Kymberly Hunt
ISBN-13: 978-1-58571-440-7
ISBN-10: 1-58571-440-2
$6.99

The Finley Sisters' Oath of
    Romance
Keith Thomas Walker
ISBN-13: 978-1-58571-441-4
ISBN-10: 1-58571-441-0
$6.99

September

Except on Sunday
Regena Bryant
ISBN-13: 978-1-58571-443-8
ISBN-10: 1-58571-443-7
$6.99

Light's Out
Ruthie Robinson
ISBN-13: 978-1-58571-445-2
ISBN-10: 1-58571-445-3
$6.99

October

The Heart Knows
Renee Wynn
ISBN-13: 978-1-58571-444-5
ISBN-10: 1-58571-444-5
$6.99

Giving It Up
Dyanne Davis
ISBN-13: 978-1-58571-446-9
ISBN-10: 1-58571-446-1
$6.99

November

All I Do
Keisha Mennefee
ISBN-13: 978-1-58571-447-6
ISBN-10: 1-58571-447-X
$6.99

A Love Built to Last
L. S. Childers
ISBN-13: 978-1-58571-448-3
ISBN-10: 1-58571-448-8
$6.99

December

Fractured
Wendy Byrne
ISBN-13: 978-1-58571-449-0
ISBN-10: 1-58571-449-6
$6.99

Everything in Between
Crystal Hubbard
ISBN-13: 978-1-58571-396-7
ISBN-10: 1-58571-396-1
$6.99

Other Genesis Press, Inc. Titles

Other Genesis Press, Inc. Titles (continued)

Other Genesis Press, Inc. Titles (continued)

Do Over	Celya Bowers	$9.95
Dream Keeper	Gail McFarland	$6.99
Dream Runner	Gail McFarland	$6.99
Dreamtective	Liz Swados	$5.95
Ebony Angel	Deatri King-Bey	$9.95
Ebony Butterfly II	Delilah Dawson	$14.95
Echoes of Yesterday	Beverly Clark	$9.95
Eden's Garden	Elizabeth Rose	$8.95
Eve's Prescription	Edwina Martin Arnold	$8.95
Everlastin' Love	Gay G. Gunn	$8.95
Everlasting Moments	Dorothy Elizabeth Love	$8.95
Everything and More	Sinclair Lebeau	$8.95
Everything but Love	Natalie Dunbar	$8.95
Falling	Natalie Dunbar	$9.95
Fate	Pamela Leigh Starr	$8.95
Finding Isabella	A.J. Garrotto	$8.95
Fireflies	Joan Early	$6.99
Fixin' Tyrone	Keith Walker	$6.99
Forbidden Quest	Dar Tomlinson	$10.95
Forever Love	Wanda Y. Thomas	$8.95
Friends in Need	Joan Early	$6.99
From the Ashes	Kathleen Suzanne	$8.95
	Jeanne Sumerix	
Frost on My Window	Angela Weaver	$6.99
Gentle Yearning	Rochelle Alers	$10.95
Glory of Love	Sinclair LeBeau	$10.95
Go Gentle Into That Good Night	Malcom Boyd	$12.95
Goldengroove	Mary Beth Craft	$16.95
Groove, Bang, and Jive	Steve Cannon	$8.99
Hand in Glove	Andrea Jackson	$9.95
Hard to Love	Kimberley White	$9.95
Hart & Soul	Angie Daniels	$8.95
Heart of the Phoenix	A.C. Arthur	$9.95
Heartbeat	Stephanie Bedwell-Grime	$8.95
Hearts Remember	M. Loui Quezada	$8.95
Hidden Memories	Robin Allen	$10.95
Higher Ground	Leah Latimer	$19.95
Hitler, the War, and the Pope	Ronald Rychiak	$26.95
How to Kill Your Husband	Keith Walker	$6.99

Other Genesis Press, Inc. Titles (continued)

How to Write a Romance	Kathryn Falk	$18.95
I Married a Reclining Chair	Lisa M. Fuhs	$8.95
I'll Be Your Shelter	Giselle Carmichael	$8.95
I'll Paint a Sun	A.J. Garrotto	$9.95
Icie	Pamela Leigh Starr	$8.95
If I Were Your Woman	LaConnie Taylor-Jones	$6.99
Illusions	Pamela Leigh Starr	$8.95
Indigo After Dark Vol. I	Nia Dixon/Angelique	$10.95
Indigo After Dark Vol. II	Dolores Bundy/	$10.95
	Cole Riley	
Indigo After Dark Vol. III	Montana Blue/	$10.95
	Coco Morena	
Indigo After Dark Vol. IV	Cassandra Colt/	$14.95
Indigo After Dark Vol. V	Delilah Dawson	$14.95
Indiscretions	Donna Hill	$8.95
Intentional Mistakes	Michele Sudler	$9.95
Interlude	Donna Hill	$8.95
Intimate Intentions	Angie Daniels	$8.95
It's in the Rhythm	Sammie Ward	$6.99
It's Not Over Yet	J.J. Michael	$9.95
Jolie's Surrender	Edwina Martin-Arnold	$8.95
Kiss or Keep	Debra Phillips	$8.95
Lace	Giselle Carmichael	$9.95
Lady Preacher	K.T. Richey	$6.99
Last Train to Memphis	Elsa Cook	$12.95
Lasting Valor	Ken Olsen	$24.95
Let Us Prey	Hunter Lundy	$25.95
Let's Get It On	Dyanne Davis	$6.99
Lies Too Long	Pamela Ridley	$13.95
Life Is Never As It Seems	J.J. Michael	$12.95
Lighter Shade of Brown	Vicki Andrews	$8.95
Look Both Ways	Joan Early	$6.99
Looking for Lily	Africa Fine	$6.99
Love Always	Mildred E. Riley	$10.95
Love Doesn't Come Easy	Charlyne Dickerson	$8.95
Love Out of Order	Nicole Green	$6.99
Love Unveiled	Gloria Greene	$10.95
Love's Deception	Charlene Berry	$10.95
Love's Destiny	M. Loui Quezada	$8.95
Love's Secrets	Yolanda McVey	$6.99

Other Genesis Press, Inc. Titles (continued)

Other Genesis Press, Inc. Titles (continued)

Other Genesis Press, Inc. Titles (continued)

Soul to Soul	Donna Hill	$8.95
Southern Comfort	J.M. Jeffries	$8.95
Southern Fried Standards	S.R. Maddox	$6.99
Still the Storm	Sharon Robinson	$8.95
Still Waters Run Deep	Leslie Esdaile	$8.95
Still Waters...	Crystal V. Rhodes	$6.99
Stolen Jewels	Michele Sudler	$6.99
Stolen Memories	Michele Sudler	$6.99
Stories to Excite You	Anna Forrest/Divine	$14.95
Storm	Pamela Leigh Starr	$6.99
Subtle Secrets	Wanda Y. Thomas	$8.95
Suddenly You	Crystal Hubbard	$9.95
Swan	Africa Fine	$6.99
Sweet Repercussions	Kimberly White	$9.95
Sweet Sensations	Gwyneth Bolton	$9.95
Sweet Tomorrows	Kimberly White	$8.95
Taken by You	Dorothy Elizabeth Love	$9.95
Tattooed Tears	T. T. Henderson	$8.95
Tempting Faith	Crystal Hubbard	$6.99
That Which Has Horns	Miriam Shumba	$6.99
The Business of Love	Cheris F. Hodges	$6.99
The Color Line	Lizzette Grayson Carter	$9.95
The Color of Trouble	Dyanne Davis	$8.95
The Disappearance of Allison Jones	Kayla Perrin	$5.95
The Doctor's Wife	Mildred Riley	$6.99
The Fires Within	Beverly Clark	$9.95
The Foursome	Celya Bowers	$6.99
The Honey Dipper's Legacy	Myra Pannell-Allen	$14.95
The Joker's Love Tune	Sidney Rickman	$15.95
The Little Pretender	Barbara Cartland	$10.95
The Love We Had	Natalie Dunbar	$8.95
The Man Who Could Fly	Bob & Milana Beamon	$18.95
The Missing Link	Charlyne Dickerson	$8.95
The Mission	Pamela Leigh Starr	$6.99
The More Things Change	Chamein Canton	$6.99
The Perfect Frame	Beverly Clark	$9.95
The Price of Love	Sinclair LeBeau	$8.95
The Smoking Life	Ilene Barth	$29.95
The Words of the Pitcher	Kei Swanson	$8.95

Other Genesis Press, Inc. Titles (continued)

ESCAPE WITH INDIGO !!!!

Join Indigo Book Club©
It's simple, easy and secure.

Sign up and receive the new
releases
every month + Free shipping
and
20% off the cover price.

Visit us online at
www.genesis-press.com or
call 1-888-INDIGO-1

Order Form

Mail to: Genesis Press, Inc.
P.O. Box 101
Columbus, MS 39703

Name _____
Address _____
City/State _____ Zip _____
Telephone _____

Ship to (if different from above)
Name _____
Address _____
City/State _____ Zip _____
Telephone _____

Credit Card Information
Credit Card # _____ ☐ Visa   ☐ Mastercard
Expiration Date (mm/yy) _____ ☐ AmEx   ☐ Discover

Qty.	Author	Title	Price	Total

Use this order form, or call 1-888-INDIGO-1	Total for books	_____
	Shipping and handling: $5 first two books, $1 each additional book	_____
	Total S & H	_____
	Total amount enclosed	_____
	Mississippi residents add 7% sales tax	